Whilst places and buildings in this story may be real, the histories and facts have been altered to suit the author's needs and should not be regarded as fact. All characters are a work of the author's imagination and any resemblance to persons living or dead is purely coincidental.

978-0-9557503-1-1

Printed by the MPG Books Group in the UK

Typeset by Lisa Simmonds

www.craigphoenix.co.uk

Cover photograph by Laura Trevail
Cover artwork by Trudi Couldridge

Acknowledgements

Lisa Simmonds – Thank you for your help, advice and expertise in setting this book out and getting it ready for printing.

Trudi Couldridge – Thank you, you have come up trumps again.

Mel Newham – Thank you for your help, advice and comments.

Ellan Parry – The subject of the photograph.

Laura Trevail – Thank you for allowing me to use your photograph.

Dad – Thank you for your help with this book, it's been great having you on board to help me.

1

"So what do you reckon? Old Ship? New Ship?"

"Don't actually like either actually, Pete"

"'Don't actually like either actually' that's good English James" Suzi mimicked.

"Yeah alright Suzi, and yours is so perfect" James replied sarcastically.

I turned up the volume on the car radio as Madness 'Our House' came on to cover the noise of my two friends arguing over English grammar; a playful heated discussion which no one would win. Part of it I thought was because they had once dated, about three years ago, for several months and knew each other quite well. They never really split more drifted into being 'just good friends'. They were a lot closer now.

I certainly preferred it as we were; all single and friends. All the time they had been together I had put up with them smooching. Physical chemistry was probably all they had going for them at the time and they didn't worry about rubbing my nose in it. They didn't seem to care that I had been mostly single. Anyone else and I might have taken offence, but I couldn't with these two. I liked their company. James and I had been friends since we were twelve. Suzi joined us when we were in secondary school when the board of governors decided to mix the girls and boys schools; then we became a group within a group.

Suddenly James's right arm flew up nudging my elbow. The car swerved to the right forcing me across the central white line. Panic swept through my mind for the briefest second but luckily there was no oncoming traffic.

"Watch it!" I said in good humour, I knew it was accidental.

"Sorry Pete! Suzi flicked my ear."

Glancing at James I caught Suzi doing it again.

"Don't do that!" James was obviously getting agitated, each knew they were pushing the other too far, but it never stopped them.

"Otherwise what?" Suzi replied playfully.

"Pete, tell her to stop" James pleaded impersonating a child. He turned as best he could with the seat belt holding his bulky frame in place and I could make out the snapping noises as they started slapping each others hands repeatedly in quick succession, which is what they did when an argument was not going to be resolved. They started laughing and I knew everything was alright.

"You two are worse than kids" I smiled.

"Yes Dad!" they both said mockingly before sticking their tongues out at each other.

As James turned back he caught my shoulder. The car swerved to the right and I over compensated, veering towards the pavement. I heard and felt the car go over a drain cover in the gutter and only just avoided clipping the kerb.

"Sorry Pete" James felt abashed. Still Suzi mocked him from the back seat, where I could see her in my rear view mirror, her soft features looking so beautiful framed by her long hair.

"I would like to get to the pub in one piece you know" I responded sarcastically.

"Well I thought it'd be more interesting to go in pieces. You know it is Wednesday after all" James retorted.

"Yeah. And that means what James?" Suzi replied sharply, "you're so stupid!"

"Oooh get you! Anyway I don't know" James shrugged his broad shoulders.

"Well you can go in pieces if you want."

I jerked the steering wheel sharply left causing the car to swerve but in my haste had been over zealous and the near side wheel hit the kerb spinning the steering wheel rapidly through my fingers and allowing the car to mount the pavement. Before I knew it the driver's side front wheel hit the curb and a split second later the wheel spun out of control. In my panic I pushed hard down on the accelerator instead of the brake, my inexperience kicking in; I'd only been driving three months. Desperately I grabbed at the steering wheel, a thousand reactions flying around my head. The far edge of the pavement loomed up and I could see the steep bank beyond getting closer. We were on an open stretch of road that ran down to Leigh Station from Leigh Broadway. On the right side of the road were neat well manicured gardens leading up to the houses above, on the left, the side we were about to head down, it was a rough waste ground littered with small trees and thorn bushes in amongst the tall uncut grass which hid other obstructions and discarded rubbish.

My friends were shouting and screaming. Taking my foot off the accelerator I stamped it on the brake. Everything was happening too quickly.

The car jolted as the rear wheels mounted the pavement. I couldn't make out what my friends were saying; I was concentrating too hard. Sweat formed droplets on my forehead. In desperation I yanked at the handbrake but we were over the brow of the steep grass bank and nothing could stop the inevitable.

The cars' momentum launched it down the bank at a terrifying speed. In vain I tried to steer the car but it just followed the course of the ground and we headed down the bank. Small bushes and trees appeared in front of the car before disappearing underneath. In vain I tried to bring the car to a halt, re-applying the handbrake and jamming my left foot on my right foot and pushing the break pedal even harder as if that would make a difference.

The noise was awesome as we grazed past a rock hidden by the long grass, gouging into the side panels of, this, my first car. We were being tossed around like rag dolls. It didn't matter which way I turned the wheel, I had no control. It all happened so fast yet it seemed like a slow motion replay. The ground underneath was rough, bangs and knocks made me think that any second now the car would break into pieces.

With an almighty crash we hit a tree stump, the back reared up like a horse before finally coming to rest. My seatbelt gave way under the immense strain and my head hit something hard before it was flung back as loud explosions filled the car and the airbags were deployed. At last silenced consumed us.

The full moon shone into our metal box making the twisted metal and shattered glass sparkle.

The air bags in my Renault Clio had done their job for James and I, but not Suzi. I couldn't see her. I desperately wanted to turn around yet something seemed to be holding me firmly in place, even moving my head was difficult. I struggled to look at James only managing to view him out of the corner of my eye, I saw the slow deliberate movements as my friend seem to check that he was still alive.

Quite suddenly I found myself free from whatever had been holding me but I was numb. Turning round I saw Suzi, blood streaming down one side of her face. From the stains on the rear side window I knew she had smashed her head against it. I tried to speak yet no sound came out. A second later I realised I heard nothing at all. Just silence. Suzi looked at me dazed, questioningly, almost as if to ask 'what had happened?' Her head then became too heavy for her neck and lolled to one side. A few moments later she raised it again placing one hand to the wound on the side of her head, lowering it she looked at the blood before her eyes rolled back in their sockets and her body went limp.

James was panicking, struggling to get free, scrabbling at his seatbelt. It wouldn't come undone and he shouted something at me, his mouth articulated his anger although I couldn't hear it. I was watching a dream sequence with the volume turned down. My body movements were sluggish and heavy, a haze started to cloud my vision.

The windscreen looked like a piece of frosted glass, a million tiny cracks. The passenger door was open slightly and James's feet were outside of the car, but the seatbelt still held him fast regardless of how much he struggled. Using his body as a dead weight he tried to break it, relentlessly jerking backwards and forwards; still it held tight, despite pure adrenalin driving him on. The car rocked gently under his efforts and finally the seatbelt tore free of its holder and James scrambled out tripping over his large feet in his haste to get clear of the wreck, panic finally subsiding.

Sitting down on a rock a few feet away he held his head in his hands, the moonlight highlighting his roguish facial features against the dark backdrop of trees. I could see his warm breath rising into the cold air, yet I didn't feel the cold.

Time seemed to be standing still.

After what seemed like ages James got up and came back to the car. Moving the front passenger seat forward he reached in to check on Suzi who was still out cold in the back. Undoing her seatbelt he lifted her almost effortlessly out of the car, I reached out to him yet he ignored me and I watched as he carried Suzi clear of the wreckage.

Lethargy made me feel that I was part of the wreckage, part of the car itself, numbness mastering my body. Mentally I checked my body; nothing seemed to work.

James was attending Suzi and slowly she came round, held tightly in James's arms. I knew she'd be alright.

A few minutes passed before they both came back to the car and eyed me up and down, they were talking to me; I could see their lips moving but every word was silent. I was sure I was talking back to them yet they didn't seem to hear me. The more I tried, the more they ignored me. I pleaded for them to drag me free from the wreck but they didn't.

James got out his mobile phone and dialled a number.

In the moonlight the trees and bushes looked strangely ominous and threatening, James's and Suzi's shapes blended into the background. I couldn't understand why they were pretending I wasn't there. Slowly I resigned myself to the fact that I was stuck where I was. I couldn't feel the cold, in fact I couldn't feel anything, my eyelids grew heavy and gradually they closed letting James, Suzi and the scene outside disappear from sight.

"You can't let him get away with it" a young innocent voice spoke to me, seemingly from nowhere.

I looked around. I heard the voice again and replied "Let who? Let who get away with what?"

"You can't let him get away with it. You must stop him."

Trying to see where this voice came from I undid my seatbelt, opened the door and effortlessly got out of the car. The grass was wet. Turning around my car was gone, so were James and Suzi.

It was daylight. The sun beat down whilst the remains of the morning dew glistened. There were people sitting on blankets with picnic hampers. Children playing ball, flying kites. A plane roared overhead.

It was the Airshow, the Southend Airshow. I'd been to it many times, never intending to go as I wasn't particularly a fan, yet every year I went because various friends wanted to and rather than be left out it was easier to go.

"Over here."

"Where are you?" I asked.

I was led to a thicket of brambles surrounding a small tree, too dense for me to walk into.

"I can't go in there" I said.

"You can't let him get away with it. You must help us."

"Help who? Do what?"

"Protect us. He can't get away with it."

Then I noticed a child standing in the midst of the brambles, she was no more than six or seven years old and wearing an old Victorian style child's dress. It seemed completely out of context to the rest of the scene.

Spinning round I viewed the surrounding scene again, no one else could see what I could see; they were gleefully enjoying their day watching the aircraft. There was a family nearby that was familiar but I couldn't understand why. I whirled back to the girl, she was pointing to the family. Staring at them I turned back to her, she was gone.

"He took me away and hurt me."

Opening my eyes I was engulfed by flashing blue lights and busy people all around me. The roof from my car was missing three or four firemen were carrying it away. Masses of people were working in silence as I was pulled free and put onto a stretcher, which was then carried with difficulty up the bank to a waiting ambulance. James and Suzi clambered in after me and sat on the other side. A paramedic attended to me. I still couldn't feel anything.

The journey was just images played out silently and I wondered if I was actually still alive. I could feel the rocking of the ambulance as it sped its way back to the hospital and the thud of the trolley as they wheeled me into the casualty department. But no associated sounds. Lots of bodies around me, men in masks, bright lights. It was like I wasn't really there. I caught the glint of metal instruments and slowly shut my eyes. I had had enough. I didn't want to see anymore.

"You must help us. You must stop him. Don't let him hurt us."

I was back on the cliffs. The Airshow was in full swing.

The familiar family were sitting just in front of me and didn't seem to notice I was there. A mother, a father, two girls and a boy, two older folk, possibly grandparents, completed the happy unit.

"Please, please" the voice pleaded with me.

I tried to think through the fogginess in my mind "I don't understand. Who are you?"

The grandfather looked over at where I was standing. I stared deep into his intense eyes. Getting up he slowly walked towards me. For some unknown reason I felt terror and as quickly as the scene had appeared it was gone.

I was staring into the eyes of one of the nurses before slipping into unconsciousness.

2

I woke early the next day on a hospital ward, the events of the previous evening sketchy in my fuddled brain. The sky outside was just breaking into daylight. Struggling to sit up a throbbing pain in my head caused me to wince and placing a hand to my head I found a bandage there. Gently I searched it with my fingers; I didn't know exactly what for, just searching. Then I felt the wound and was surprised that it didn't hurt, just felt warm under the slight pressure. Everything ached as if I'd gone twenty rounds in a boxing ring and lost.

In the ward there were twelve beds, seven of which were occupied including mine. I tried to recollect what had happened but nothing would come into focus. Remembering a little girl I wondered if I had hit her? It was a strange image that didn't seem to fit the whole picture. The Airshow! How did that figure into everything? That was months away.

My throat was dry and hoarse; I spied the water jug that had been left on the bedside table with a glass upside down next to it. Reaching over I tried to pour some water but my arms were too heavy, concentrating I managed to summon up the strength to lift the jug. I only drank a little as my head began pounding like a pneumatic drill from the exertion.

Wearily I slunk back down and drifted into sleep as nausea made its presence known and every ill was magnified by the simplest task.

"Help us. Don't let him get away with it. He hurt us"

The girl was standing in the thorn bushes again. I remembered! She pointed behind me to where the family were sitting, they were happy

9

having fun, enjoying the sunshine. I looked intently at them, they seemed so familiar, yet something just wouldn't click; why did they look familiar?

"You have to stop him, please." I turned to face the girl. She had long brown hair below shoulder length with soft curls tucking under, her features were soft and innocent, her complexion fair. She wore black children's shoes with a buckle on them and knee high white socks.

She put her hand in mine. It was cold. The chill penetrated me making the hairs on my arms stand on end. She squeezed gently. It was comforting in a strange sort of way.

"Please help us" her voice was soft, warm and pleading.

I turned to her.

A nurse was standing next to my bed tapping my shoulder. Looking at her I said something, I wasn't sure if I was still asleep, my eyelids were heavy like iron curtains and I struggled to keep them open. Her lips moved but no sound came from them. I replied back to her, in my mind I knew what I had said, but I only felt the internal vibrations of a muffled, distant sound. I put my hands to my mouth to feel my lips and spoke again to make sure my mouth was moving and it wasn't just my imagination. Again the nurse spoke and I heard nothing. She made some hand gestures and then left.

Laying still I contemplated the situation, pinching myself to make sure I was awake and not having a nightmare. Sitting up again I tried to ignore the aches and pains. Picking up the glass I had drunk from earlier I banged it against the glass water jug, no sound. I did it again, and again, each time my panic intensified, but still no sound. The person in the next bed stirred and looked at me as though I were crazy. I tapped the metal bed head, clicked my aching fingers all to no avail. A mild hysteria swept over me as the realisation hit. I looked for other things that I knew made a noise, I didn't want to believe the truth that I couldn't hear.

Panic made me forget about all my injuries and the throbbing in my head. I still needed proof so got out of bed, almost immediately my legs gave way and I was forced to hold onto the edge of the bed to steady myself before making my way to the end of the ward looking a little drunk. At the seating area, I switched on the TV and after finding the remote turned up the volume until the gauge on the screen wouldn't go any further. I changed channels in quick succession, wondering if it was just that particular channel, maybe there was something wrong at the TV station and the sound was not being transmitted.

I felt a firm but gentle hand on my shoulder and turning saw the nurse. She eased the remote from my hand and switched the TV off. I had tears in my eyes and slowly they started to travel down my cheeks. Taking my arm she led me to her desk and sat me down. I was visibly shaking.

She sat down next to me and proceeded to scribble on a pad.

PETER, A DR WILL BE WITH YOU SHORTLY.

I said something and hoped it was what I thought it was, "What's happened?"

NOT SURE YET. A DR WILL SEE YOU. THEN A NURSE WILL TAKE YOU TO THE E.N.T SPECIALIST.

I must have looked puzzled because she then wrote:

EARS, NOSE, THROAT.

I was guided back to my bed, not sure what to do or make of this new situation. Frightened. I curled up in a ball and stayed like that until the doctor arrived.

Ten minutes later I was in a wheel chair and being wheeled out of the ward. Wild thoughts started to whizz through my head a continuous bombardment of feelings and anxieties, pictures of my life so far and pictures how my life might be.

The rest of day was a whirlwind of various examinations, physical and mental, pulling me this way and that. No one explaining what was going on and I didn't really care, still absorbed and lost in my new world.

By early evening I was back on the ward where James and Suzi came to visit me. We sat there, not sure what to say to each other and when they did speak they tried to communicate by gesticulating. I watched intently, staring at their mouths and trying to decipher their hand movements but I couldn't follow the shapes their mouths made, frustration started to build up inside and I became more detached. In the end they resorted to pen and paper which Suzi went and bought from the shop whilst James and I sat awkwardly in the gulf that was opening up between my old hearing world and the silence in which I now found myself.

James looked uncomfortable. I wanted to know what he was thinking as he watched Suzi do all the writing, the pen would hover for a while before she would scribble a question, I would give one word answers and with the accident a moot subject this left us with very little to talk about which was unusual for the three of us. Suzi wrote that she had spoken to my parents and they were coming in later. Soon James and Suzi left as it became obvious that I didn't really want to talk.

My parents no longer lived locally, choosing to move to Norfolk almost as soon as I decided to leave home into a small one bedroomed flat which they helped finance by paying the ten percent deposit. It wasn't much but it was mine.

I was kept in for one more nights observation, despite the fact that other than my hearing and the cut on my head there was nothing really wrong with me.

Underneath the bandage, my hair was matted with dry blood and a nurse eventually took me to the bathroom to help wash it carefully, avoiding getting the thirteen stitches wet.

Walking was very strange, the loss of hearing was making me unstable on my feet, my sense of balance skewed.

When I left with my parents the following day I was given a list of appointments and places to attend: various specialists and therapists to help ascertain whether my hearing loss was permanent or temporary and then, if necessary to help me adjust to this new life style.

Inside my flat it was like a new world. No longer could I hear the knocking of the pipes when the heating was on, the boiling of the kettle, footsteps across the laminated wooden flooring. It was like solitary confinement despite both parents being there. We communicated using notes or obvious symbols like one hand held horizontally over a vertical hand for the letter 'T', which meant either 'Did I want a cup of tea?' Or 'Tea was ready', it was cumbersome but we could get by.

Finally, Tuesday, my parents left knowing I was as well as could be expected. Work had been contacted on my behalf and a card arrived wishing me a speedy recovery. There was plenty of food in the fridge, though sooner or later I would have to leave my haven and venture to the supermarket. I had internet access but preferred to shop physically rather than online, although internet shopping was looking more attractive now.

In the afternoon, I sat on the settee staring out of the window, the TV was on, subtitles flashing up on screen. I couldn't be bothered to read them and wasn't that interested in what was on either.

The silence was deadly, a man made prison. I lay down on the settee and tried to remember all my favourite songs and films, trying to fill my head with as many sounds as I could.

"Please, help us"

The girl was there again holding my hand. It was cold, my breath forming clouds in front of my face. We were standing at the corner of the road that ran down to Leigh Station. It looked different. The road was single track with grooves cut where it had been used so often. The bank that my car had gone down the previous night was now well kept, with neatly cut grass, flower beds full of colour, trees of different varieties, small bushes. It looked nothing like the overgrown mess of the previous night.

A man dressed in a collarless shirt, leather waistcoat, and grey trousers was working the gardens, tending to their every need. The little girl pointed to him.

"He must be stopped" the girl tugged at my hand, her voice pleading.

"But I don't understand."

"He hurt us all, you must stop him."

"But I don't know what I can do. How can I help?"

The little girl walked me over to an area near a group of trees about twenty feet from the man; an area I had never seen this neat and tidy. It had always been waste ground ever since I could remember.

The girl pointed to the ground.

A small well clipped Holly Bush occupied the ground under the canopy of a Birch tree, next to them were some Chrysanthemums and Rose bushes of different colours.

The girl spun me round gently on the spot to take in the view. The scene changed and I was standing near where my car had come to a halt the night of the crash. Again she spun me round to see the view and it changed back to the neat gardens.

Suddenly I was back in my flat and puzzled by what the little girl was trying to explain. None of it made any sense. Why was she talking to me? What had I done? I'd never been one for believing in ghosts or spirits. I'd never even seen a ghost before. I always sat on the fence in discussions whenever the subject came up. What was the reason behind the visions and voices? Whatever it was it had something to do with the crash. It had to! Maybe I was hallucinating, a mild concussion. But in a sense the visions and the little girl's voice drew me in, compelling me to believe and know that I was not going mad. It eased my frustration of being in a silent world. I didn't know what I should be doing or even what my next course of action should be. Maybe I was meant to go and investigate where we crashed. Maybe something there would answer my questions. According to the girl there was obviously something that I was supposed to see or do.

Leaving the house did pose its own set of fears. Everyday situations scared me now; crossing a road, walking along a pavement, not being able to hear what was going on around me. I knew there would come a time when I would have to bite the bullet; I just wanted to put it off for as long as possible, isolated in my flat. I couldn't use the phone, I didn't know if the doorbell rang. Even cooking dinner wasn't the same, I used to be able hear the 'ping' as the timer stopped on the microwave, now that had changed.

I wanted to contact my two closest friends, wanted their company, but the few times they had been round, in the last few days, had been awkward; communication was slow and frustrating. They had ended up talking with my parents instead.

I loafed around on the settee for the rest of the afternoon just letting the night-time draw in, making me feel even more dejected and depressed.

A vibration in my pocket disturbed my contemplation and pulling out my mobile phone I saw I had a message.

CAN U LET US IN PLEASE SUZ

Sluggishly and reluctantly I got up to let Suzi and James in who looked pleased with themselves. I made tea for us all and we sat down in my small front room. James immediately went over to my computer and flicked the keyboard, the screen sprang to life.

Opening up Word he began to type. Conversation became much easier now as we could all type efficiently, they could hear my replies and as we barged each other out of the way to type, it became a sort of game and for the first time since the accident we were all laughing. I finally asked if my friends would drive me to the scene of the accident as I wanted to see the area. They were hesitant and curious about my request and to my reasons, which I didn't want to tell. They obliged after a little convincing.

I trusted these two people and felt safe going out in public with them, they would keep me safe. It was early evening and light was still good. Possibly another hour and a half before dusk, and it was warm.

Near the scene of the accident it all became quite clear in my head as the night before replayed in my mind, a recollection that made my heart pound inside my chest and my hands become clammy. We parked up on the opposite side of the road, got out and stood on the footpath that the car had crossed before careering down the bank. It was a strange moment as we stood mesmerized. It had been quite an event and now, looking down the bank we realised how lucky we were. The deep gouges my car had made were still visible although the police had had the car towed away.

It was eerie not being able to hear all the everyday intrinsic sounds that I had taken for granted in the past.

My legs began to tremble as I remembered how it felt. I took deep breaths to calm myself inside. All three of us took in the scene for a few long minutes until I felt a hand on my shoulder, it was Suzi's, I looked at her and she smiled, I reciprocated.

Without sound to help me my legs were still a little wobbly as I made my way down. James put his hand on my arm to steady me, I glared at him and he let go. He meant well, but I wanted to do everything as normally as I would have done before the accident. My friends followed me down. The grass was damp and I slipped a couple of times, my deafness seemed to confuse my brain making it misjudge distance and I twisted my wrist as I put my hand down to break my fall. Arriving at the point where the car had stopped a chill ran down my spine. In my mind I could see some of the images how the moon had made everything appear.

Scanning the area I tried to map out the image I had seen in my dream of the little girl, figure out the positioning of everything, the bushes and trees, where she had been pointing to, and where she stood. I searched the ground diligently, not sure what I was looking for, just an overwhelming confidence that this was what I was meant to be doing. Nothing seemed out of the ordinary; earth, rocks, twigs, and odd bits of rubbish and debris from my car. The cliffs, as they were affectionately referred to had been the subject of two landslips, only minor ones but enough to change the landscape and expose some giant boulders.

"This way" The little girl took my hand and led me to a spot a few feet away "Help me" she said pointing to the ground

"What! I don't understand" but she was gone

Turning and looking at my friends they were puzzled by my actions. Had I just fallen asleep standing up? Had I really seen the girl and felt her hand? I pointed to the ground and my friends made their way to where I was standing. Pointing to a spot on the ground I told them 'she's here'. My friends looked at me as though I had gone mad. I ignored them, feeling compelled to carry on, so grabbing a thick stick from nearby I knelt down to started digging, pulling the dirt out of the way and within a few inches hit something solid. Throwing the stick to one side and I started to clear the area with my bare hands. It was just a rock, quite large, but just a rock. I could feel my friends' eyes piercing my back wondering 'What the hell I was doing, had I gone insane?' I dug round the rock to get a purchase on it so I could heave it out of the way. It was too heavy to move on my own and I asked James to give me a hand. He looked uncomfortable, first glancing at Suzi, looking for her approval. She said something to him before he reluctantly helped, between us we managed to move it out of the way.

Underneath was a hessian sack which I stared at for the briefest of moments before lifting it up. It was dirty with something loose inside. The sack only came away so far as a corner was snagged on something. James and myself yanked at it and suddenly it came free, throwing us backwards and scattering bones on the ground as it ripped open.

James looked at me, then I at Suzi, none of sure what to make of it. James and Suzi suddenly became very wary of me, physically taking a step back, their faces questioning me.

3

I stared at the bones strewn across the ground whilst still holding the sack in my right hand, fighting the queasy feeling in the pit of my stomach. Morbid curiosity drew my attention to the bones which were small, and for a moment I was relieved as I thought they might actually be from an animal, inside I knew they were not. Something heavier still remained in the sack and I hesitated for fear that I knew what it was. A skull.

Impulse after impulse shot round my body but not one of them could make me move, all the documentaries I'd ever watched about gruesome discoveries, human remains buried, paled into insignificance now I was actually confronted with the very situation that I always believed would never affect me. I looked to my friends for support.

They had retreated a safe distance not sure anymore what to make of their friend, who seemed to know where to locate bones. Suzi had her head on James's shoulder, his arm around her for comfort.

I understood their reluctance to take any further part, yet they were my friends. Was I asking too much? It seemed so. A moment later they appeared to be arguing with each other. James angry and upset, his long arms gesticulating emphasizing his mood. He turned to leave and Suzi grabbed his arm which he easily shook off shouting something at her. She watched as he went back up the bank to his car and drove away.

She looked directly at me and I held her gaze for a few seconds before returning to what lay in front of me, still unsure of what to do, whether to look in the sack or put it down.

Quite suddenly I was disturbed from my questioning thoughts by a hand on my shoulder, turning I saw Suzi's face, her hazel eyes reflecting the light from a distant street light that had come on as dusk fell. She pulled her mobile from her back pocket; pressed a few buttons and then showed me.

POLICE? Is what it simply read. Nodding my agreement she duly rang. I placed the sack back on the ground where I found it and then stood up.

A squad car turned up within minutes followed shortly after by another. Within an hour a forensics team had appeared and the whole scene was cordoned off.

The scene resembled one out of the murder documentaries I so enjoyed watching, men in white overalls wearing masks, surgical gloves, and rubber boots. Tape was used to make a perimeter fence then setting to work they scoured the ground looking for other remains.

Back on the pavement above two policemen took us to one side to ask their questions, eyeing us both suspiciously. From the actions of Suzi I guessed she had explained that I was deaf and therefore was not being obstructive by not answering any questions – this calmed one particular officer who had been getting annoyed by my apparent indifference. I found myself struck dumb so let Suzi do all the talking, although she couldn't answer the questions fully because she didn't know why I had brought them to this site so unexpectedly. Standing there I almost felt like a bystander.

Suzi typed another message on her phone.

STATION US 4 QUESTIONS. OK? I agreed with a nod of the head.

In the sterile interview room we were each given a requisite cup of instant coffee from the machine. It was obvious from the way we were being treated they didn't really suspect us of anything sinister, but were merely intrigued by our discovery and what we might know. Questioning lasted for nearly two hours, partly due to the fact they had to write down any questions for me. Eventually though, they had a statement from both of us, which we duly signed and dated before they released us. It was now midnight and we were both tired.

From the look on Suzi's face she also wanted answers although I knew she would leave these for another day. She typed another message on her phone, STAY AT MY PLACE? I agreed. I didn't fancy a night in my flat on my own not after tonight, it also made me feel as if she hadn't lost faith in me, as a friend. James, I wasn't so sure, discovering the bones had obviously rattled him.

Suzi lived at home, like James, her parents were relaxed about her having guests stay over in her room, male or female, and preferred the fact that they knew where she was and who she was with. Suzi had a spare mattress which she slid out from under her bed. It was already made up. Normally we would have talked but under the circumstances this was not going to happen. My mind was in turmoil but even that couldn't keep me awake any longer.

"Don't let him hurt us, please stop him."

The little girl took my hand, we were still standing on the cliffs, as she turned we moved at breakneck speed to another location. I didn't quite recognise it at first, but after a short while it came to me and I knew exactly where we were. There were less houses than I knew it to have but it was definitely Highlands Boulevard, and a small grassed area about half way along. Today it was a neatly kept council garden with a bench. Here I was viewing a scrap of land, not even the side street existed. The waste land stretched up to Belfairs woods, which in my time did not come this far. This was obviously before the development had taken place. She pointed to an area and turned to face me.

In an instant we were standing in St Clements church in front of a grave stone, it read 'Lillian Francis Hall – Aged 8, taken from this world on 9th June 1886.'

If I didn't understand before, now I was even more confused.

"If you don't help us more will go."

"I don't understand. I don't know how I can help you?"

"You must stop him from hurting us".

"But how? Who? This is the past you're showing me".

There was a tug at my shoulder, I opened my eyes and saw Suzi staring at me. She had put on the bedside light, her eyes were weary and bloodshot, she said something to me and then remembered I couldn't hear her. She got up and grabbed a pen and paper from her desk in the corner by the window.

WHO R U TALKING 2?

She wrote.

Looking at her I thought of what to say without sounding as though I had completely lost my mind. I had managed so far to avoid any explanation, to both the police and my friends, of everything up to now, how I knew where the bones were buried on the cliffs. I knew the questions would start soon. In my dream I could only surmise I was being shown another burial, what was confusing was that there was a grave as well. None of it made sense to me.

Suzi pointed at her piece of paper again. I still didn't know what to tell her

"It was just a dream" I whispered.

WOT GOING ON PETE?

Suzi dabbled in spiritual things but I still didn't feel comfortable talking to her, telling what was really happening. It was new to me and I was feeling uncomfortable with it all.

"It's just a weird dream. Don't worry about it".

She put her finger to my lips to quieten me down.

IS MORE. U NEW ABOUT BONES. HOW?

There it was. The question that I knew was coming. I couldn't fob her off anymore. I sighed and although we were both tired I made myself comfortable and began to explain the missing details. Occasionally, when getting too loud she would put her finger to her mouth then I would go to the other extreme, it was very frustrating trying to gauge ones own volume when you couldn't hear. It was nearing four in the morning when I finished. Suzi had listened intently and not laughed, or disbelieved me, which deep down I knew she wouldn't and talking did actually give me a sense of relief. Now I didn't feel like such a freak.

We settled down for sleep.

In the morning, after breakfast, I headed home, whilst Suzi went to work although she'd contemplated phoning in sick as she was tired, but decided against it as she had a few errands to run. I spent the day surfing the net looking for any relevant information regarding 'Lillian Francis Hall, 1886' trying various searches: 'St Clements church' 'newspapers 1886' 'Southend library' 'history' 'murders in Southend' and endless others strings of characters. Nothing I entered brought up any information of use, just thousands upon thousands of irrelevant pages about anything except what I was looking for. I knew a visit to the library sieving through hard copy information was probably my next port of call.

Being at home was starting to make me restless; I had been out of school nearly three years so had broken the routine of short days and in truth I enjoyed my job. I missed the friendly faces and daily banter. My appointments with various specialists had been scheduled and they would help me come to terms with my deafness and with nothing specifically wrong, no physical reason for it, I just had to learn to live with it. There was a possibility it was temporary, but the longer it remained the more likely I would stay deaf the rest of my life and would need to adjust my lifestyle accordingly.

I was stuck in a kind of limbo, not working, not studying, just, existing. Suzi was keeping in contact with me via text, this at least made me feel part of the real world. Everything else was just... nothing. Emptiness. A sense of being a stranger in a foreign land, unable to speak the dialect.

It was late afternoon I knew the library would still be open and so that was where I was heading. 'Who was the little girl that was haunting my mind? Was it Lillian?

The Library proved surprisingly fruitful. Backdated copies of local newspapers gave enough information to determine that Lillian had been murdered in 1886, the culprit was never caught but her grave was found September 1886 by local workman turning a bit of wasteland into a public seated garden area in Highlands Boulevard. The girl disappeared on June 9th that year. They showed a sketch of the girl, and although it was rough I could see it was not the little girl in my dreams. How did this girl fit in with the one in my dreams? Why show me Lillian's gravestone? None of it made any sense.

Suzi came over that evening and I told her all that I had found out. James preferred to keep his distance.

There appeared to be no logical reason for thoughts of the girl intruding in to my subconscious. The deaths had occurred so far in the past there was very little that we could actually do to prevent them, or even bring the culprit to justice. So why the pleas for help? We toyed with various scenarios but none could offer any sound basis to work from. It was all history, past. What affect could the present have upon it? As much as we would like to help, we couldn't, our hands were tied.

Suzi retrieved from her shoulder bag a little box barely three inches square and gave it to me and opening it I saw a small pendant hung on a short silver chain. She wrote on a note pad:

AMULET HELP PROTECT FROM EVIL SPIRITS. GARNET

"What? I don't understand".
Holding it up I studied it closely, in the light it looked beautiful,

an orangey red crystal that had many different levels within it. This sort of thing I was always sceptical about. What power could an Amulet have?

Suzi wrote some more;

AMULET WARNS OF IMPENDING DANGER, RE-ENERGIZES CHAKRAS.

I grimaced even more confused.

Suzi was doing her best to make me feel easier and she knew that I was worried by this sudden talent for being able to talk with the deceased. She had experienced similar things many times in her life. She stated that her Nan had told Suzi she was a channel. Her special gift was something to be treasured as not everyone could harness such a gift or even handle the power that comes with it. Her Nan had given her the Amulet in order to protect her through her early experiences in case evil spirits tried to toy with her.

I looked at her thankfully, if a little hesitant. The little girl was disturbing my dreams but not in an awful way, in a strange way she kept me sane; if only I could figure out the purpose and why she had chosen me. If this was in part due to the car wreck, why hadn't she chosen Suzi who already possessed this gift and knew how to use it wisely?

I gave Suzi a hug, in the last few days she'd proven to be more of a friend than she had ever been before and because of that felt closer to her.

4

After Suzi went I ambled off to bed, not really tired only fed up with my world of silence and laying in the dark appealed. Holding the amulet I contemplated whether to wear it or not. The dreams and the girl gave me a sense of reassuring peace, a connection with my old world. The intrusions meant I could hear clearly again and hold a relatively normal dialogue. I placed the amulet back on the bedside table, that way I knew it would be there if I needed it.

A strange kind of irony existed; now I couldn't hear the usual night-time chorus I found the thought of sleep a little unnerving. I wasn't specifically listening for the unusual sounds of the world at night but subconsciously was prepared for them. I had got used to hearing doors close and footfalls across the floor in the upstairs flat that normally littered the night. My brain would register them yet ignore them, but now I couldn't hear them paranoia could quite easily set in, if I let it. My sense of danger was inhibited by the lack of sound and that presented its own set of risks, fire alarms. At the other end of the spectrum it was nice not to be disturbed by spurious intrusions from the outside world.

Sometimes in nights since the accident I had woken up believing I'd heard something, my imagination playing tricks. Of course, there was nothing except the world that I was in, devoid of sound.

Restlessly I slept, tossing and turning, my eyes opening just to check whether I was asleep or not. The hours passed, dark and silent, but eventually I drifted off to sleep.

"Come with me, I need to show you something." The little girl took my hand. She was standing next to my bed.

"Where are we going?" She did not answer but the scene before me changed.

Standing outside a big house she looked at me, I observed the familiar street, large Victorian houses with timber frames, a long line of them fresh and new. The road - I knew. Just not in the state I was seeing at this moment.

A solid wood front door sprung open and a family came out, a husband, wife and three children; two girls and a boy. The children were all aged between five and ten, dressed in their Sunday best. The children walked in an orderly fashion behind the parents with the wife linking her arm with the husband.

Quickly the scene changed to St Clements Church, Leigh-On-Sea. The family entered the churchyard through the gate in the perimeter stone wall running along Church Hill, a narrow street paved with cobbles. From the direction they had come I knew where their house was, Leigh Road, which ran into Highlands Boulevard once it crossed the London Road. There weren't so many of the Victorian houses left now, which was why I hadn't recognised it immediately.

The church had crowds of people surrounding it, all talking in groups and with children running round chasing each other. The church bells started to toll and everyone looked up at the clock on the bell tower which showed it was half past nine.

The scene changed again this time people leaving the church, the children running off, en masse, across the narrow street of cobbles, Church Hill, then disappearing through a gateway into the walled Library Gardens. Library Gardens is a massive expanse of nicely kept gardens, landscaped and stocked full of a myriad of plants both exotic and home grown. We followed. The kids separated into groups, starting their own games some had skipping ropes, others were playing tag.

The little girl took me over to the far end of the gardens where there were stone steps leading down to a lower grassed area that was hidden from view by trees and shrubs. This was just past the building that I knew as Leigh library, however, it did not look like the library I knew more like a grand residence of some kind.

We headed down the steps to the garden area. A solitary girl, one of the three children we had observed earlier, wandered about on her own taking in the sweet scent of the flowers. This section of the gardens was still unfinished; some beds were almost empty with the exception of a few tall shrubs and trees but nothing like the upper section. A gate in the far corner swung in the summer breeze. The grating of the metal hinges echoing round the gardens.

Following the girl through the gate I watched her exploring. Curiosity leading her along, moving her away from the place where she knew she was allowed. Beyond the gate was an alley I hadn't seen before and didn't know existed, certainly not today. In the alley there was a medium built man wearing a black leather waistcoat and dirty collarless shirt; he was busy fiddling with a canvas sack. The little girl wandered up to him innocently. He turned round, looking flustered at having been disturbed, trying to hide what he had been doing. The little girl asked him a question. He grabbed her and with one powerful hand pulled her tight to his own body smothering her mouth with his other hand stifling her attempt to scream. The little girl could not break free, twisting and struggling she fought bravely. The man dropped the sack on the ground allowing the top to open. Inside was the body of a young boy. The little girl froze as she caught site of the body thus allowing the man to twist the girls head sharply to the right in one swift movement, her body immediately going limp.

I went to lunge forward, but the little girl stopped me. I was stunned to witness such brutality; for me this only happened in films. How could someone do such a thing?

The man seemed to be quite calm and casually continued to tie the canvas sack with the body of the boy inside as if it was just rubbish. The sheer audacity was incredible.

I turned to the little girl who had led me here and did a double take as I looked more closely at the face. The girl that held my hand was the girl we had followed; Even more sickened, the bile in my stomach started *to rise and I had to fight the urge to vomit. I wanted to turn away in disgust but felt compelled to watch on, to see the events unfold.*

The man had a narrow wooden cart that looked like a primitive wheelbarrow with short sides and was perfect for the tight dirt-track alleyways which ran behind the Library Gardens. The tall brick wall which was the boundary to the gardens hid us from the view of the residents of the Library. The gradient of the hills should have allowed the cottages below to view the scene that had taken place but the fact that it was Sunday I concluded meant that the residents were at church.

The man opened another canvas sack and placed the girls body inside and without a care lifted it onto the cart which also held some gardening tools and a few plants. He effortlessly pushed the cart onwards.

I stumbled forward, the enormity of the crime and the ease with which it was carried out was mind numbing. We followed.

The alley came out onto Leigh Hill, the road where we had crashed in my car. No one was about.

He pushed the cart towards the seafront. One of the sacks fell off and without thought he stopped and lifted it back on, adjusting its position so it wouldn't fall off again. The man wheeled the cart halfway down the slope, then stopped and lifted off the two sacks, throwing them easily over his powerful shoulders and picking up a shovel walked further down the grass bank. He stopped, let the sacks fall to the ground and proceeded to dig. Some people walked by and waved from the footpath, he acknowledged them then carried on with his task.

I awoke alone and back in my room, eyes wide open, my breathing laboured, sweating and my throat was dry.

The clock on my bedside table read "5.17" Picking up the amulet I placed it around my neck and held it for a minute or so until my breathing had returned to normal. It was almost as a reflex to the ghastly images I had seen and in vain hope that it would keep them from me. I fetched a drink of water from the kitchen.

Wide awake I paced the lounge until I decided to make the best use I could of my time and search the web for any information in relation to Leigh Library, if there was any available.

Punching in 'Leigh Library' the central website for all the local libraries came up, 'clicking' on history, it detailed all relevant buildings. Scrolling down I found the page I was looking for, 'Leigh Library'. A brick built three storey house of huge proportions, it had a double pitched roof and large traditional Victorian chimney stacks reaching high into the sky. Double oak doors were set in an imposing stone archway, simple in design. Three wide steps led up to the heavy doors. Originally it had been built as a Rectory in 1836 and was not converted to the library as it now stands until 1928, once it had been purchased by the town council of the day.

The Rector, liked to open the gardens to his congregation after Sunday mass. He felt it would bring them all closer, allowing them to enjoy the sanctity of this peaceful and beautifully kept garden for which he felt privileged to be responsible for. Tea Parties were quite frequent during summer months as he strove to make his church the social centre for the area.

Three hours had passed and I had to get ready for my appointment with the specialist who was arranging for me to have lessons to learn sign language and lip reading.

By mid afternoon I was home again. A vibration in my pocket just as I closed the front door told me I had a message, it was from Suzi asking if I fancied going out that evening for a drink, I replied 'yes'. First I would have an afternoon nap as I was quite exhausted from the intensity of my session and the realisation of the enormity of the task ahead. I lay down on the settee.

I was standing outside the Victorian house once again. The little girl was standing on the doorstep beckoning me to follow her in as she disappeared through the door.

"He has to be stopped. You have to know."

"I have to know what?" I followed her.

"Everything. You have to know everything. Make him stop hurting us."

"Make who stop hurting you? Can't you just tell me who?"

"I don't know who he is."

"If you don't know who he is, how am I meant to know?"

"You must! You must stop him!"

"But I can't change what's already gone. It's impossible" I could feel my frustration rising inside.

"Please help us. Don't let him hurt us" the voice was always calm and gentle but pleading, the sort of voice that it is hard to say no to.

Standing in the hallway of this elegant character house, all was tranquil. People moved about their business, hardly a sound being made. The expressions on there faces was solemn.

In the dining room the evening table was set, only four places. I started to piece together in my head all the information I had acquired. Sometimes it was a slow process but I got there eventually. I looked at the few pictures around the room, mainly family portraits. The family were obviously fairly wealthy to have so many photos.

The mother was standing at the table, tears streaming from her eyes. The father was doing his best to look masterful and controlled. The children didn't seem to understand fully the consequences of what had happened.

The little girl then led me into the sitting room where a fire had been lit and was burning brightly, flooding the room with its glow. A newspaper was lying on the armchair in the corner by the bay window. The little girl pointed to it and I went and read the front page which lay face up:

LITTLE GIRL GOES MISSING

Has anyone seen Sarah Couper aged six, who went missing last Sunday week. She was last seen playing in the Rector's garden after morning mass. Local residents and police have searched the local area but thus far no trace of the girl has been found. Police are asking for anyone who may have seen the girl to come forward.

Sarah looked at me and for the first time since she had come into my dreams I saw sadness in her eyes rather than just innocence.

I woke with a start, the sky was darkening outside and looking at the video clock noted it was '7:03', Suzi was picking me up in half an hour and I hadn't had dinner.

As I rushed about thoughts of Sarah pre-occupied my mind. I still didn't understand how she wanted me to help. I really didn't think there was anything I could do. History is past and we were talking almost 120 years ago. Why didn't she tell me what she wanted me to do? Showing me riddles only managed to confuse me. I wondered whether somehow the accident had caused my brain to malfunction and all this wasn't real. But that wouldn't explain the remains and how I knew where to look.

5

Suzi turned up early as usual. I had been dashing around like a maniac trying to get ready in time and was ready to sit down to eat my dinner when my phone vibrated with a message to say she was outside. Letting her in, we both sat as I ate. In between mouthfuls I filled her in on what I knew about Sarah and all that I'd seen.

She just smiled at me. At first I couldn't work out why, it was a strange sort of knowing smile and when I reached up to my neck to scratch an itch I realised why. I was wearing the amulet. I thought a bit more about the amulet. It hadn't stopped Sarah coming into my dreams. Why? Suzi was looking curiously at me and I responded with a puzzled frown.

"I need to talk to you about the amulet." I said. She carried on smiling "I don't understand why Sarah can still enter my dreams; you said it would protect me from spirits"

SARAH?

She typed as we sat at the computer after I'd eaten, half a bum cheek each on the seat.

"That's her name. She is six..was six years old. She died in 1886"

Suzi's eyes showed her surprise.

1886????

I nodded

AMULET WILL PROTECT U FROM BAD SPIRITS, STILL ALLOW GOOD SPIRITS TO TALK. THIS STRANGE, NOT HEARD OF BEFORE. SARAH DOESN'T SEEM TO WANT TO HARM U. JUST GUIDE U

She paused and then added

LET GO PUB

Suzi was evidently also baffled by events.

Leaving my flat we headed to The Old Ship in Old Leigh, a favourite haunt of ours. It was strange to sit in Suzi's car and not hear all the usual sounds that I associated with it, it was like sitting in a vacuum. However, I started to notice other nuances, the vibrations through my hands and feet that reverberated from the bodywork, the rumble of the road as we drove over the cobblestones, vibrations rather than sounds, more exaggerated than previously. My senses seemingly more acute compensating for the loss of one.

We sat at a table over looking the murky sea. Suzi had brought a pad with her and to an outsider it must have looked peculiar, I was still very conscious of people's stares.

SO FAR, WE KNOW 2 MURDERS, NO REASON, OR WHO. KNOW WHEN?

I raised 3 fingers.

3?

"Yes. Lilian. The girl in Highlands Boulevard, the boy, and Sarah."

OK. BOY? WHAT BOY? OH YES BOY. STILL PUZZLED. Y U? WOT OUTCOME WANTED?

"I don't know, I can't think of one single reason for any of this."

SOULS SOMETIMES DON'T REST TIL SCORE SETTLED. Y WAIT TILL NOW!! MURDERER WOULD HAVE DIED AT LEAST 80 YRS AGO. MAYBE SHE JUST WANTS U 2 FIND BODIES, SO THEY CAN B BURIED PROPERLY AND SPIRIT CAN FINALLY REST.

"I don't think so, because one of the dead girls had been found and correctly identified. I saw her grave, remember? Okay, the little boys' remains, as far as we know, still haven't been found. I'm sure he was buried with Sarah. I followed the man to where he dug the grave."

DID U ACTUALLY SEE HIM PUT BODY IN HOLE?

"No."

MAYBE HE DIDN'T, PUT IT SOMEWHERE ELSE?

"Maybe, But why? Surely that would be more risky."

YES. DOESN'T SEEM TO CARE ABOUT RISK.

"True. I still don't understand why?"

MMM...

We sat and drank the drinks Suzi had bought on the way in. "How is James?"

OK. BEEN BUSY.

"Busy doing what?" I detected Suzi was covering for him.

Although I couldn't hear the change in her tones, her face and manner in which she wrote said a lot.

JUST STUFF

"Just Stuff! What's his problem? Why doesn't he come out with us?" Suzi motioned to me that my voice was getting loud again.

Suzi hesitated before writing again

DON'T KNOW. WON'T SAY. HAS STARTED ACTING STRANGE LATELY THOUGH

"How do you mean?"

DON'T KNOW, JUST STRANGE

We sat in silence for a few minutes.

WALK??

Finishing our drinks we went for a walk along the seafront towards Chalkwell. A cool breeze blew, but as long as you were sheltered from it the night was mild.

The absence of noise was unnerving, the pathway was mainly unlit and the darkness enveloped us like a cloak. Out of the corner of my eye I saw Suzi move suddenly a cyclist whizzed past throwing me off balance. Suzi grabbed me to stop me falling. I held on tight. Visibly shaking, Suzi rubbed my arm compassionately. Her lips moved but I didn't understand. I stared at her and for the briefest moment we caught each others' gaze. The world stopped spinning, Suzi's hand slid down my arm and into my hand where she held it tightly, reassuringly, remaining there whilst we turned round to head back to the car. For that few seconds I felt really close to her, something I had never contemplated could exist. A warmth ran through me and I wanted to hold onto her hand forever.

I wasn't sure if what I was thinking was one way, mutual, or just brought about by the situation. Maybe she was just confirming that she was there for me, like a true friend, unlike James who seemed to have deserted me when I needed him most. Was I reading into this friendship more than there was ever going to be? In truth I'd always been attracted to Suzi, but over the years had just put it out of my mind as the three of us were a close group and happy that way.

Suzi dropped me back home and I asked her in for coffee which she declined. The moment I asked, I knew I was trying to change the state of our relationship. It had been a leading question. When she declined I felt I had passed one of the imaginary boundaries that had been there from the beginning. Would I lose her too?

Inside I settled down with a coffee and reflected on the evening. My eyelids grew heavy. I contemplated sending James another text message; I needed a friend here and now, I needed to talk. He hadn't replied to my previous texts so why should this be any different. In vain I text him anyway and solemnly drank my coffee before going to bed.

Voices appeared in my head. Children's voices. Too many of them to understand what they were saying, an amalgamation of noise reverberating round inside. I was standing in what could only be described as a large garden centre, rows and rows of flowers and shrubs, neatly organised, people tending to them, taking great care in what they were doing.

There was a horse and cart over in the far corner being loaded up with various shrubs, tools already lay to one side of it. A man turned round and looked directly at me. My heart jumped a few beats. He looked straight at me, his eyes appeared calm, yet devious, it was the same man as earlier.

"You have to stop him. Only you can stop him." Sarah appeared at

my side.

"Who is he?"

"He is bad, he hurts us" Her voice became almost tearful as she pleaded with me.

Sarah took my hand, the next second we were back in Leigh, this time the other end of the Broadway which was the main shopping street that ran from St Clements Church, to the Grand Hotel where we now found ourselves. Everything looked so different to how I knew it. The Hotel occupied a large plot of land whereas in my time it barely had room for a small car park and a beer garden.

Sarah led me into the grounds and into what is now the beer garden but then was just a grassed area with carefully planted flowerbeds. Into the garden walked the figure of the man we had seen earlier, carrying plants. On his second journey he carried a sack which I guessed was manure. Again he went back out of the garden.

Sarah took me to the sack which lay on the ground and pointed to it. I looked at her eyes. They looked hurt

"You?" I uttered unsurely.

The man picked up the sack and I could make out the outline of a body inside.

I reached out to grab the sack as if that would help matters, as if I could prevent what was about to occur or what had already happened.

I turned as someone else walked into the garden. I felt instant relief, I believed our man was about to be caught in the act. The second man went over to speak to the 1st man, who had dropped the sack on the ground with a thud. They remained in conversation for a few minutes. I was willing the other man to take a look in the sack, but he just seemed intent on discussing his plans for the garden. He walked away oblivious to what was going on under his nose.

In disbelief I shouted "WAIT!" but it was futile.

Sarah took my hand and next we were standing in a house. A woman and man sat at a dining room table. Tears welled up in the woman's eyes and she wiped them away with a hanker-chief, the man sat holding her hand, a newspaper dated 18th June 1886 lay in the middle of the table, on the front page there was an article about a missing person.

MISSING

Peter Mark Daniels, missing since last Tuesday. Police have made enquiries but thus far have no leads. They believe this to be associated to the disappearance of young Sarah Couper aged six who also disappeared a few weeks ago. Police are baffled by the disappearances but Chief Inspector Collins promises he is doing his utmost to find the missing children.

"He takes us, and hurts us. You can stop him. You have to stop him."

"But Sarah I don't know how."

"You are the only one that can help us" Her voice seemed to go quiet as tears snaked down her cheeks.

Suddenly we were in a room of some sort, a meeting place with no windows, possibly a basement. The door behind us was flung open. In walked our man barely recognisable, dressed in a heavy robe, blue with red trim round the cuffs. The robe stretched down to the floor hiding his powerful build but making him look huge. He busied himself lighting candles and a few minutes later more people entered dressed the same way. Four of them were carrying something between them, it was a young boy. Was it the young boy that could have been in the sack? No, I answered myself there had been no movement from the sack. Was Sarah showing me events that led up to that scene? I turned to ask but she put a finger to her lips. The boy was alive, struggling to break free. I felt useless as I couldn't help him. He was carried to the centre of a circle drawn on the floor and gently placed inside.

The boy curled up into the foetal position and hid his face as if this would protect him. The man who we had been watching stood nearest the head of the boy not entering the circle; he raised his hands above his head and the others took up various positions around the circle kneeling down, taking hold of the boys arms and legs, forcing him to lay face upwards. He was clearly terrified although he daren't make a sound.

Kneeling down the man held the boys head still before a woman dressed in another robe, this time red trimmed with blue, entered the room. She knelt down close to the boys head forcing the man to edge sideways. Placing both hands on the boys' cheeks she lowered her face to his. The boy visibly relaxed, almost reassured by her sight and stopped fighting. The woman leaned forward and put her mouth to his, there was a pause.

The boys' chest rose significantly before falling again. Every muscle then went into spasm before his tiny body became limp. The woman stood up, her eyes wild and manic. She then walked out of the room. The man we had followed so many times before brought over a canvas sack and bundled the boy into it; hoisting it over his shoulder then left through another door.

I didn't quite comprehend what had gone on, or what it all meant. I faced Sarah who looked at me with hope in her eyes.

"I don't know how to help. What do you want me to do?" It sounded hopeless.

I was in my bed again. For a few seconds I glanced around the room checking it, before sitting up. I searched my bedside table for the amulet then I realised I was wearing it. Holding it tight I laid down again. Did I feel safer? I didn't feel I was being threatened anyway but knew I was getting into something dark and was not sure what I should do. I was afraid and doubted that I really wanted to go on with this anymore. But how could I stop it?

After a long restless time I drifted off back to sleep. An uneasy sleep, my mind plagued with unconnected thoughts. Why did I feel guilty about these crimes? They were in the past. And who was this man?

6

Waking up late, the sun broke through the gaps in the curtains. I had an appointment later with my specialist who was meeting me at a special lip reading and sign school in Rayleigh. I didn't fancy going back to school but it was necessary. I had hated school and was so happy when I left. These lessons were essential if I was going integrate back into the world in spite of my new disability.

After switching my phone on the little envelope appeared informing me there was a message; It was from Suzi.

SORRY DIDN'T COME IN LAST NIGHT, WAS TIRED, C U 2NITE SX

Smiling I allowed myself to entertain the thought that maybe there was more to our relationship, then again, maybe I was just reading into it what I thought I wanted.

Eating breakfast I watched morning TV. The subtitles flashed up as usual but I wasn't really interested, just let the flickering house and DIY programmes ramble on interspersed with adverts.

Despite the moving pictures time seemed to go really slowly, somehow sounds made the days, each taking up precious seconds. The midday news kicked in and I saw pictures of somewhere I recognised. It was a report about the discovery of the bones on the Cliffs. I reached for the remote to turn the sound up out of instinct. I sighed inwardly, a momentary lapse that made me wonder how many times I was going to make that same mistake. Some of the subtitles had gone already and I had to piece together the remaining ones to make up the complete story.

The police could not identify the person whose remains had been found. They had carbon-dated the bones back to around the 1880's. Records of the time were not specific enough to tie in the remains with any particular person but they believed they were for a girl aged between six and nine years old and the cause of death was a broken neck. Records showed that there were a few girls around that time that had gone missing and have never been found but with no accurate records for the time period it looked as though her identity would remain a mystery.

Inside I felt smug as I knew who it was, but also I felt sympathy for Sarah. It would have been nice to lay her to rest in a marked grave or even find a relative and put an end to a family mystery that may have been passed on through generations.

I couldn't exactly go and tell the police; one, I didn't think they'd believe me, and two, they'd want to know how I knew and that would be difficult to explain.

The visit with my specialist went well. The teachers and their assistants seemed friendly enough and did their best to make me feel at ease and make it feel like fun rather than an onerous task. I watched a couple of the pupils working with their assistants and saw how they worked together and also the frustration that was still experienced in the process of adjusting. It was an awesome task and I didn't know if I was up to it. Time would tell and what choice did I have.

By the time I left, I was tired and emotionally drained. Physically all my wounds were healing nicely. I'd worn a woolly hat to hide the bandage around my head but even that wound only ever gave a niggling throb, occasionally making me want to scratch it. I put this down to that fact that I couldn't wash my hair as often as I usually did. Only a few more days and the stitches would be out. I would be able to wash my hair properly. I hated wearing hats normally.

Going home I emailed my parents, a daily routine, then

spent rest of the day puzzling over the identity of our murderer and how to go about establishing who he was. I had two bits of information; what he looked like, which was great if there were picture records somewhere, and that he was a gardener. Did he work for the council or private? Nowadays photo ID's were normal for council workers but in 1886 photographs were very much a luxury for the wealthy.

How to access the councils' records would be another difficult problem! Much as I thought about it no solution presented itself, I would need a name in order to spin a line about it being a distant relative and that I was trying to trace my family's working history; but if I knew that I wouldn't need to search anymore.

My phone vibrated in my pocket. I had a message! This time it was from James. I was stunned; it had been a few days since he'd had any contact with me, I pushed the view button.

HI, REALLY SORRY MATE. CAN WE TALK? CAN I CUM OVER AFTER WORK

Relief flooded me. Finally my best mate wanted me again. I immediately replied

YES. C U THEN

I text Suzi to let her know, she replied simply saying

GOOD. TXT ME AFTER. I'LL COME ROUND. S X

James turned up from his job as a car sprayer at about a quarter to six. At first he still seemed a bit awkward, almost clumsy. I made the usual chat, 'How are you?' he nodded for 'good' 'What you been up to?' He shrugged his shoulders – which I took it as meaning 'not much'. I made coffee before we sat at my computer.

SORRY HAVEN'T BEEN IN CONTACT, I DIDN'T NO HOW TO HANDLE IT, EVERYTHING FROM THE ACCIDENT. I BLAMED MYSELF REALLY. AND THE BONES???

He hesitated as he typed the last word and question marks as if he was scared they would jump up and bite him.

"Why? It was my fault, not yours" I said staring at the screen as if the words would magically appear in front of me. "It's been hard for me, I just need my friends around me." I paused "I don't know what to say about the bones. I have more questions than answers." I guessed James didn't really want to talk about them, 'the how's' and 'wherefores' so I left it at that. "Anyway" I continued "It's not the same playing 'Rally Driver' on my own and Suzi's no good! You've seen her driving"

YES. WELL I THOUGHT IT WOULD GIVE U CHANCE TO GET BETTER, U NEED PRACTICE.

"Do you want to try your luck, ace?"

I WOULD BUT I'VE SEEN WOT U DO 2 CARS.

He looked at me pondering what my reaction would be.
"That was below the belt"
We both laughed.
Everything was back to normal now. We communicated via the computer for another hour before switching to computer games. Sometimes I asked James to speak the words so I could try to read his lips rather than the words on the screen. It was so difficult, I only managed the odd word, if I was lucky. It was useful; I knew I would have to do more of this eventually. I still felt a little deflated when he left because I was on my own again. For a few hours things had seemed normal again. I had my friend back and that was important.

Texting Suzi about 11pm I was surprised when she said she

would come over.

I told her everything about the dream the previous night and James, in no particular order. Trying to read Suzi's lips I kept drifting off, imagining myself kissing them, so gave up and resorted to the screen again. I was relaxed with life and by the time Suzi left, about one in the morning, kissing me on the cheek, I felt really good about everything. I watched until her car pulled out of sight willing her to change her mind, park again, and come inside, she didn't.

For the first time since being home I went to bed feeling happy and content, sleep coming easily as I let my thoughts paint pictures of Suzi and I together.

A little hand slid into mine and looking down I saw Sarah. We were in Southend, standing at the top of Pier Hill, looking at The Royal Hotel. It looked amazing in its regal splendour. I'd only ever seen it in its current state, when it was used as a place for the homeless and immigrants. Here it stood, like a palace looking over the worlds longest Pier which as I viewed it was barely 400 yards in length and only just running to the Pavilion where I knew the bowling alley used to stand before a fire destroyed it.

People were bustling about and there was a buzz of excitement in the air. The gardens were being tidied and planted. Everything about the hotel was being cleaned and polished, more excessively than you would expect for a normal day. Suddenly a man came out calling the people to order. They quickly finished what they were doing, put their tools and cleaning equipment away and disappeared.

A carriage pulled up flanked by riders on horseback. Everyone was immaculately turned out, every button polished, every piece of lace carefully placed. Out stepped Queen Victoria on one of her regular holidays to the area and in particular that hotel.

Sarah led me to the Cliff-top gardens just a short walk along from the hotel. The Queen was out with her entourage, followed by reporters, there was obviously a specific reason for the occasion but it was not obvious to me. In the background, a man was working, pruning some roses. As he turned I recognised him straight away. It was our man! He was dressed in smart, clean work clothes for the occasion. The Queen briefly spoke with him before moving on again.

Sarah took my hand and the image around me changed. It was early evening, the sun low in the sky. The shops were all shutting their doors and our man was buying an evening paper from a newspaper seller standing on the corner of Alexandra Street. On the front page, there was a headline that read, 'Queen visits Cliff-top Gardens to see a new species of Rose named in her Majesties honour'. I skimmed through the article as best I could, but it became too difficult to read as the man walked away.

The scene changed again. I was standing in the Kursaal Gardens. Our man was walking away holding a young boy's hand. I looked around expecting to see some parent looking out for their child, but was presented with a calm and tranquil scene with no anxious people anywhere. Did nobody care? I asked myself.

I awoke but wanted to sleep, take in more of the dream see what happened next. I tried to relax and surrender to sleep. I prayed for Sarah to show herself. The more I tried the less tired I became and the less likely it was I would drift off. I didn't know why it bothered me so since there was nothing I could do. It was all still in the past.

I must have fallen asleep for suddenly it was the next morning. Initially I was stricken with panic; what had happened to the boy? Knowing I could do nothing only renewed my energy and gave me a new resolve. I had an idea of how to find out who our man was. I needed to go to the library.

Leaving my flat I didn't think twice about my deafness and in my excitement almost got run over at the first road I had to cross. Only because of the fact that I saw movement out of the corner of my eye was I saved, the car drove passed, the driver shaking his head disapprovingly. Knowing I might be able to uncover the identity of this mystery man had rallied my thoughts and made me careless. I was sure that the newspaper article would hold the final clue or even the answer. I couldn't be sure why, it was just a feeling I had.

It took me a while to find the paper I needed since I didn't have the exact date. When I did, I found the information I wanted.

QUEEN VICTORIA VISITS CLIFFTOP GARDENS

Queen Victoria takes in the local sights spending time to visit the luscious gardens that Southend has to offer. I spoke with the gardener, Thomas Richfield, who not only keeps the gardens so well ordered, but has also bred a new rose in honour of her majesty Queen Victoria, The Victoriana. Thomas said 'It makes it worthwhile to see the Queen appreciate Southend's great gardens. She said she liked the Rose.

I skimmed through the rest of the article which was brief but important to the local town.

I text Suzi my findings, she shared in my excitement and replied saying she had a few ideas of what to do next.

7

Suzi came round about half past six. She had suggested getting a take-out and I stupidly said I would cook dinner. For the first time since I moved into the flat, a year before, I was actually going to cook a proper meal for two, nothing flash or spectacular, just pasta and a side salad. At least that way it was going to be edible.

It did mean I had to visit the supermarket, a prospect that filled me with dread. On my own for the first time since my mother had left having stocked up my fridge and freezer. I knew this time would come eventually, my confidence had grown slightly over the past week and although I didn't usually talk that much when shopping, the thought that I might be asked something or need to ask for something was a concerning factor, at least in my dream world that wasn't a problem. Thank God for Sarah! Deep down I knew I had to do it. If my life was ever going to get back to as near to normal then I had to go and no amount of putting it off was going to disguise that fact.

It proved to be less traumatic than I had built it up to be, and walking home I was pleased with myself, a new spring in my step. I was looking forward to cooking for Suzi. To make the meal special I'd bought a bottle of red wine. This was the first time that we had ever shared a meal without James being present.

It was pleasant, if a little strange, to sit in complete silence, some conversation was usually good.

Afterwards we sat at the computer with our glasses filled, the alcohol made me feel relaxed.

"So what are your ideas?"

Suzi started to type before I had chance to indicate for her to look at me, I wanted to read her lips, at least attempt to. She started to but again I found myself getting distracted by temptation to kiss them. In the end I suggested using the screen saying 'it would be quicker', Suzi was adamant, now that I had initiated it, that we started my rehabilitation process to help me master this new skill. In the end we used a combination of both, the drink not aiding us at all and the more we drank the more we used the computer, thankfully.

"I have an Aunt who works for the council" Suzi used hand gestures to help my understanding of words "If you give me his name I will ask her if she can find out anything about him. It should be okay as it was so long ago. We can find out how long he worked for them and where exactly, maybe we can cross reference all that with missing person reports of the time."

"That sounds good but I still don't understand how all this is going to help. She pleads that I have 'to stop him because he hurts them'." I raised my hands up and made speech marks with my fingers. "This is all in the past; nothing we do now can stop what happened then."

"She obviously means you no harm as the Amulet is charmed to protect you from evil spirits. Although it is difficult to stop spirits if they want to communicate with you. You can tune them out, just like most people have to tune them in."

"How do I do that?"

"Practice. And control. Do you want to?"

I thought about it briefly "That's the strange thing actually, no. I can hear her. I suppose I find that reassuring in some way."

"Kinda makes sense. That was the doorbell." She had to repeat the word 'doorbell'.

James had decided to visit; he knew Suzi was there because her car was outside. I got another glass and he joined us.

As we started to relax Suzi and James started talking like we all did before the accident. Instantly I felt out of it, they were forgetting to type things and I couldn't lip read to even a degree of competency, and therefore found it difficult to follow what was being said. They were laughing and giggling and talking it was like watching a tennis match with words. I drank my wine solemnly and felt guilty when Suzi noticed immediately apologising for not thinking.

They devised a game using paper and pens, they would sit directly opposite me and point to who was going to speak next, they would ask me a question and I had to tell them the answer. Simple things; What is your name? Favourite colour? Then we swapped round and would put cotton wool in the others ears to make them deaf temporarily reversing the situation. This provided quite a lot of fun although the other had to write what the others had said in reply to questions. At least we were once again playing and laughing.

It was eleven thirty by the time James got up to leave. Suzi had told him about the dreams and the events. He didn't really comment. He said he would see us the following day and asked if we fancied getting a couple DVD's out, having a few beers and basically 'vegging'. We agreed.

Alone again Suzi asked if she could stay the night on the sofa as she didn't think it wise to drive after drinking. James had cycled round. I suggested she have the bed and I the sofa. She was adamant the sofa was fine as she had to get up for work. She kissed me goodnight on the cheek and we both went to our separate beds.

She'd left by the time I got up in the morning. I decided go to the library and see if I could find all the dates for the missing children between 1880 and 1920. I used a tenuous story of a great, great, grandfather who had vanished around 1886. The librarian pointed me in the right direction and didn't seem to have any problem making me understand her, although she tried sign language and I had to explain that I couldn't read it, she looked miffed that finally she had been able to use the skill only to find a person couldn't interpret it.

I had not had a dream that night and it felt strange, as though I had missed someone, a companion.

Only two references of missing children occurred in that time, where remains were never discovered. There were quite a few deaths but no notable murders of children that remained unsolved; it seemed to be a dead end.

Suzi came round early that evening after speaking to her Aunt who was delving into it and would let her know. Accurate records were a bit scarce at the time. Between us we seemed to be making little progress.

James joined us about an hour after Suzi arrived and we went out to get the DVD's, some beers and snacks then spent a thoroughly enjoyable evening doing nothing, reading the subtitles meant the films lost their edge. James and Suzi were staying over, James and I sharing the bed which left Suzi on the sofa again. James and I would normally have talked for a while, but under the circumstances it was not going to happen and I was disappointed.

I slept fairly restfully until I thought I heard a voice. I wasn't sure if I was dreaming or not, it sounded so real. I wondered whether my imagination was playing tricks on me. It told me '*Run, get away from him*'. Resting up on my elbows I took in the room, James was sprawled across the best part of the bed and had most of the duvet, luckily my flat was quite warm.

Forgetting my deafness I listened intently, but could hear nothing, reluctantly I lay back down and closed my eyes.

"*Get away from him. He is dangerous. He hurts us. He'll hurt you too.*"

"*What? I don't understand. Sarah, I am trying to help you but I don't know how I can help. This is history to me.*"

"*He hurts us*" Sarah's voice sounded distraught, it had always sounded so innocent, there was real fear there now.

"*Thomas Richfield, is dead. There is nothing I can do.*"

"*He is not dead.*"

I was perplexed by her answer, how can he not be dead? Sarah was standing beside me, I felt her hands slip into mine, she tugged lightly, pulling me to the right. We were standing in a park. The time seemed different from before. People were walking and children were playing. The clothes they were wearing looked to be from a different era. Behind the trees I caught a glimpse of a motor car. From the little I knew, I would have said 1920's.

"Is he in my time? Where are we?" I didn't recognise the park, it was large, stretching as far as the eye could see, trees lining the perimeter and they were the only visible signs of a barrier separating the play area from the streets beyond.

She took me to a sign nearby, 'Bonchurch Recreation Ground'.

As I studied the grounds it became clear but the area that I now knew as Bonchurch Park was a mere fraction of the original colossus that it occupied, as I saw it here.

A family walked by, Sarah pointed to the man.

"He hurts us. He is not dead. You must stop him. You are near him."

"But how? I don't understand."

The family, man, woman, and two kids became part of the revellers enjoying the summer sun. The man looked behind and smiled malevolently at us.

I immediately felt uncomfortable, the hairs on the back of my neck stood on end

I was back in my bedroom, groping for the amulet around my neck. I held it tight in my hand – it was warm, very warm, to the point where I thought it might burn me. I was wide awake. I knew I wouldn't get back to sleep so got up and made myself a drink doing my best not to disturb James – which is difficult when you can't hear the noise you're making. The kitchen clock showed the time as 5.37, closing the door I switched on the light, then the kettle. I stood there thinking about my dream, puzzling through it all. What had Sarah meant; 'He's not dead' and who was the man?

I jumped as a hand touched my shoulder, spinning round I saw Suzi looking slightly bleary eyed.

"You frightened the life out of me. What are you doing up?"

"Sorry. I saw the light on" She ran through the actions to explain what she had said, before I understood.

"Sorry, didn't mean to wake you. Do you want a coffee?"

She nodded 'yes'. "Couldn't you sleep?" she pointed to me and then put her hands together resting her head on them.

"Had another dream" I told Suzi about the dream whilst I finished making the drinks before we went and sat down on the settee, pulling the quilt over us, sitting shoulder to shoulder, our feet hooked up under our own bodies.

"He's dangerous. He is near. You must stop him."

"Where?"

I found myself awake again and the centre of attention. Suzi was staring at me, James standing in front of us. Their mouths moving in fast repetition but I couldn't follow the conversation between the two of them. My head felt weary and I let it rest on cushions behind allowing myself to drift off again.

I was standing in a garden, a long narrow garden, a back garden that belonged to one of a string of terraced houses. It was late evening; there was a deep hole behind some bushes in front of a short wooden fence that marked the boundary of the garden. The man we had seen earlier was just lowering something into the hole. A canvas bag of sorts, with a drawstring top, like the type I'd seen sailors carry in old films.

The man stopped what he was doing and looked directly at me, deep into my eyes, I felt unnerved. Could he see me? I didn't think that was possible, but he was staring right at me, almost penetrating my soul. Then he carried on as if nothing had happened. We watched as he bundled the bag into the hole, covering it over. He distributed the extra soil around other areas of the garden and planted some flowers and a small tree. By the time he had finished it looked like a normal garden that had just been dug, turned, and planted; no visible sign of the grizzly secret that it held.

I looked around hoping to recognise the row of houses but it didn't look familiar. Next, we were standing by a newspaper seller. On the 'A' frame board that stood in front of the stand was the headline

BOY AGED NINE MISSING

Over the shoulder of someone purchasing a paper, I briefly read the story;

Peter Smith – aged nine disappeared whilst playing in Bonchurch Recreation Ground, Saturday last. The Police are concerned about his safety. This is the first disappearance of a boy in the local area for nearly fifteen years.

The man whose shoulder I was reading over turned and faced me, our eyes met. Locked in confrontation; it was him again.

8

I was being shaken awake.

"Are you alright?" Suzi mouthed, it took a couple of attempts for me to understand her.

Suzi and James explained that I had been dreaming with my eyes open, my face showed that I was petrified.

"He saw me" my voice broke.

"Who saw you?" James asked putting his hand in front of my face and pointing to his eyes and then to me to help explain what he was saying.

"The murderer! The Man! But it's not Thomas Richfield." Their faces portrayed puzzlement.

"Who was it?" Suzi enquired, accentuating the movements of her mouth so I would understand.

"I don't know. Everything was different, different time. Not the 1880's, it seemed like the 1920's"

Suzi spoke next.

"What?" I couldn't follow her speech; she grabbed a pad and begrudgingly wrote out what she had said, I could see it was frustrating for them as it took so long to talk to me, whether writing or speaking.

DOESN'T MAKE SENSE. UNLESS GROUP OF THEM?

"None of this makes much sense anyway" I told them. Then in detail told them my dream and what I'd seen. It still left us at a dead end.

55

SO SHE ONLY COMES WHEN ASLEEP?

James wrote. I nodded agreement. He turned away in thought briefly before spinning round again to say something which I completely lost, he resorted to mime. I told him to write it down and then he became insistent that it had to be done this way it would help me. Now it was my turn to get frustrated as I was forced to play along. "Why don't you get hypnotised or whatever it is. You might be able to pick up more info." It took me ages to follow what James said, so many words that I didn't understand but James did his best, even if it was crude. Hypnotised he spelt by pointing to his HIP, then his NOSE, then EYES, and where I really couldn't get it, he wrote the words down. Suzi used the same format, it was painfully slow. I believed they thought they were helping and I suppose in a way they were but the conversation dragged along at a snails pace. How would I ever be able to communicate properly?

"It's not really that straight forward, Sarah obviously chooses when she wants to come, we can't force her. You've got to be careful not to upset the spirits - they can do a lot of harm" Suzi's reason was always sound advice.

I was taking this all in, but could see James was sceptical. We'd never really discussed this sort of subject before, Suzi had always been into witchcraft and spiritualism, she was quite frank about it, but she didn't force the subject onto people and unless it came up in conversation you would never know.

"There are charms and spells that you can do that help someone connect with a spirit. You have to be careful that the spirit doesn't take control."

"So why don't we try that then" James said as he turned away and I had to tap him on the shoulder.

"It is easy for you. It is not you that will have to face the consequences." Suzi replied.

"Yeah, but maybe it will give us more clues and answers. I

mean what have we got to lose? You can control things can't you Suzi?" James was almost goading Suzi, daring her, but it was me who would be taking the risk.

I didn't know how strong Suzi's power was, or whether I was prepared to put it to the test.

Suzi looked at me and I at her.

"I can if you want?" She let that sink in. "I will need to get a few things first though. I don't know what it will achieve in the sense of answers, but you'll be able to communicate with her more readily. It's like opening a door and depending on how strong the spirit is it might be difficult to close straight away. It's possible though. Once open it will take a while for you to learn how to control it. You must remember, if you let her she will take over. Do you think you can cope with that Peter?" I read that last phrase a few times, letting it sink in, thinking about possible consequences.

Both Suzi and James looked at me awaiting my answer.

What was being suggested sounded like a good idea. I didn't have a bad feeling about Sarah but did feel uneasy about the man that I had come into contact with who seemed to know about me. The amulet protected me from evil spirits but how would it react under these circumstances. I was wary. I'd seen films both documentaries and Hollywood style stuff, that showed the power that could be released. I thought to take all these with a pinch of salt would be foolhardy. I was only a risk-taker when I believed the outcome could be judged to be pretty certain or if it failed, the consequences would not be too detrimental.

This was a subject where I was in unfamiliar territory. Suzi would do her best, I knew that, and would not risk anything if she felt it was out of her league. But! What if things got out of hand? Would she be able to cope?

"Shall we go for breakfast down the arches, my treat? This is far too heavy a conversation for this time in the morning" That was my solution – postpone the answer.

We all agreed and left an hour later to have our full English breakfasts down at the seafront café. Our favourite eating place occupied one of the many arches underneath the road which ran down to the seafront.

We managed to waste the whole day doing nothing in particular which was nothing unusual. But we did avoid the main issue even though it raced round my head all day. We picked up take-away pizzas and headed back to mine for the evening to watch Sunday night TV rubbish.

Out of the blue I announced "I'll give it a go. If you feel you can control the situation, Suzi?" They both considered what I said for an instant before realising what I was agreeing to. What was I agreeing to? To open communication with Sarah! Was I being brave or just stupid? I prayed I wouldn't regret it.

"Are you sure?" Suzi asked looking as though she wouldn't have minded if I change my mind..

"If it will get the answers we require and you are confident that you can stop it at any time, then…" I stared at them both "… yes."

James seemed quite excited by the prospect as if it was a game. I suppose it was to him, to a certain degree. I noticed Suzi looked wary just before she left to go home to gather the things she needed.

James and I played Fifa 2000 while we waited for Suzi to return. Inside I turned over again and again what I had agreed to allow, questioning whether it was the right thing, and whether I would be safe, even though I trusted Suzi one hundred percent.

As usual, I won.

Suzi returned and started to prepare the room, moving the coffee table out of the way and pushing the settee back further against the wall to give us more room. Suzi started to stick masking tape to the floor and continued placing objects, mainly candles and a few coloured stones, around the shape she had marked out. Finally she put some bowls of spices or leaves or something in position. I watched with bated breath feeling a little anxious now it all was so real. James looked amused and excited. I had complete trust in Suzi, but when it came to things like this, I just felt uneasy. I had heard many horror stories of people who had messed around with spirits, stories where once the gateway was opened it had driven people to insanity or even, in some cases suicide. Whether these stories were true or not I could only guess. I had never been witness to anything like it.

She took her time to explain exactly what she had done writing down the procedure she would be following so I fully understood what was going on.

"I've set up the Star of Galesick." She pointed to it in the book she was reading from. It has eight points with a blessed candle on each point, between each point and the edge of the Octagon outlined in the centre. I've placed Rhune stones that represent the three levels of time, past, present, and future. At the top, set out perpendicular to the top point are three crystals representing the three levels of life. At the dead centre of the star, I've placed the Codah of Ixler for protection.

"Codah of Ixler?"

"It is allows communication and gives control of the flow, keeping out any evil that could be lurking in the area.

It looked like a lump of misshapen metal from a breakers yard.

"Pete if you sit just behind the Codah of Ixler."

"Cross legged? Or, on my knees?"

"Whatever is the most comfortable." Once I understood I did as instructed

"Now there is an incantation I have to say. If you just close your eyes and concentrate only on Sarah Couper. Clear your mind of all other things. If at any time you feel uncomfortable with anything, just say so and I can end it. Whatever you do don't leave the Star of Galesick or you will leave the gateway open. That can be quite dangerous depending on the spirit."

I gulped. I could feel the anxiety rising inside.

I looked at James, he had taken a seat in the armchair to the right of the chimney breast, with a beer in his hand looking almost bored. Suzi had resumed writing everything down and therefore was taking a long time to explain. I took up position, preferring to sit cross legged. The star was nearly six feet from point to point providing just enough room to take up residence. The heat from the candles made me even hotter than I already was so took off my shirt leaving my T-Shirt exposed.

Suzi took up position directly in front of me, also cross-legged. She placed the book in front of her and then took my hands in hers.

Suzi started to speak and I closed my eyes to concentrate.

This was it I thought.

In my mind I could see Sarah's face. I concentrated harder, emptying my mind of all the little things that seem to enter it at times like this, stupid things like my last holiday or the family dog, Max, that we used to have. Shortly the atmosphere around me changed and I couldn't feel Suzis' hands. It didn't feel as though I was in my lounge anymore. My eyes opened automatically.

I saw Sarah's parents grieving and felt a chill even amongst the warm glow of the candles.

A swirl of voices seemed to come at me from every direction, different children's voices. I couldn't make out what they were saying until a solitary voice spoke clearly amid the furore, beckoning me closer. It was Sarah.

"I need more information as to how I can help you" I said following my instincts.

"He hurts us. Only you can stop him."

"I know but he is in the past and I cannot change the past, Sarah; you must tell me more."

"He lives on."

"I don't understand." I could sense my voice rising, I wanted answers not riddles.

"I have shown him to you."

"You showed me two different people."

"They are the same."

"How? They can't be. It's impossible."

"He knows you are here. Help us. He hur...."

Sarah's voice broke and I felt a tight grip around my heart, a crushing grip, squeezing the life force out, I found it difficult to suck in air.

"Go now, he knows"

I struggled to speak, the breath from my body all but gone. I wanted to alert Suzi to bring me back, but I couldn't, I felt myself gradually losing consciousness.

Everything was quiet, dark. I was lying on my back facing a ceiling. I was being held down and could see figures out of the corner of my eye - all dressed in ceremonial robes just like the ones I'd seen before. A woman was just getting up from being bent over me. She stretched her hands as high as they would go and said some strange words. I watched her as she got up and walked over to another area where a second woman was being held on a table. The second woman was still, she seemed reposeful, and looked heavily pregnant. The lady in the robes bent over her and said some words that I couldn't make out. Then slowly put her mouth to the woman's. I saw the chest of the woman raise slightly.

The woman awoke and let out an ear splitting scream before sleeping again.

The grip on me loosened and I got up. When I looked back down I saw a body lying where I had been. It was Thomas Richfield.

I looked around the place. It was a large hall with no distinguishing features just a normal run of the mill hall. Various doors ran off the main area, probably leading to kitchens and toilets.

The body of Thomas was carried out through a door at the far end; I followed. A large furnace was already roaring away lighting the room. Carefully the two large doors were opened and the body tossed in like a discarded piece of rubbish.

I walked back out of the room. The pregnant woman was still lying on the table seemingly unconscious. The woman in red robes stood at *one end chanting from a book she held, it was a language I couldn't understand. I reached to grab the book; I wanted to take it and run.*

Sarah appeared beside me, she tugged at my hand.

"Twenty one......" was the last thing I heard

Back in my lounge I sucked in air as if I had been holding my breath to set a record, the air rushing down tickling my throat, I coughed and spluttered regaining my composure. Suzi pulled at my hands. I looked at her. Sweat was pouring from me.

"Are you okay?" she was asking although it took a while for me to comprehend.

"I think so. Sarah was just about to tell me something. What happened?"

"You were trying to get up. I had to bring you back. You were going to leave the Star of Galesick. I couldn't let that happen" Suzi spoke facing me trying to enunciate each word clearly but she still had to grab the pad and pen.

"Something about twenty one. She didn't get a chance to finish."

MAYBE SHE KNEW IT WAS MY BIRTHDAY SOON!

James imparted, writing it down for me with a smiley face underneath. I gave a sarcastic smile.

"Yeah right! You never did take this seriously" Suzi said.

YOU ARE NOT SURE WHAT SHE WAS RELATING IT TO?

she asked me.

"Well, it's all mumbo jumbo really" James interspersed.

"So what do you reckon happened here tonight then?" Suzi retorted, I could see her getting annoyed with James.

James didn't reply to that, I think he just preferred to pretend not to believe. It made him feel more comfortable.

PROBABLY TWENTY ONE VICTIMS.

James wrote and spoke at the same time.

"Maybe" I replied.

I explained to them everything that had happened, and all that I had seen. Suzi knew of many cults that did unusual things and said she would see what she could find out. James sat there, except for the odd comment making mockery of it all, although the comments lost their impetus as he had to write them down.

As it was getting late James got up to leave.

"While we on the subject of twenty one, it is my twenty first in two weeks, I thought we might go away for the weekend, if you fancy it. Whizz over to Amsterdam? I've got a voucher for a car and up to four adults. We can find somewhere to stay once we're over there."

We both agreed.

After helping Suzi clear up the things on the floor, once James had gone, we sat on the settee not speaking. I was still a little unsettled. Suzi held my hand reassuringly, finally I asked her to stay over; she agreed.

"I'll get the duvet."

"I'll just share your bed if that's alright with you. I think I can trust you by now."

9

I watched Suzi sleep until I too was taken. Knowing she was beside me made feel comfortable about the silence of the night. I let images of what I'd seen replay in my mind, trying to decipher what it all meant. Twenty one, the pregnant woman, Thomas Richfield; Why had Thomas' body just been burned like that? Why not a proper funeral? Who were those people? Sarah said 'he knows'; knows what? How could he know about me? She was still showing me historical events, their timeline had gone. Nothing I did now could change them, I was merely viewing. Yet there was something strange about this second man, he looked directly at me. Who was he?

Thomas was dead, I saw it, yet Sarah says he isn't and he needs to be stopped. There were so many open ended questions. Suzi would have been my reference point but she didn't seem to be able to shed any more light on the subject.

The ceremony, I believed was of significance, otherwise why was Sarah showing me? She didn't seem to be giving me answers, only clues, yet she wanted me to stop him. Why didn't she just give me the answers? Was something stopping her? I couldn't think of what, unless there was an unwritten rule about what information spirits could pass on. Was it like an elaborate game?

A hand on my arm jarred my thoughts, I opened my eyes. Suzi was asleep next to me. I could just make out her body shape under the duvet in the dim moonlight that shone through the thin curtains. I scanned the room, searched every nook and cranny. The hand felt so real, and I didn't think I had been dreaming. I had kind of hoped it was Suzi's but I knew it wasn't. I lay back down and closed my eyes, holding the amulet in my right hand.

"I know who you are. You can't stop me, so don't even try" came a voice thick with malice which chilled me to the core.

Sitting bolt upright I searched the room with my eyes, disbelieving caught between reality and dreams, part of me knew that I could not be harmed by a spirit from eighty years ago, but a part of me was beginning to wonder if that was true. Had we opened the gate, as Suzi suggested was possible? Or, was this just my imagination being over-active in the night?

"He knows who you are. You are in danger now as well. You must stop him"

Was this real or a dream? The borders were beginning to blur.

"Who is he? I don't recognise him. I need more information to track him down. What were you going to say about twenty one?"

"I can't tell you. I am not allowed. You must find out."

"Where can I find out what I need to know?"

"You have all the information near you, now just open your mind"

I was standing at another gravestone 'Peter Michael Stane – 1912 – 1919' I looked around; Sarah was nowhere to be seen. The man was there. He was looking straight at me from behind the gravestone. I could feel his cold and heartless stare penetrating my being. He smiled a dirty, horrible, evil smile, then turned and walked out of the cemetery. I followed.

When I reached the corner of the road he had disappeared from view. I studied the area. It was unfamiliar to me. I didn't recognise the church. Even though I wasn't a church goer I knew them as landmarks, and as most of them don't change from one century to the next, I thought I should recognise this one.

I carried on walking and came to an intersection I did recognise, in Rochford, not far from Market Square; this was a turning which I never knew had a church. I was not far from the Scout hut that occupied an unusual shaped plot, just before the Old Ship Pub.

I walked away from the square for want of a better place to go. It was early evening and the sun was low in the sky.

Sarah, was by my left side, "You are in danger. Leave!" I ignored her plea, drawn on by curiosity. I wanted answers to the many questions and as I wasn't getting them in the real world then I would have to search for them here and now. I wasn't sure how much control I actually had, or if I would be able to run from danger should it occur.

"I don't...How?"

A mass of people appeared to my right. I felt safe, because I wanted to believe that. Sarah tugged at my arm.

"Go now, you are not safe."

Hands suddenly grabbed at me pulling me in all directions.

"No. Let go!" I shouted. My words were empty and hollow.

I was hoisted off the ground and into the air. Men and women all around dressed in the red robes I'd seen before. There was a symbol on the front of each, it looked like a backwards 'C' with a cross through it. I was being carried passed the Old Ship Pub and down an alleyway to the side of the scout hut. I could see Sarah standing, watching helplessly. An overwhelming sense of betrayal came over me for not heeding her warning.

"You must leave now" she said to me. She was far away yet when she spoke she sounded so close. I was being controlled by the throng of people; no matter what I tried they held me tight. I couldn't get free.

Still Sarah hastened me to leave before it was too late.

I was carried into the hut - it was the hall I'd seen before - and laid out on a table, held firmly in place. I tried to reach for my amulet but their grip was too tight. I couldn't understand how they could have a hold of me, it was all too strange. To me this was a dream, yet this was happening. I couldn't fight my way free.

I was shaking, physically shaking. A woman at the top of the table was chanting words in a different language. My breath was short. Sarah was urging me to leave. But how?

My body became sluggish. I was succumbing to whatever enchantment or spell they were casting. I could feel my will power failing me.

"Go now before it's too late" Sarah said "Your friend is trying to help, let her in."

"But I can't h…"

"Peter, come back to me" said a voice that was familiar yet it wasn't Sarah.

"I can't break free, help me please…" I heard myself speak wearily

The chanting was louder and stronger, all the men and women around the table had joined in.

Everything went black, and silence resonated around my head.

Taking in a deep breath I re-inflated my lungs which felt as though a vacuum had occupied the space, coughing as the air passed down my dry throat. Reaching over I grabbed the cup of water from my bedside table drinking as if I hadn't drunk for a week. The clock read '3.57am'. There was a tug at my arm, Suzi was sitting upright. Laid out on the bed was the book she had used earlier, two candles on saucers, and a sign drawn on a piece of paper that was an eye in the centre of a square. In her hands she held two of the Rhune stones. She smiled and cleared the bed.

Placing my hand on the amulet, it was hot. I lifted it slightly, the skin underneath was still warm. Suzi pushed my hand slightly to one side and touched the skin where it had been, she told me it was red and I understood her. I got up and looked in the mirror in the hallway. Sure enough it had left a mark from the heat.

Suzi followed a couple of minutes later carrying the book, wearing one of my shirts as a nightshirt. She didn't have a model figure, but she looked every inch as sexy as I had painted her to be in my head. The shirt hung on her perfectly, accentuating all the right places. I glanced back in the mirror.

"I thought you said this would protect me. I don't understand what was happening" I was frightened and my words came angrily.

U WERE TALKING TO SOMEONE. WHO?

Suzi thrust a piece of paper towards me.

"Sarah. She was there. She was telling me to go. But I couldn't get free. I was being held down. How was that possible? I thought it was only a dream and I was just viewing past events. How can I be part of that?"

I DON'T NO.

Suzi walked back into my room and retrieved the book, she opened it at a page and indicated for me to read. The Amulet was 'The Ochma of Ophidia' The god of protection against evil spirits. Ophidia was said to have battled Zentab the Gatekeeper of Hell and won, as Zentab died a great rockslide buried Ophidia. He survived, this mark was left on him as a permanent reminder of the battle and it is said that that is what saved him from death under the tons of rock. Despite being just a myth, it has been proved to work over the centuries.

MIGHT NO SOME 1 WHO WUD NO Y DIDN'T WORK AND Y BURNT LIKE THAT

"Who's that?"

MY GUIDE NANCY. I'LL SPEAK TO HER LATER TODAY

"Sarah said 'my friend knows'. She can't tell me directly. I think she meant you"

Suzi looked puzzled. I told her about the symbol on the robes. It didn't ring any bells with her, but she had some reference books that we could use at her house. She suggested I come round after she finished work.

It was half past six by now so we had breakfast and she left to go home and get ready for work.

That night at Suzi's house I sat on her bed sifting through the books to see if I could find the symbol I'd seen, whilst she rang her friend Nancy. I found nothing that looked familiar to me. There was some interesting stuff which I glanced at, but not relevant. Suzi was on the phone for about half an hour.

NANCY LOOKED INTO. NOTHING SPRANG TO MIND. PUZZLED Y AMULET DIDN'T WORK. WILL CALL ME LATER. U HAD ANY LUCK?

"No. Nothing"

She asked me to describe the symbol again. I drew it on a piece of paper instead. We searched every book she had to no avail. Finally we fired up her laptop and surfed the web. There were some specialist sites she knew where she could look up unusual information. Then she scanned in my drawing and sent a few emails. All we could do now was wait.

"That's weird" I said startled a little. The amulet had started to get warm

As Suzi held it in her hands, her face showed her puzzlement. She picked up the handset of the phone from her bed where she had left it.

"It's James" she mouthed at me
"Say 'Hi'"

BOWLING TONIGHT??

"Yeah fine with me."

With James and Suzi around I had all the confidence I needed to face the outside world and act as normal. We arranged to meet at 9pm. We hadn't heard anything from Nancy by the time we left Suzi's. I was in a funny kind of limbo, I had certain knowledge, limited to what I was allowed to know. The answers were to be found somewhere and right now that lay with Nancy who I'd never heard of before, but who was obviously close to Suzi.

On the car journey the Amulet was making its presence known, it had been fine all day. I couldn't understand why now it was so alive.

"You must get away, he is close."

My head and shoulders shot backwards into the seat, I hadn't realised that I'd drifted off. I hadn't been tired all day but alive with nervous tension.

We parked behind The Kursaal Bowling alley and went inside. I found the flashing lights of the arcade machines a little disorientating at first, hushed in silence. Balance was my biggest hurdle; I know I had been a little unsteady on my feet but now it seemed as though I was completely drunk, I kept bumping into Suzi and James. I began feeling self conscious and didn't know if I would be able to bowl without causing injury to me or someone else. We went to the bar after paying for the lane; we were a little early so we found a table to sit down at. The amulet seemed to be getting hotter.

"Danger, you must leave" Sarah said.

This time I was awake, I knew I was. James and Suzi were looking at me. I held the amulet.

I could now see Sarah standing in front of me, she had something in her hand.

"Go, his power grows." She turned to go and dropped what she held. I made an immediate attempt to grab for it.

The table hampered my progress and I managed to send the drinks flying, the table righted itself and James put his hand out to steady me. The amulet sent a shock wave into my body as it became instantly red hot. I ripped it from my neck throwing it onto the floor where it landed in the spilt drinks sizzling, sending small steam clouds into the air, the glass shards shattering.

I gave a shocked look to Suzi who was perplexed. Other people were staring at me and I became uncomfortable, not sure what to do. I did the only thing I could and battled my way past everyone to head out into the night, not sure whether I was scared or annoyed. Frustration was brimming out of me, driving me along. I ran across the road to the sea wall and just stood there staring out to sea wondering whether I was going mad.

A minute or so later I felt a hand on my shoulder. I turned and saw Suzi standing there. I immediately hugged her, she reciprocated. James followed a few seconds later stopping short of where we were shooting a look of disdain at me that could have stopped even a ferocious animal in its tracks. He turned and walked away.

Suddenly I felt so safe and warm in Suzi's arms. I held her tighter. She didn't break away. Then after a while she withdrew slightly, looked at me and without saying a word, kissed me gently on the lips. A flood of emotions ran through me making me forget everything that had just happened.

I was surprised as much as pleased. Watching James walk off in the distance I still couldn't stop myself, her warm lips enticed me further, the kiss was deep and lingering.

10

I stayed the night at Suzi's for the most part wrapped up in each others arms. For her parents, Martin and Vanessa, having boyfriends staying over was not a problem as they were quite liberal-minded people. They countered any arguments saying, 'I would rather know that she is safe', and, 'it takes the pressure off the sexual side of things' meaning they felt that having the sanctuary of your own home to experiment in you would be more likely to take the relevant precautions. They didn't want Suzi's life to be any more difficult than it had to be. They preferred it if she didn't, however, they lived in the real world.

Refreshed and alive I was full of the joys of spring. I hadn't admitted to myself how much I had wanted to be more than just friends with Suzi. She was curled up in the foetal position, her naked back facing me, my right arm around her waist with my hand on her left shoulder, her hair like a dark mane down her back. She stirred only to put her right hand on mine our fingers intertwining, a gentle squeeze, life couldn't get any better. Her sweet essence and soft skin was heaven; she softly kissed the back of my hand. A smiled oozed across my face and I inched even closer and lay lost in the tranquillity of the moment.

I thought back to the previous night, after the Bowling Alley and came alive as the warm feelings swarmed over me again. We'd walked along the seafront holding hands no need to exchange words we just let the evening wash over us, before heading back to Suzi's.

Suzi had had a message from Nancy on her phone asking us to go round Tuesday night about seven thirty. Abruptly the alarm went off and as Suzi stirred I knew this moment had to end, how time flies. Reluctantly I let her go, she glanced back at me as she left the room and smiled an encompassing smile. After coming back from the bathroom I watched her get dressed, her playful curves disappearing from sight. We kissed goodbye, a long lingering kiss and she left to go to work. She didn't eat breakfast all the time, she offered me some but I declined; too happy to be hungry.

She picked me up at about seven to go to see Nancy, who lived in a one bedroomed flat in Southchurch, Stromness Road, a road that had, like many in the area, gone through a radical state of flat conversions in the 1970's & 1980's. We rang the doorbell and waited. I was unsure what to expect of Nancy; Suzi had never talked about her before yet it seemed they were close. It's surprising how little you can know someone.

The woman that appeared at the door was in her mid thirties, short cropped hair, about 4' 8" and wore jeans and an Iron Maiden T-Shirt saying 'Can I play with Madness?'.

"Hi come in" she mouthed and I found her lips uncannily easy to read - she made the point of looking at me directly when she spoke, a part of my brain seemed to fill in the silence and it was as though I wasn't lip reading at all, almost like she was using ESP.
Her flat was very modern, no fussiness and the furniture purposeful. Rugs strategically covered the wooden laminate flooring that ran throughout every room we saw as we were led into the lounge where we sat down on a Settee.

Nancy and Suzi started conversing, I tried to follow, but kept getting distracted by the little nik-naks scattered around the room.

Suzi nudged me and indicated she wanted the sketch of the symbol I'd seen on the robes; I withdrew it from my pocket and showed it to Nancy, her brow furrowed as she studied it intently, seemingly thinking about it as if in a deep dark recess of her mind she held a memory of it. She clicked her fingers in confirmation and disappeared from the room. Suzi squeezed my hand gently, smiling reassuringly. Searching her pocket with her other hand she pulled out the amulet which I'd forgotten all about. I touched my neck and could feel the raised skin where it had burned me. Suzi held it but did not try to give it back to me and I didn't try to take it.

Nancy reappeared a few minutes later carrying two books, one fairly small like a paperback novel, the other a large encyclopaedic type bound in leather with faded gold embossed writing on it. She passed me the smaller of the two which was wedged open by one of her fingers, opening it I saw the symbol. Underneath were listed its titles 'Drysidium Cross or Hultatim Jistata'. There was a short passage which I read:

The Drysidium Cross represented the order of the Hiotym. Muthia was their High Priest and they prayed to the god of Avaron, offering sacrifices every full moon. Part of the sacrificial rituals involved drinking the virginal blood of the sacrifice which would be a child under sixteen. This ritual was known as 'Ghanuti' or 'Transcenden of Souls'. 'The Circle' consisting of the High Priest; The Vexicon, the bringer of the sacrifices; The Numeratist,(who studied the ancient Germanic Alphabet where each rune would have it's own magical significance), aligned the points of Gafta; they would all gather at the Acratic Altar at the eleventh hour of the full moon.

The first part of the ritual was held in private with just the three present, then after the first Orbitol they would be joined by their followers and proceed with the second and third Orbitol.

When any of the circle came to the end of their life then the ritual of 'Nankamari' or 'Breath of Life' would be performed. This allowed the spirit of the dying member to pass into the body of an unborn child. The child when born would be protected by the Circle, until the age of twenty one when the child would be taught to perform 'Hijolter' or 'The Rising of the Soul' which brings to life the resting spirit within and then takes over the carrier.

The Hoitym existed in 18th century Mongolia. When King Kansu came to the throne in 1737 he outlawed the Hoitym and hunted them down until many switched their worship to either Tibetan, Buddhism, Muslim, or Shamanism, to avoid execution.

For about another five years after there were references found, but they were relegated to the history books.

Nothing about them is known to exist today.

I looked at Nancy and then to Suzi. "What does all that mean?"

"That, we don't know at the moment. But this is what that symbol represents. What the connection is between them and your dreams, I'm not sure" said Nancy speaking clearly to me, unusually clear. I was pleased with the relative ease with which I understood her.

"What's the other book for?"

"If you are willing I'd like to try something, a little experiment. I think there are some strange forces at work, strong forces Suzi was not expecting" Suzi looked a little put out. Nancy turned to her and smiled, said something that placated her, then continued "Is that okay?"

I sat and thought about it a little wary after my last experience yet resigned to the fact that if I was going to do anything then it had to be now, hopefully with more to gain, this time. Every apprehension in me wanted to say 'no', reluctantly I agreed.

Nancy disappeared from the room again. Suzi smiled at me, I reciprocated letting my affection show, my eyes wandered over her body, I had started to look at her in a different light and it was nice - a warm fuzzy feeling.

Nancy returned carrying a few of what looked like trinkets beckoning me to sit on the floor cross legged in front of her, as she did the same.

Around her neck she was wearing a large necklace that I hadn't noticed before. It looked like a giant silver eye. She turned my hands palm up and rested them on my knees, in each she placed a different stone, one that looked like black Onyx to me but was actually Hematite, the other a luminous red stone which I was told was Carnelian.

She spoke something I couldn't follow as her words no longer echoed in my head. She placed more trinkets in between us, in one long line, five items, all silver in colour, non-descript lumps of metal.

Nancy repeated what she was saying. I glanced at Suzi, who sat watching. A strange feeling shot down my spine making my eyes go wild, the muscles in my hands contorted and became engulfed in an irritating warmth. The smell of burning filled my nostrils, a putrid smell that made me cringe. I went to say something but found the room around me had disappeared, a grey mist encapsulating me. Swirling clouds, dark grey, hints of black. I looked down at my hands; the black stone was glowing, radiating an immense white light. The Carnelian stone emitted a shard of light that made contact with the mark the amulet had burned on my skin, it was freezing cold but still caused a burning sensation. Immediately my breathing became difficult.

Back in Nancy's lounge she was looking at me. The Hematite stone was scorching my hand and I released it, studying the area where I expected to see a mark, there was none. Nancy turned her head to Suzi and spoke. Suzi nodded and left the room, barely thirty seconds later returning with a book. Nancy took the book and searched through. Dazed and bewildered I looked at Suzi who shrugged her shoulders.

Nancy showed the book to me.

For confirmation that a person may be possessed by a spirit use:
Rites of Passage:-   Deal of Division
                         Entira Con dryduis escalata

Place the Marks of Trino out in a long line in front of the subject, placing the Stone of Aquaritum in right hand and Stone of Equimartum in the left. Repeat incantation above. The Stone of Aquaritum will glow white if victim is not possessed, burning cold and will not leave a mark.

If possessed the The Stone of Equimartum will glow red and burn, leaving a blistering burn in the palm"

Nancy and Suzi both seemed pleased with themselves and quickly became embroiled in a conversation I couldn't follow, I started to feel tired and looked around the room slowly drifting off.

"Time is running out. He will be again. He'll hurt us" Sarah's scared voice penetrated my thoughts again.

She showed me another grave, 'Henry William Smith, 1923-1931'. From what I could see we were standing in the Church yard in Rochford, not far from where I had been dragged off. I walked slowly to the hall, ever conscious of what happened last time, surprised by my own actions and nervous that I was here again. The streets seemed tranquil, like a Sunday afternoon. I could see the hall in front of me. I watched the area closely, prepared for any movement. Sarah was by my side.

Walking down the narrow alleyway that led around the building I looked for a way in. The door was locked but a nearby sash window was slightly ajar, pushing it up silently I checked there was no one in sight, all was quiet.

The window was higher than normal from the ground but with only a little struggle I was in, standing on the floor of a kitchen. A large wooden table occupied the centre of the floor space and a dresser was at one end with crockery neatly stacked. A sink was in the corner to my left with a wooden draining board. Serving hatches were opposite the window and they were of mottled glass, again sash type, a door was to the right of these.

The door led into a corridor which had various other doors leading off. The walls were wood panelled, the floor parquet. No one was about which gave me an uneasy feeling, Sarah was still behind me. It was bizarre, I was looking for something and I didn't know what, Sarah was observing, like a teacher does sometimes to make sure you are doing it correctly.

Trying the first door on my left - it was locked, as was the door next to it. Another door further along on the right was ajar. I pushed it open slowly keeping a watchful eye for any movement, there was none. It looked like a normal sitting room, a few armchairs, a couple of occasional tables with lamps on, the few windows that there were all had patterned curtains neatly tied back.

A shove from behind sent me hurtling to the floor, my breath knocked from me. I became icy cold. I tried to turn but a foot crashed down on my right leg deadening it. I was hauled up to a kneeling position, my calf muscle feeling the weight bearing down on it.

A firm hand on my throat left me fighting for breath. A face loomed up close to mine and looking deep into the eyes of the man before me I saw they were dark and cold; void of emotion.

Something silver flashed in his free hand and a knife was thrust to the hilt into my chest. Shock registered as I felt the initial burn of the wound. He let go of my throat. I stood looking at the handle of the knife that protruded from my chest.

My assailant smiled and turned to walk away.

Sarah was in the doorway but the man just walked straight through her and out of my sight.

11

A hand landed on my left shoulder. Sarah was still watching at the doorway as another landed on my right. Gently but firmly I was pushed to the floor face up. My consciousness was fading, a fogginess clouding my vision. A woman wearing the robes I'd seen before looked down at me, her eyes warm and kind, in an instant they changed to pleasure and cunning. Kneeling above me she leant over and put her lips to mine. Already too weak to fight I could hear chanting in the background, soft at first, slowly it increased in volume. I became aware of more people surrounding us.

I started to go numb as everything faded to black. The discomfort from my wound dissipated and cold entered, life was leaving me. I wanted to fight, to struggle, but it was beyond any strength that I could muster and I entered into a sort of limbo.

Opening my eyes, it was dark. I was in bed. Was it my bed? It felt strange and unfamiliar. Sitting up I tried to decipher the shapes in the room, an alarm clock sat on the bedside table, it was round with bells on top.

Was I still dreaming?

This was more real. The bed covers were not of the softness of my quilt, more coarse, they were heavy blankets. The dark unfamiliar silhouettes resembled pictures I'd seen in books, a 1920's style wardrobe stood in one corner, a deep chest of draws against one wall.

I was wearing thick patterned rough feeling pyjamas. Once out of bed I pulled the thin curtains aside. The sash windows had tape running diagonally from corner to corner of the individual square panels. I turned and switched on the light, the room was sparsely decorated, pale green wall-paper, a threadbare carpet, and a small chest of drawers with a mirror on top. I walked over to the chest of drawers and looked in the mirror. The reflection was not me.

The face that came back was young, thick black hair, pale skin, piercing brown eyes. In confusion, I touched my face to see if it was real, I touched other objects in the room. They were all real. Outside I heard a siren go off, louder than anything I had ever heard before. I rushed to the window to see what was going on. The door to the bedroom was flung open and in marched a tall male figure wearing a plain dressing gown.

"What do you think you're doing? Get down to the air raid shelter now!" the voice was urgent and firm, but friendly. Before I had time to move I had been grabbed by the arm, a powerful grip biting into the muscle, my dressing gown taken off the hook on the back of the door and thrust into my arms. I was bundled down the stairs and out through the kitchen door into the garden with what, I assumed were the rest of the family. The next door neighbour joined us and we all scurried into the corrugated tin shelter at the bottom of the garden.

My mind was lost in the confusion of the situation. This was a vivid dream but very real, the sounds, the smells, the touch. I desperately looked round for Sarah half expecting her to appear and give me her stark warnings that 'he' must be stopped.

The air raid shelter was cramped and barely hospitable, each person vying for whatever space they could find. Pushed into a corner I was told to look after my younger brother. This eight or nine year old boy was thrust into my arms. With the door shut, all fell silent, listening, waiting in the darkness.

From my history lessons I guessed we were expecting a bombing raid and the year must have been sometime between 1939 and 1945. Who I was, why was I here? It was all a mystery.

We all huddled in the cramp conditions for what felt like hours, all remaining hushed as if it made a difference to the planes flying overhead. Cringing as we heard the whistling of bombs when they came hurrying down from the sky. They sounded far away, but when they exploded they seemed so close and dust would fall from the roof of the shelter. Suddenly I felt very vulnerable. Strange place, strange people, strange circumstances. Inside I was wishing that Suzi or Nancy could extract me from this dream that was fast becoming reality. In hushed tones I called their names repeatedly, they never came and the dream marched on. More dust fell from the roof of the shelter as another bomb landed close by. My supposed younger brother buried his head into my chest and I could feel muted sobs as each bomb exploded.

After a long period of nothing another siren went off and everyone left the shelter, the daylight dazzled me.

"Well son, not a good way to spend your twenty first birthday. Happy Birthday!" My supposed father patted me on the back then gripped my shoulder in a very fatherly acknowledgement.

"Thank you" I said half heartedly still disbelieving the reality I was in.

Where was Sarah?

Back inside the house we sat down to breakfast prepared by the mother. I was handed a package wrapped in brown paper and string. A bewildering and underwhelming experience for a 21st Birthday, I thought, but guessed that this was what it must have been like. Opening the package I let myself get taken in by the situation.

Suddenly knowledge started to flow into my brain, as if someone had cleared a blockage in my memory. Details of 'who' I was, friends, family. I had friends. I knew of them but it seemed so strange to go and see them because I didn't really know them. But my 'so called' parents asked if I was seeing them and I felt obliged to say 'Yes'.

I left the house after Sunday lunch, which was good, bearing in mind the rationing, but modest by the standards that I was used to. It humbled me.

I walked through the streets, not knowing where I was going but instinctively heading there as if led by another force. In a conversation earlier, with my so called mother, I discovered that I was born at 7.47 in the evening at Rochford Hospital on 28th June 1923 and I worked in the local printers.

I was walking along what I knew as the London Road when a friend came up behind me and tapped me on the shoulder. William, peculiarly

I recognised him, asked me if I wanted to go to the pub; we headed to the Cricketers.

We'd been in the pub a while when two more friends came in, John and Peter. Although money was short we still managed to have a good time and celebrate my birthday in a good old fashioned way, drinking. I was surprised how cheap everything seemed and found it confusing to use shillings. The barmaid was staggered by my obvious confusion with the change from a round of drinks.

Unexpectedly I started to feel strange, not ill. A dark mood settled over me and I was eyeing everyone with suspicion. I stopped laughing, made my excuses and abruptly left.

Walking back home, I became inexplicably contorted in pain, doubled up on the pavement. All my insides became cramped with uncontrollable spasms. The streets were dark as the streets lamps were not lit. I managed to crawl onto the entrance steps of the nearby Church where I lay in the protection of the giant stone arch that framed the entrance. I tried to call out for help but everytime I did, nothing came out, words in a vacuum. I lay there for some time.

At last the pain subsided as quickly as it had come. I had never suffered anything like it before and afterwards I felt invigorated, alive and strong, almost invincible. I checked my watch by the dim light of the night sky, a little after eight. Physically I was better, still a little peculiar almost as if I was not in control of my own body. In my mind I wanted to walk home but found myself walking in the opposite direction, positively, without hesitation. I turned right at the next junction and headed towards Hamlet Court Road, crossing over I turned left into Ditton Court Road stopping at the third house on the right. I looked up at it, sizing it up before opening the front gate.

The door was opened before I reached it and quickly I was guided inside without a word and led into a back room lit only by candles. A make-shift altar was erected in front of the drawn curtains. I knelt and placed my hands on the bottom of the Drysidium Cross.

"Ascoutar Resimure Detucteen Retarcus"

On the floor in Nancy's flat I was cringing as a burning

sensation manifested on my chest. I doubled over. Suzi rushed to my aid and I gripped her hand tightly, tears streaming from my eyes. The pain was intense. Suzi shouted something to Nancy who sat there and did nothing. A split second later the pain was gone and relief filled me. Wiping the tears away I was curious about my experience and more than a little scared.

Sitting up Nancy offered me a cup of water which I took and drank quickly quenching my thirst. Suzi helped me onto the settee.

Explaining what had happened Nancy gave a knowing look which I found curious and unnerving. Not once did Nancy seem surprised by the events, as if she expected no less. In return I expected some sort explanation.

Suzi expressed her shock at what I'd seen, Nancy remaining calm. Then she spoke to both of us.

"I knew there was more to this than what you had described, so the 'Deal of Division' was just part of the spell that proved you were not possessed. What I added at the end after you were under were the words" she wrote them out on a piece of paper 'Hifdeoto Likgotda Jigmata'

"It's nothing to do with the Drysidium Cross but part of the Faith of Glatheus. It binds you temporarily with the spirit that is trying to hurt you." Rage burned inside me how dare she take me further than I was prepared to go, the anger almost burst out. I thought this person was trying to help me.

"What?" I stammered too incensed to get my words out clearly "I thought... you were meant to be helping me, not making things worse" I stood up as if to go and stumbled as my legs gave way. Reaching out I clung to Suzi who had lurched forward when she saw me fall. I had so many questions yet was so angry that I wanted to leave.

Nancy got up and put a hand on my arm. I went to shrug it off, but her eyes calmed me, the rage leaving me. "Wait. By taking you deeper I could find out more. You were in no danger, I would not have done it otherwise. It merely binds you to the spirit. If I had seen you were distressed at any point I would have brought you out."

I felt betrayed and uncomfortable. and was not sure whether it was just down to the fact that I knew so little about this dark stuff that I now found myself embroiled in, or whether I didn't trust Nancy.

Half taking in what was being said between Suzi and Nancy I let my own thoughts distract me. Slowly it dawned that I could look up the person whom I'd temporarily taken up residence with as I knew his name and address. I could find out what had happened after that night of his twenty-first birthday.

Walking home with Suzi, I was cold towards her; something nagged at the back of my mind, a thought I couldn't quite work out. I decided I would do a little investigating on my own tomorrow, after work at the library.

12

It had been agreed that I would go into work at about 9.30am the next day for re-orientation with my department head, Phil. Although most off my work was on a PC apprehension still lingered at the thought of returning. How were people going to be towards me? If I needed more time off they had said that it was fine but maybe it would be best if I came back sooner rather than later, allowing time off to attend any appointments I might have.

When I arrived I could see Phil from the door, he was looking on edge and that made me peculiarly more comfortable, he was normally such a confident guy. It was strange being back; it looked the same but the peacefulness made it lose some of the warmth, the hustle and bustle didn't have the same charm. The office was open plan and when my colleagues saw me walk in they acknowledged me from their desks. If they said 'Hi' I couldn't tell, I just saw their mouths move. The post-room clerk was the only person to come over and shake my hand to welcome me back, nothing phased him.

I sat down at my manager's desk which was behind a wall of filing cabinets with only one side open to the full view of the main door.

He shook my hand muttering what I thought was an incomprehensible greeting. He wasn't a popular man but he was fair and looked out of sorts as we briefly sized each other up waiting for the first bite at communication. I watched as he nervously shuffled papers about his desk and wondered how he was going to tackle this tricky situation.

Phil, at first, tried to articulate his words, carefully and methodically, I tried to follow but we seemed to be getting nowhere so I asked him to use a word document on the computer. He was an efficient typist so it speeded things up and he visibly relaxed.

My duties as office administrator had been adjusted to suit my new condition. I could no longer answer the telephone or talk to my customers, people I had built up good relations with over the last year. The company was doing its duty by keeping a job open for me as I was now considered disabled in their eyes. They knew their obligations. I was lucky to live in such modern times, I thought, where email was used extensively, I enjoyed the communication with my customers, it was one of the points that attracted me to the job in the first place.

I decided that it might be best to stay rather than delay it another few days feeling it would aid my rehabilitation and integration.

Back at my desk I sifted through the mountains of paperwork that had been left for my return, most of it non-urgent matters. Some of it, over the course of the day I found had been dealt with. I smiled at colleagues who sat opposite, they returned the greeting but didn't try to converse with me, instead they looked awkward before fidgeting in their seats. That in itself made me self conscious.

Gradually through the day I ignored the occasional stares from people who didn't realise they were doing it, and enjoyed the steady flow of frowned upon internal E-mails, welcoming me back, asking how I was. My surroundings, which hadn't changed, felt completely different. I blamed the silence. A couple of times when I saw numbers I recognised flash up on the little display screen on the phone, I answered, expecting to hear a cheerful familiar greeting before remembering that it was pointless. I had to make my excuses and hope that I was understood.

Some colleagues came to say hello. It was difficult; lip reading was a skill I needed to learn and found people almost expected me to be able to do it already, like it was a seventh sense! People use their mouths in such different ways that at times I wondered if I would ever learn the skill. Simple things like 'Hi' looked so different for different people. Sometimes, when I didn't answer, people made their excuses, as if I would understand that better, smiled graciously and left. Phil checked on me a few times to make sure I was settling in okay. I was glad when the day had finished.

Suzi text a couple of times during the day to make sure everything was going well.

Mentally I was drained by the end of the day finding myself concentrating harder than I ever had done before, just to do simple jobs I knew backwards. Still, I was determined to go to the library. At least there I wouldn't feel so out of place. Silence was king.

Leigh Library was not as extensively stocked as the main library in Southend, but it had good links with it. I wasn't sure what I was looking for. 'Witchcraft' carried a large stock of titles. I narrowed my search to 'Drysidium Cross'. The information that I found was similar to what I had already read at Nancy's. Time was getting on and my stomach was rumbling so finished with a quick search through the history of the area via past newspapers.

The life scene I had been part of was 1944 but I didn't really know what I was looking for, just anything untoward, my name had been Charles. Although I didn't know the surname I flicked through the images that were thrown up on screen, nothing seemed to stand out and I was getting ready to leave as the library was due to close soon.

SUSPECTED WITCH CRAFT RESPONSIBLE FOR RECENT MURDERS

Was a side heading in one column. Taking the paper to a nearby photocopier, a message flashed up that I had to insert money. I fished around in my pocket and couldn't find any small change. Typical! Out of the corner of my eye I noticed a lady walking towards me, it was the lady from reception. I glanced at my watch and immediately realised that it was closing time. I put a pound in the money slot and the copier light flashed into operation and slowly an A4 sheet spun out.

The lady said something to me but I didn't pay attention just quickly thanked her and headed out of the building, paper folded in my hand. I tried to read as I walked but it was difficult to follow the words and look where I was going. My balance was still poor anyway although I didn't look as though I was drunk anymore. I folded it up and placed in my inside pocket.

At home I put a frozen lasagne in the microwave and read whilst I waited the eight minutes for it to cook.

The four children's bodies recently discovered in Westcliff, near the Railway station are thought to be the work of a local coven of Witches. There has been widespread rumour over recent months that a coven of witches has been operating in the local area. Strange goings-on have been reported, sightings of people acting out ritualistic ceremonies in the vicinity have been reported to the police, although no arrests have been made.

Police questioned local residents but nothing could be confirmed that is until the grim discovery on Monday of last week. Inspector Marshall wanted to keep it quiet initially until they had more information to act upon. No conclusions have been drawn yet and now police are appealing to the public for assistance with their enquiries.

The bodies were discovered by Stan Hummington in the early hours of the morning whilst walking his dog on the wasteland that runs alongside Westcliff Railway Station. Here he made the shocking discovery of a child's hand protruding from the ground.

Police scientists have not been able to discover a cause of death. The bodies were intact and showed no obvious signs of mutilation. One of the children, now known as Robert Simpson, aged ten, had been reported missing two weeks previously and feared dead in the bombing raid that took place around the time. Robert was said to have been holding a black shiny stone in his hand which must have burned red hot as it left it badly scarred.

The other children, Heather Rose, aged seven, Juliette Harris, aged nine, and William Jones, aged seven, have all been identified by their parents and the funerals will take place in individual ceremonies over the coming week.

The police are asking for any information to be directed to Chief Inspector John Marshall of Leigh Station.

The microwave timer showed zero and I grabbed the Lasagne, for some reason being deaf had made forget how hot it was still going to be and I nearly dropped it on the floor. Sitting down in the lounge to eat the lasagne my mobile vibrated in my pocket. Suzi was on her way round. A part of me wanted to text back and tell her not to come, still shaken by events of the previous night but I didn't know how without causing her to question my decision. It would have been easier if we were still 'just friends', so much had changed and I wasn't sure whether it was still for the good.

When she entered she gave me a hug and a kiss, I reciprocated but not whole-heartedly. I made her a cup of tea and as she sat on the settee I sat in the armchair, she gave me a little querying look and for an instant guilt ran through me. But before I could explain she started talking.

"What are we going to do for James's twenty-first?" Suzi spoke slowly still trying to help me with my lip reading, I wasn't in the mood.

"Oh god, I'd forgotten about that. When is it?"

NEXT WEEK, FRIDAY

she wrote on the pad from the coffee table

"What were you going to get him?"

"I don't know, I thought we.." she persisted with the lip reading but then saw I wasn't into trying and reluctantly continued on paper

JOINT PRESENT

"Could do. Don't know what though?..Hold on! Weren't we meant to be going to Holland for his birthday?"

YES. JAMES FOUND VOUCHERS OUT OF DATE. CAN'T AFFORD EITHER

"Oh"

U MUST NO WHAT? U SPEND NUFF TIME TOGETHER

"Yeah, but. I don't know, I'll have a think about it. Have you seen him recently? I haven't seen him for few days"

SPOKE YESTERDAY. A COUPLE OF RUSH JOBS OVERTIME

The more we talked the more I forgot about the previous day, her lips looked so luscious and there was a sparkle in her eyes that I couldn't resist and conceded by sitting next to her. The rest of the evening was spent huddled up on the settee watching TV. This was pleasant enough but I missed not having music in the background and talking normally.

"Time is running out, he will be loose again, you must be stop him."

"Sarah" I turned and saw her running off in the distance, I tried to follow but I found myself rooted to the spot on the pavement, a hand

on my shoulder, I turned and it was gone. I turned around again and standing there was the man I'd seen at the paper stand, he looked deep into my eyes and a chill froze my heart. I tried to make a sound but didn't have enough breath. I was weak and disconnected.

Reaching out I placed my hands on the mans shoulders to hold myself up. I was too far away, fading fast, vision was blurring.

"Go now before it's too late", the voice was faint but I knew it as Sarah's "you're stronger. You can fight it."

I wanted to answer, the grip on my heart was excruciating, like nothing I'd ever felt before. I mustered every last sap of energy. This was one of those vivid nightmares you get when falling and all of a sudden you wake before you hit the deck. However, that didn't seem to be happening, this was very much real and it was going to be played out to the bitter end. I scrabbled at the man's clothes, trying to shake myself loose. He just laughed an evil resonating laugh. The streets were empty around us and we were locked in combat. I was losing. Losing my life.

He came in close to me, his face a few inches from mine, my eyes were closing, his image becoming a blur. I felt his lips touch mine and my life force seemed to ebb away. All the muscles in my body relaxed.

Back in my lounge I was pushing Suzi away from me "What are you doing? What's going on?" I stated urgently, scared and unsure.

She grabbed the pad, whilst I stared at her confused

TRYIN TO KISS YOU!

She came in close to me again.

Looking at her in disbelief I gently held her back before getting up and walking away from her.

My breathing was rapid, my heart pounding in my chest. Suzi followed and turned me to face her, her hands gentle but firm on my arms.

"What's wrong? I was only trying to kiss you" she mouthed and I could follow it.

I stared at her for a long moment

"I think you'd better go"

Suzi looked hurt and as soon as the words had come out I wanted to retract them. It was too late. Suzi hesitated for a brief second looking deep into my eyes for an explanation, which I couldn't give. I had acted on impulse, irrationally, the real consequences I wouldn't know until tomorrow. Suzi gathered up her things, and left without looking back.

I headed to the front window and watched her walk to her little maroon fiesta. She got in and instantly accelerated down the street without hesitating. I turned to face the empty room, which now seemed cold.

I sat down heavily on the settee.

"You're safe now" came the quiet voice.

13

"What do you mean? 'I'm safe now!' Stop speaking in riddles. Tell me what I need to know" I said angrily, tears welling up in my eyes.

"You are safe now."

The emotional rollercoaster was making me tetchy. I had no solid answers as to what was going on or why. Hearing voices in my head and being deaf didn't lend itself to speaking openly to people. Suzi, whom I thought I could trust was the only person that understood. Sarah was saying that she is danger and only once she had gone was I safe. Who could I believe? I found it hard to believe that Suzi would harm me. My whole world had been turned upside down in the last couple weeks, changing beyond all recognition. One silly mistake had wreaked havoc and now my sanity was being toyed with. Why should I believe a ghost more than a friend?

I was beginning to doubt that Sarah was real, maybe just a figment of my imagination that came from banging my head too hard when I crashed. Maybe I was in a coma playing out some nightmarish reality. It was all getting too much and grabbing a beer from the fridge I slumped down in front of the TV, the subtitles flashing up over the blurred images.

I missed the sounds I wanted so desperately to hear again, my favourite music. I was never really interested in watching the news but I would have given anything to be able to hear it now. Finishing my beer I got another. My mood darkening, drinking only succeeding in blurring reality, I wanted all this to end. 'I want my hearing back' I shouted as loud as I could and then in an act of desperation I switched on the stereo, cranking up the bass, resting my hand on one of the speakers to feel the vibrations. Closing my eyes I concentrated as hard as I could, trying to allow my imagination to fill in the melody of 'Madness – Our House'. A song I knew well since a friend's elder brother had managed to brainwash me with their music when we were younger and our families had been on holiday together in Devon. I played the video through in my mind.

I couldn't stand the silence. I found myself getting more and more wound up, I rolled the volume switch to its maximum mark. I could only feel the bass. I missed the music. I launched my beer across the room in frustration, the bottle smashed into a picture, sending debris to the floor. It all seemed to be going wrong. Eclipsed by my own self-indulgent misery I grabbed my coat and stormed out slamming the door as hard as I could behind me.

Stomping down the road my destination was unknown, hands thrust deep into my pockets as anger boiled over. I started to run, punching the air. I had never been an angry person, always laid back and calm. Today, all that changed. Thoughts pulsing round my brain, adrenalin numbing my screaming muscles as I pushed them as hard as I could.

It started to rain, a few spots at first, then drizzle until a torrential downpour started and I was forced to take cover in a bus shelter. My trainers were soaked through. I'd come out with little thought or preparation and as the rain continued the colder I started to get. The adrenalin was losing its effect and the cold from my damp clothes entered my now sore muscles. Looking round I saw The Elms Pub, finding it hard to believe I'd come so far. I found a few pound coins in my pockets and headed into the pub for a drink and to warm up. I ordered a pint of lager, stating quite clearly what I wanted, something where I thought I wouldn't have to answer any questions and could just hand over the money, a pint of Stella, taking it to a booth in the corner where I could sit unnoticed, observing the comings and goings of others all wrapped up in their own lives, jealous of how easy they appeared to have it.

I was on my second pint by the time I reflected more sympathetically on what had occurred and how I'd treated Suzi. 'How could I have doubted her?' was the resounding thought that rattled inside my head. I got my phone out to text her and hesitated at the first words, not sure what to put.

Leaning back on the headrest I stared at the ceiling, looking for inspiration, everything seemed to blur. Closing my eyes I tried to concentrate, think of how to apologise. Nothing flowed in a way that sounded rational.

A chill went down my spine and suddenly the pub was gone.

I was standing in a children's playground, I recognised it, Blenheim Park. It looked very similar to how I knew it. I felt a tug on my hand and looked down to see a little boy barely six years old looking up at me. He pointed to a gate in the far fence and we walked to it, swiftly, effortlessly, at the gate, turning right towards the fire station stopping a few yards further up. On the other side of the road was a piece of land where a house was being built. He looked up at me, tugged at my arm beckoning me closer and I bent down.

"I'm in there" he spoke shyly, barely audible.

"You live there?" I said not grasping what he meant.

"I'm in there, they never found me" I could hear the sorrow in his voice.

I reeled slightly retracting my hand instinctively.

"I want to rest, please find me."

"Wher..How..I don't" I stuttered" Where are you?"

He took my hand and led me across the road and into the site. We stood close to where the foundations were being dug.

"I'm here" he whispered into my ear.

Suddenly the site changed around us, the building going up in double quick time. We found ourselves standing in the garage.

My shoulder was being nudged and suddenly I found myself back in the pub, a glass collector trying to get my attention.

Another man standing next to him said something but I didn't follow what it was, he repeated again. I still didn't follow, he was getting agitated. I was still a little dazed and confused from the vision, unsure whether I had fallen asleep, too dumbstruck to explain. Suddenly he put the glasses he was holding down and grabbed me by the upper arm to haul me from my seat. The second man took a hold of my other arm as I stood up. I tried to resist, they were talking at me but I didn't know what they were saying. I finally managed to tell them I was deaf but they weren't listening to me and I was forcibly ushered to the door, through it and pushed heavily out into the night air. Straightening my clothes I made my thoughts known emphasizing the fact that I was deaf, asking 'whether they were stupid?', they didn't seem to care, just turned and went back inside.

In disbelief I stood, astounded that I had been thrown out, wondering why? I wasn't causing a nuisance, just sitting minding my own business.

Luckily the rain had eased off and I took a moment to gather my thoughts, wanting to go back inside to make my feelings clear but deciding it was futile.

I thought about the vision or dream, or whatever it was, not sure what I should do with the information.

I needed to speak to Suzi. How could I talk to her now? Searching my pockets I couldn't find my mobile, frantically I rechecked. It was gone. Then as if reading my mind my left hand was grabbed and a mobile phone rammed into it by the glass collector. Before I had a chance to say anything he had gone again. Looking at the drink covered mobile I hoped that a message would appear from Suzi, nothing. I wiped it down with my hanker-chief, relieved I had got it back as this was a lifeline for me.

I hesitantly pressed the buttons to enter a message. Again lost for the words to write and eventually put in back in my pocket.

"You need to discover his body."

Sarah was standing beside me. Turning swiftly round I was still standing in the street outside the pub. If anyone was watching, I must have looked crazy.

"How can I discover the body?"

I noticed a couple leaving the pub looking at me strangely before quickly wandering off.

I wasn't sure if I was hallucinating, I knew I wasn't asleep. Something cold covered my right hand and looking down Sarah held it in hers. My mind became an incoherent mass of thoughts making me uneasy on my feet. I decided the best thing to do was to head home and have a coffee convinced I must be drunk.

Walking along the London Road I could still feel Sarah's hand in mine, I tried to ignore it, but it was there, a cold sensation as if I were holding a block of ice. As I was about to pass Cricketfield Grove she tugged on my left arm, indicating for me to head along that road.

"But I live this way, it's the quickest route" I uttered my mind unsure now what was reality and what wasn't.

"We need to go this way. We have to discover his body."

"Whose body?" I shook my head trying to clear it.

"William's. He wants to sleep."

"William?"

A second or so later I realised who she was talking about, the boy in my vision. Numb inside, tired and fed up with all the riddles, and not knowing what it was I was meant to be doing or who it was that was harming them I reluctantly complied with Sarah's wish. In reality I just wanted to go home in the hope that tomorrow I would wake up and find that the accident had all been a dream. In fact, all of this had just been a bad dream.

I knew where the place was in relation to where we were and headed there directly and in about twenty minutes, walking slowly, we were standing opposite the house in question.

I had no idea how to explore and discover the body without risking getting arrested for trespassing and even then I guessed the garage floor would be concrete so there would be very little I could do.

The house did not seem to have changed much in its short life, appearing dated now, but well looked after. The lights were on in the front room. The time on my phone was '12.13'. It occurred to me why I had got thrown out of the pub. It had been closing time and they must have thought I was a drunk sleeping it off. Now it made sense and I felt a little embarrassed.

"You have to discover him, so he can sleep."

"But I can't just go in there and start digging the place up." This seemed like such a futile conversation to have. What could I do?

The walk had cleared my head and I was a little more relaxed feeling less dejected.

"You must discover his body so he can sleep."

"Yes. But I can't just enter the garage, I'll get arrested" I thought for a second *"Is this still to do with the others?"*

"Yes."

"Oh right." I sighed.*" Still. I can't enter the premises. I'll have to think of another way of doing things."*

She looked at me, sadness in her eyes and as I turned away from her gaze I saw William standing in front of the garage door before disappearing. Guilt riddled me then.

"I promise I will do something. Just not yet! Okay?"

Sarah was disappointed. I had made her a promise that I would do something, but I needed time to think about how. Sarah said nothing but disappeared herself.

Making my way home I puzzled the predicament, trying to fathom a solution. My thoughts soon ran back to Suzi.

At home I found a note lying on the doormat inside the outer door. I knew the writing; it was Suzi's and picking it up I was expecting the worst. Then I noticed light under my front door, coming from my lounge, flickering light, it was not the central light, more like the TV.

Opening the door quietly and slowly I crept into the lounge, my pulse racing. My parents had keys, but I was not expecting a visit from them.

Peering round the doorframe the room was empty. The TV was playing some programme on monkeys. Cautiously I walked around the rest of the flat, everything was as it should be and I realised in my frustration that I had left the TV on when I went out. The lights were also blazing away on the stereo so this confirmed my thoughts, luckily the CD indicators showed that it had stopped as I suddenly saw the volume knob on full.

Switching on the light I sat down to read Suzi's letter.

Peter,

I don't know what that was about earlier, but hopefully you will tell me in your own time. I thought we had something special. We've known each other a long time and I know this is a difficult time for you, but I am there for you. I thought you could talk to me, maybe I was wrong.

I really like you, I always have done. I never thought anything would ever happen between us because of James. I'm glad we got together and I like you very much. If it is all moving too fast, you only had to say and I would have backed off a little.

If you want to talk you know where I am.

Lots of love

Suzi

XXX

Immediately I wanted to text her but something held me back, a niggling thought that I couldn't justify. In the end I gave in, asking her to come round after work tomorrow night so I could try and explain, and to apologise. Relief coursed through me and without solid reasons for any doubts I wanted to make amends and put it all down to the unnatural circumstances that I found myself in.

Thursday found me rushing home from work and waiting for Suzi. It was a little awkward at first so to break the ice I explained about the dream. Not wanting to talk about the niggling doubts I had about Nancy and the spell they had performed on me on Tuesday, best leave that for the moment.

Suzi suggested that we find out when William was murdered, or when he disappeared then we could ring the police anonymously stating the location, name and age of the victim, they would be forced to follow up, especially if their records confirmed the details and the case had remained unsolved. She explained the police had x-ray equipment that could detect bones buried underground without necessitating digging. Therefore, if it was true, they would dig and William could at least be put to rest.

14

Saturday spun round, Suzi had stayed Friday night allowing us to make up properly which aided with my second night of restful sleep, the dreams/visions abated as if Sarah knew we were on the case of William and was giving us time to work out the next clue. I still found the quietness of my world, particularly at night, a little strange and hard to get used to. Occasionally I'd wake worried I'd overslept. My relationship with Suzi was back on course and we planned to go out for a drive, if we had time, after we found what we needed at the Library.

It was wet and windy but the forecast said the sun was meant to be making an appearance at some point. We text James 'happy birthday' but didn't receive a reply. It was only 9.30am on a Saturday.

James had been absent from our lives for a few days, no sight or word from our friend. Arrangements had been made to meet him in 'The Hogshead' at four that afternoon, from there we didn't know where we would go. James knew he would take a lot of stick about the vouchers for Amsterdam, even more so once we all started drinking. It was likely we'd end up in a club.

A part of me was nervous about the evening, it was the first time I had been out in a big group of our friends and I wasn't sure how I would cope with the flow of the conversation. If it was any other occasion I would probably have pulled out, letting my lack of confidence gain another point, making my excuses. However, this was James's twenty-first and I didn't want to be a party pooper. I also didn't want to ruin Suzi's evening.

We had bought James a DVD box-set of series one of 'Little

Britain', which he absolutely loved watching, and a beer jug with his name and age engraved on it.

The Library quickly gave us what we were looking for;

William Thorpe aged nine had disappeared from Chalkwell Park, June 14th 1964, whilst out with his parents.

The article had made the front page of the Evening Echo.

Parents, Keith and Eileen, are worried and would like anyone who has any knowledge to contact the Westcliff Police Station, Detective Pierce. Police are concerned about the boy's safety'.

We left the library and walked back to Suzi's car.

"Where are we going to ring from?" I asked.

"Yours" she motioned.

"Woah! Then they'll know my number."

"No" she nodded and spoke the words "dial 1472" she held up her fingers to recount the numbers "before the number and that withholds it." It took me a while to guess the rest of her actions as they confused me.

"Oh right. I wondered how people did that."

Suzi looked at me in astonishment but I had never had cause to worry whether my number was seen or not.

By the time we got to my place we decided it would actually be best to use a payphone just in case they had technology that could still trace the call. The phone call was made near the Punchbowl in Paglesham followed by a walk before having lunch there. The police naturally were reluctant to investigate a new lead on such an old case. Detective Pierce had retired six years previously. The police were more interested in how Suzi had come across such information and what her connection was.

Suzi played it cool and simply explained that she was not wasting their time, that it was legitimate information starting to spin a story about an old letter she'd found in her grandad's possessions after he'd passed away. In it there was reference to a murder and the boys name was mentioned, he was confessing to it, it looked like the letter was going to be posted but never had been. She told them how disgusted and upset she was by it all but wanted to do the right thing for the boy's parents, should they still be alive. Saying who she was would only bring shame upon her family and nothing would be gained from doing so. Her memories had all been shattered and she couldn't bring herself to do that to the rest of the family. Suzi had tears starting to well in her eyes by the time she had finished her account.

I was starting to recognize the odd word Suzi used, she used her mouth to great effect and in my head I placed my memory of her voice with them. Although if she spoke quickly I could easily lose those, she had patience to try and help me attain this skill, which would prove to be so useful for the rest of my life.

Begrudgingly the officer had given in, even though he still tried to get contact details. All we had to do now was wait and hope that the local newspapers would broadcast the discovery.

Outside the Hogshead apprehension was growing inside me, this my first time out in a loud music bar, although that was not going to be an issue, since the accident, Suzi picked up my vibes and gripped my hand reassuringly, I smiled back, she looked stunning with her long brown hair gently flowing in the evening breeze exposing the shape of her beautiful face with very limited make-up. Standing outside you could normally hear the hullabaloo going on inside – I was unnerved by the silence of my world. Inside, the regular crowds jostled around with the same energy and high jinx that one would expect at this early hour, knowing full well it would be worse later on. We saw Claire standing by herself and went to join her.

The bouncers padded us down on the way in, this time I was more aware of it the silence of my world making me more conscious of other forms of communication, like touch.

Immediately inside a slightly large girl, who seemed to be bursting out of her very skimpy outfit, looking rather worse for wear bumped into me. She turned and mouthed something that I couldn't understand, I guessed, or rather hoped, she was apologising. Suddenly I felt very conspicuous and awkward. Suzi saw my unease and gripped my arm tightly, hugging it closely to her body, kissing me on the cheek.

Suzi and I went outside to the beer garden to grab one of the hexagonal tables that easily sat eight, as it was a warm night, whilst Claire bought some drinks before joining us. Immediately Suzi and Claire got engrossed in conversation, catching up, as they hadn't seen each other for a long time and although they didn't mean to cut me out I was at a loose end. I occupied myself by observing the other tables one by one, wondering what they were talking about, relying totally on visual clues. Some appeared to be talking quietly, whilst others were animated and boisterous, and judging by the way other people were looking at them being very loud.

Suzi tapped me on the shoulder and asked if I was alright. I watched her lips produce the words, she spoke so beautifully, and for a moment I didn't register what she said, only when she repeated did I nod, acknowledging that I was fine, even though I really wanted to go home. Suzi held my hand and carried on talking with Claire. Another twenty minutes passed before Alan, Paul, and Teresa turned up, James obviously running late, as usual.

Standing up I shook hands, as expected, with Alan and Paul then kissed Teresa on the cheek. Teresa looked at me strangely then her mouth moved soundlessly. I must have looked dumb struck as I could see the annoyance building up in her eyes but could not make out anything she was saying. Explaining that I couldn't understand her didn't make any difference she carried on talking as if the more she spoke the more I'd understand her. I shrugged my shoulders, starting to dread the night ahead, looking for Suzi who was deep in conversation with Paul. Teresa tried again making sure that I could see her mouth moving, but I didn't understand. Suzi interrupted, easing the frustration that was building up in Teresa, who was an impatient person at the best of times, and thought she was the best at everything – including someone being able to read her lips. She couldn't understand that maybe it just wasn't that simple. Teresa gave up and sat down to speak with Paul. Suzi touched my arm, I smiled half-heartedly and hoped the world would open up and swallow me even wishing that Sarah would talk to me. Taking my seat again I let the conversation drift on without my participation, sinking back into my own world.

Half an hour passed before I realised my frustration was turning to anger, seemingly fuelled by the drink, I had had two pints of Stella drinking them quickly, I tried to quash it. I was nothing more than a hanger on; I couldn't join in the merriments of the occasion. No one noticed me and this gave me more cause to let the anger build up. Suzi had got carried away enjoying herself without giving me a second thought and that, in truth made me feel guilty for thinking such a thing.

Quite suddenly, all my friends stood up. Out of the corner of my eye I caught the figure of James striding purposefully towards us. I reluctantly stood up as well, if a little unsteadily. People around turned to look at us.

James greeted everyone and paid me some attention, this lifted my spirits briefly but, all too easily, I faded into the background again. Another round of drinks appeared and the celebrations started in earnest.

Leaving the Hogshead about half past nine we headed to the Chinese in York Road, a brief five minute walk. By this time Carla, Denise, Michael and another friend Jamie, had joined us.

Everyone, except me, was having a good time, Suzi had made the odd conscious effort to keep me involved by holding my hand or arm but it was difficult, being surrounded by friends she knew well, catching up on each others lives, whilst I meandered alongside. I became more and more detached as the evening dragged on. Suzi was enjoying herself.

The meal was nice even though I had only picked at my food. Finally the bill was on its way. James attempted to stand up, he had had quite a lot to drink and was rather the worse for wear. I found it difficult to follow anything he said but guessed what it might be when he pointed at the clock that hung above the bar opposite our table: it read '11.20'. He had another twenty-seven minutes before he was officially twenty-one.

Upon leaving the restaurant there was a discussion on which club to go to, TOTS 2000 or The Mezzanine. James had the casting vote, as it was his birthday. I watched Suzi as she giggled and talked to our friends, struck by how beautiful she was, I wanted to drag her to one side and spend a little time on our own feeling her body close to mine. The Mezzanine came out on top. Even at this time of night there was a queue to get in and we fell in line. Reluctantly I queued not enthralled at going to a club preferring to go home. The drink only made me feel withdrawn from everyone yet I didn't want to disappoint Suzi who I knew liked to go clubbing, and it was a special occasion. There was a lot of giggling and drunken behaviour going on in our group; all seemed good humoured and all exempted me.

We were about six people away from getting in when James stopped larking about and became very deadly serious. It caught everyone by surprise, even woke me from my stupor.

I didn't know what was said but he started to walk off, various friends went to grab his arm, he violently shook them free and carried on up Alexandra Street.

What followed was a short discussion about James, which again I wasn't part of, everyone's faces conveyed puzzlement and it put a damper on the evening. I thought for a few seconds and whilst the others including Suzi entered the club I decided to head after James, making my excuses and telling Suzi I'd see her back at my place. Not waiting for a response I ran off down the street after James. I was relieved at having an excuse to leave and knew Suzi would enjoy herself more now.

By the time I saw James he was walking along Cambridge Road towards Hamlet Court Road. I shouted after him, he turned, looked at me and carried on walking faster. A few seconds later a cab pulled up and he got in.

I knew our friendship had chilled since Suzi and I had got together but I didn't think it had affected him that badly he hadn't voiced any problems and was not normally one to hold back. In fact he had been in good spirits – literally – all evening, so this sort of reaction from him was completely alien.

I headed home as there was little else I could do except stay up until Suzi came in, which was about three in the morning. She'd had a good time and was quite drunk, tripping over anything and everything finally ending up on the floor, which made me laugh. When I went to help her up off the lounge floor she dragged me down and that was where stayed until she fell asleep and I then carried her to the bedroom.

15

I was walking along a street, the night lit by street lamps, their light reflecting off the few parked cars. A cold hand was in mine and Sarah was walking by my side, we were in Rochford, walking past where the old scout hut used to stand, not far from Market Square. A shudder went down my spine as I remembered that far too real experience a few nights ago.

We turned right down a narrow street, Rocheway, the houses seemed to change from new buildings to older style cottages and then to bungalows. Passing Mornington Avenue we came to a large farmhouse set back from the road and occupying a huge road frontage with grounds that stretched back into the night. Taking a well trodden path we walked past the Farmhouse to the back where a barn stood some two hundred feet from the main house held in seclusion by trees on three sides. Through cracks in the barns timber cladding I could see light emanating from within.

Edging up to the barn I peered through a slither of a crack in the cladding, there was someone standing at a makeshift altar, wearing a long dark red hooded robe which concealed their identity, and holding a book which lay open in one hand. The other hand was hidden from view as the person was standing with their back to me.

I couldn't see or hear the presence of anyone else. All around me the night was peaceful.

Watching, the person put down the book on the altar which was covered in red material that looked lavish and expensive. They then picked up something else raising it above their head. It was a dagger with a curved blade, like a miniature cutlass, barely eight inches in length. Placing the point of the blade into the palm of their hand, the person *quietly and without warning pushed the blade slowly and effortlessly through to the hilt. I recoiled briefly with shock before curiosity drew me on to watch again and I saw blood stream from the wound, down the forearm and into the sleeve of the cloak. The person showed no sign of pain or discomfort. Then in one swift motion the dagger was withdrawn again. I could feel the pain they should have felt. The blade smeared red, the wound oozing crimson liquid. The person moved to one side and laid the dagger on the table. There was a tall church candle burning bright in front of the robed person, grabbing the wrist of the injured hand the person held it over the flame. The blood dripped onto the flame causing it to flare. Suddenly a shaft of flame shot vertically through the hand, the person emitted an ear splitting scream and I cringed from the sound, the hairs on my neck stood on end and I turned away.*

When I looked again the person was huddled on the floor buried beneath the robe. Two more people had appeared wearing similar red robes. They picked up the slumped figure on the floor and the hood fell away.

Overwhelmed by the feeling of physical sickness I had to stand back from the timber clad wall, taking in deep urgent breaths, waiting for the feeling to pass almost gagging with shock.

When I peered again through the crack to confirm I'd seen what I thought I'd seen. Disbelief rattled inside me. The place was empty, all the robed people had disappeared – I wondered whether I'd imagined it all and pinched my arm – it hurt, this was real. The dagger still lay where it had been placed on the altar, the candle burned bright, and the book lay closed next to it.

Turning to Sarah I said "I need to see the book. Can we go in?"

She took my hand and led me to the door of the barn. From there I took control and stole forth into the barn. This was a dream but it felt so real, the texture, the coldness of the night air, the smell of the burning candle with its citrus infusion. I almost forgot that it was just a dream.

The barn was constructed of giant Oak beams with a daub wattle in-fill, the floor of bare earth was covered with straw – the ceiling rose high above disappearing into darkness, possibly fifty-five feet or more. In one corner to my right was a single door, closed, but I guessed it led to an ante room.

Staring at the altar I could not see any blood stains. Easing myself further in, all the time expecting someone to suddenly catch me, I could no longer feel Sarah's hand in mine. I turned and saw her waiting at the door.

The barn was lit by a string of household light bulbs hung round the walls on metal eyes. I inched my way to the altar careful not to make any sound. The book was A5 size, bound in two-tone brown leather with faded black lettering on the cover. Picking it up I was surprised how heavy the book was and transfixed by how old it looked – centuries. It felt so real in my hands, too real for a dream. Out of the corner of my eye I saw a movement near the door of the ante room. Then it was gone. I became aware that I was very vulnerable. Maybe I had outstayed my welcome so I hastened my exit with the book, closing the door quietly behind me.

Sarah looked horrified, yet she remained silent as an arm reached around my neck and pulled me backwards, leaving me gasping for breath. I only just managed to hang onto the book. I was wrestled back into the barn and losing my footing, I fell backwards onto the person behind and we both went crashing to the ground. I heard a crack followed by a scream of pain and the grip around my neck loosened. I rolled off to one side onto the straw, adrenalin pumping through my body and without giving the person a second glance I sprinted out the door into the night still holding the book tight in my hands.

Upon reaching the end of Rocheway I slowed my pace to a jog, taking time to look over my shoulder to see if anyone had given chase. No one. My heart was beating a tattoo inside my chest telling me to stop but I knew I couldn't stop, not yet. Abruptly, a cramp took over my left calf muscle and I was forced to halt. Sarah was beside me.

"You are in danger, they know! You must go now."

"Know what?" I gasped in between sucking huge gulps of air, struggling onwards whilst rubbing my calf muscle to ease the cramp "And, yes, I guessed. Why does this feel so real? I don't understand. Why can't I leave this dream? How can all this be happening? What was he doing?"

"He has to be stopped."

"Really, I would never have guessed that!" sarcasm ringing in my voice, covering up how scared I was.

Sarah vanished. "Come back" I shouted, all the frustration coming out at once. I hadn't realised how much there was. I threw the book as hard as I could to release my anger. The instant I let go I knew I shouldn't have. I watched it make an arc, the pages fluttering in the air before it landed in a nearby front garden. The built up anger immediately replaced with a sense of guilt for throwing away something that could possibly help. I sighed, my breathing no longer laboured, pearls of sweat on my forehead.

I took a deep breath in resignation and made my way to the garden where the book had landed. The garden had a low perimeter wall, barely thirty inches high, separating it from the street, the flower beds filled with Fuschias, Roses, and a few dwarf conifers. Scouring the garden I looked for the book and with no street lamps in the vicinity the darkness concealed the book like a blanket. Leaning over the wall I fumbled in the bushes and flowers, pushing them to one side in the hope I could find it.

How stupid had I been?!

A hand gripped my right arm and I glanced round, at first expecting to see a police officer - excuses buzzing through my head, reasons for doing what I was doing - or even worse, people in red robes. There was no one. I looked up and down the street, empty, completely deserted of life. I shook my head and carried on searching for the book with increased urgency.

Again there was a tug at my arm, still no one there. A peculiar feeling went through me, a sense of being detached, no longer in control of my movements.

I saw the book at the base of one of the roses, not quite completely hidden by the sprawling branches of a fern. Reaching down to pick it up my body jolted, I couldn't feel my fingers. The book had been just in my grasp, and I could see my fingers touching the leather bound cover *curling round to pick it up yet nothing registered in my brain. I doubled up as if I was going to be sick, desperately trying to keep hold of the book.*

I fell over the wall.

I was in bed, the soft quilt wrapped around me, it was dark. Suzi's hands were on my arm, I twisted to face her.

"What!" I exclaimed.

She let go to switch on the light, she was wearing one of my collarless shirts which showed off her sexy naked legs, before returning to sit next to me. Placing her hand on my face she kissed my cheek then hugged me. I could feel her chest against mine and I pulled her tighter. My heart was pounding. Drops of perspiration were running down my forehead. She pulled back.

"Are you alright" she mouthed using her hands to emphasize the words I just about understood. She grabbed a pad from the bedside table.

U WERE SHOUTING ABOUT TO FALL OUT OF BED.

I pulled my left hand up to wipe my face and realised I was still holding the book.

Suzi looked at me strangely. I could tell she wanted to know, yet I didn't understand myself.

"I… don't know" I stammered out, dropping the book on the bed then thought for several seconds trying to recollect what had happened. "I stole it. From a barn!" my words were empty, like strangers to me, it just didn't seem plausible.

Suzi took the book and flicked through the pages, stopping occasionally to read, then continuing.

"Where did you get this?" her face showed an excited curiosty.

"In a Barn. In Rochford. I… I… just now. I… stole it" Pausing I let a thousand thoughts cascade through my brain "I was attacked. But I got away. Sarah. She led me there." Suzi turned away.

"What is it?" I urged. Then repeating my question when she

didn't respond. She turned to face me and wrote.

THIS 'BOOK OF DRYGOTSO IS WHAT DRYSIDIUM FAITH IS BASED ON. NANCY SAID NO ONE HAS SEEN THIS BOOK IN CENTURIES.

She paused and judging by the look on her face she became very concerned.

THEY NO U GOT THIS?

"I guess so. After I was grabbed, I just ran. Just ran"

WOT TIME? WOT YEAR YOUR DREAM?

"Tonight!"
Suzi's face turned pale
Suddenly, I remembered who it was I'd seen. I didn't want to believe it but it came flooding back to haunt me like a vivid nightmare, the ceremony the man had acted out, the blood. I looked at Suzi. How could I tell her? I knew I had to, she had helped me from the beginning and I couldn't hold out on her now.

Looking deep into her eyes I hoped I could find the courage that was needed to tell her what, or rather who, I'd seen. Words seem to escape me.

"There's something that you need to know. About what I saw." I bowed my head out of guilt.

WOT?

She quickly scrawled. Then placing a finger under my chin lifted my head gently.

I searched her face for an explanation, a reason, anything that would mean it wasn't true or even real.

"James" I blurted out

JAMES?

She wrote, her hand shaking.

"It was him. I saw him. I watched him in my dream, tonight. I think it was him who grabbed me but I can't be sure as I didn't stick around to see.

Suzi's face registered her astonishment. Her eyes darted to mine then the book and around the room, then back to mine.

NOT UNDERSTAND. HOW? JAMES IN UR DREAM? ATTACKED U. Y?

"Because I grabbed this book. He had performed some sort of ritual. I saw it with my own eyes" I couldn't believe my own words. I could see James again, in my mind, pushing the dagger through his hand. A wave of nausea swept over me.

16

Suzi sat dumfounded, obviously not wanting to believe what I had told her, James, who she had known for five or six years. Our friend, who was not who we thought he was. Getting up she paced the room, uncomfortable, appearing to talk to herself. I was as amazed as she was.

Like a bolt from the blue things fell into place, I now knew what Sarah had been implying when she had said 'you're in danger' whenever James was near. Taking me to Rochford was her way of clarifying the situation. I still wasn't quite sure how it all tied up with Sarah and the deaths of the children but I hoped that would become clear in time. Suzi disappeared from the room and I fell back on the bed exhausted, she returned a few minutes later carrying two mugs of tea, placing them on the bedside table before laying along side me stroking my chest, lost deep in thought still shaken by the news.

Inspired she sat up and grabbed the pad.

I'LL GO SEE NANCY TMRW. SHOW HER BOOK. MAYBE SHE CAN EXPLAIN.

"What time shall we go?"

BEST I GO ALONE I THINK.

I frowned at her "Why? This is to do with me"

I JUST THINK IT BEST. I MIGHT FIND OUT MORE.

I sat there, silent and dejected, feeling like just a piece of furniture again, that could be discarded at a whim.

"Okay" I sighed. Really I was frustrated at being kept in the dark. There were things that I didn't have a lot of knowledge of and wanted to learn about, yet, I didn't want to upset the one person who could possibly help.

Suzi leaned in and kissed me on the lips, trying to reassure me everything was okay. I smiled, but my heart wasn't in it, keeping my thoughts to myself.

It was Sunday and the thin curtains set the room in a sort of half light, the clock showed '1.37pm'. Glancing over to where Suzi should have been, I found her gone. I sat up looking for her clothes, they were gone as well. Slumping back into my pillows I contemplated what I was going to do today.

The image of James flashed into my consciousness, thoughts of what I should do beckoned, possible outcomes if I confronted him, and how I could handle them. Frustration ran around my head, Suzi had gone off to discuss the book, leaving me out of the loop, 'this involves me as well' I screamed at no one and punched the pillow. I had witnessed James perform some sort of ritual – which had disturbed me, especially after his strange behaviour the night before. What was the ritual all about?

Finally, a solution came to mind. What I though I 'should' do. I didn't feel comfortable about it, but it was the only way forward as far as I could see. I would confront James, my best friend, and not sit here doing nothing, waiting for things to be talked about without my knowledge, and after all, if he had seen me then it was best to get it out in the open rather than play an elaborate game of charades.

Leaving my flat about three in the afternoon I enjoyed the pleasant sun that hung lazily in the clear autumn sky although my confidence was starting to wane. James's house was about a mile away, I reflected on the sounds that were missing from my life. How strange the world seemed, wrapped up in silence, almost eerie. I was shaken as a cyclist whizzed past at breakneck speed, at first shock and then anger. Normally it would not have bothered me as I would have heard it coming and wasn't fussed about cycles on the pavement but in my new world I had no early warning system. My eyes and sense of smell were the only line of defence.

A car pulled up in front of me, the driver got out slamming the door shut. He looked at me and I became aware that I had been staring. For some strange reason I felt an explanation was in order and was about to give one when I decided he wouldn't have been interested. I saw his lips move, made an educated guess from his expression what he said and carried on walking I knew it was pointless to try and put my case.

I rang James's doorbell. He still lived with his parents and had no desire to move out. I was the odd one out amongst my friends, but then, I guess, I was just lucky that my parents helped me out even though they had forced it upon me. I pushed the button again and waited. There were two cars on the drive, one was James's and the other that of his parents. I started to wonder whether the bell was working or not. How would I know? I clanged the elaborate metal knocker hard on the wooden front door.

The door opened a minute or so later, a familiar face, James's mother, Elaine.

She spoke before I had a chance to say anything, I thought I caught one or two words one of them being my name and the other was James's but it was probably habit of knowing how she greeted me. She looked at her watch and I assumed she was saying something about the time he was expected back, Elaine indicated for me to come in.

Making my excuses about not wanting to wait, she looked puzzled before disappearing into the house leaving the front door open and me standing there confused. She returned seconds later with a pad and pencil and quickly scribbled:

In bed, didn't get home until nine this morning, you can go and wake him up if you like.

I smiled to her having completely misunderstood. Would lip reading ever be a skill I'd master, it seemed so alien. There was an array of facial expressions for words, intonations, everyone was so different, even shapes for the same sounds, depending who spoke them. People used their mouths so differently.

Outside James's room I hesitated, unsure what I was going to say running through the words in my head. It had seemed such a great idea originally, now I was here, my confidence alluded me. I'd run over possible starting points with possible retorts, they now all seemed to escape me.

With a sad heart I knocked twice, waited and then walked in. James lay buried beneath his quilt. Reluctantly I placed my hand on what I thought was his shoulder and gently shook him. He stirred and rolled over. I nudged him again. This time his eyes flickered open and a hundred thoughts rushed through my head, each one indecipherable. It took James a while to recognise me, looking at me blankly as if trying work out where he was, nervously and sounding rather stupid to me I said 'Hi'.

James had never been a morning person, even worse after a late night. I couldn't tell if I was just making it harder on myself, imagining that a void had opened up between us or there really was one. James looked confused by my presence and sat up exposing his naked torso. I stood my ground and watched as he flinched with pain whilst adjusting his pillows.

"You alright?" I didn't catch his response as he was looking at his ribs, there was a bruise starting to show on the right side.

"What happened?" trying to sound as innocent as possible, hoping he would come clean about last night. Was it really him I saw? Or had it really been a vivid dream that I couldn't shake down? It had to be him he had an injury which I knew about.

James reached across to his desk nearby and wrote on a

magazine cover:

FELL OVER.

"Where did you go after you left us?"

FORGOT HAD GO SOMEWHERE.

I wasn't sure if James was being purposely vague? Maybe he didn't see me last night? My confidence about confronting him was failing me. Almost as if I didn't mention it then it didn't really happen and I would still have my friend. But I needed answers. Needed to know.

Changing tack "We were concerned when you went off last night."

James smiled and scrabbled around for clean piece of paper:

GOT TXT FROM A GIRL WORK WITH SHE WANTED TO MEET. WE SEEN EACH OTHER COUPLE OF TIMES. IT WAS MY BIRTHDAY SHE HAD A TREAT 4 ME.

He smiled unconvincingly.

James had a good answer for everything I could throw at him and gradually I let the tension ease between us which made it harder for me to question my friend about what I'd seen. Like it had been two different people, twins, and this was the good one. I started to convince myself that I'd imagined it the whole thing. Except for the book? There was no way I'd imagined the book. A sixth sense told me to keep quiet about it. Secrets, a game of secrets we were playing and I didn't like it.

All the time we'd known each we'd never been secretive, a relationship built on trust and understanding, and now we had found a new level, more distant, fragmented.

We played computer games for few hours and I stayed for

dinner with his parents, always in the back of my mind the image I had seen and the unanswered questions.

The moment had passed. I'd let it pass. I was disappointed with myself.

As I left I thought it strange that I hadn't heard anything from Suzi, no texts, no calls. Over the last few days contact between us had been as regular as clockwork. It had also been strange that she left without waking me. My silence was making me suspicious of everything and everyone.

I walked home in the warm evening air deceiving myself that I had been mistaken by who I had seen in my dream, however real the book was. Taking my phone out I text Suzi asking what she was up to and how she had got on with Nancy and the book.

Putting the phone back in my pocket I headed to Bonchurch Park, I didn't know why, I didn't feel like going home straight away and that seemed a good a place as any.

A melancholy mood came over me as the park came into view, there were a lot of blue flashing lights. The whole park was sealed of with Police tape. Hoards of police vehicles scattered in the streets, parked on pavements and diagonally across roads, dog units and forensic units with men in white suits walking about. I wanted to go in and have a closer look but knew that would not be possible so skirted the perimeter of the park looking into the scene. A white tent had been erected in one corner near a group of trees. Sitting down on a bench, that was outside the opposite entrance into the park that I had approached from, I watched the scene unfolding, the minions going about their business, some milling around the tent, others with dogs presumably looking for clues or evidence.

The sun was low in the sky and warm on my face. My eyelids became heavy as I tried to keep the glare out of them.

A cold hand slid into mine and Sarah was sitting next to me on the bench.

"He's back. You're in danger. You have to stop him."

"Who is he?"

"You know who he is. You must stop him."

Sarah seemed to confirm my worst fears, the ones I had managed to hide from myself for a few hours, but now were staring me right back in the face.

"He did this." she said

"Is it just him I have to stop?" *I surprised myself with this question as I didn't know where it came from and I sounded so confident that I could do something.*

Some people walked past and looked at me, I wondered whether I was dreaming or awake now, the edges of my world were blurring. I turned to Sarah and she was gone, I didn't feel awake.

I found myself in the park, not sure how I had got there. Sarah was beside me again holding my hand, leading me to the tent.

Inside a scurry of men and women were scraping away at some remains in a shallow hole in the ground, they were only bones so I guessed they were from a long time ago.

A vibration in my pocket broke me from this image.

Lifting out my phone I saw that I had a message from Suzi:

C u at ur's. S x x'

I replied saying I'd be there in an hour or so.

17

The smell of Chinese food hit my senses as I entered my flat and although I'd already eaten I felt I could quite easily eat another meal. Suzi was sitting on the settee tucking into hers with a glass of wine poured. She turned towards me and pointed to the second plate she had brought into the lounge and the beer that sat unopened, bottle opener next to it.

I noted the book was also on the table. I was surprised how easily I ate my second meal of the day. Suzi placed a pad in front of me and I read what it said.

BOOK IS RARE AS WE KNOW. LAST KNOWN RITUAL PERFORMED 1969. 14 PEOPLE ARRESTED. THERE WAS PREGNANT WOMAN AND AN INJURED MAN WHO LATER DIED. WAS IN PAPERS AT TIME. 2 PEOPLE GOT LIFE FOR DEATHS OF 3 KIDS. 2 GIRLS AND A BOY. NANCY NOT REMEMBER ALL DETAILS AS MINIMAL INFO IN PAPERS ALTHOUGH SHE FOUND OUT STUFF FROM OTHER SOURCES.

DO U KNOW WOT PAGE IT WAS ON WHEN U SAW IN DREAM?

I thought about that whilst I shovelled in another mouthful of chicken chow mein, trying to recollect anything about the pages that James was looking at. It was James! There was no doubt now even though I still didn't want to believe it. Nothing came to mind. The pages had remained hidden from view.

"No" I said finally "I described what he was doing though. Didn't that help?"

JUST EASIER IF U SAW PAGE, BUT DESCRIBE AGAIN.

I did so. Then whilst I cleared away the dinner things, Suzi searched the book from cover to cover looking for possible ceremonies that would tie in with what I had seen.

James plagued my mind. He had acted weird on the Saturday night, yet when I saw him earlier everything had seemed okay-ish. If he was caught up in this cult then how was it affecting him and what strange things could we expect in the future. A strange thought conjured itself and I wondered if he knew what was going on. It sounded stupid, yet somehow it could make a lot of sense.

Suzi broke my thoughts with a sharp thrust of her hand into the air and a silent exultation of triumph.

She pointed to a section titled 'Bloodline'.

I leaned over the back of the settee and read:

The first part of the ceremony is to be conducted by the 1st Temple who will lead the third, fifth, and seventh Pillars and will take place seven hours before the twenty-first birthday of the Solar. This will bond the Shaddow to the Solar. The first Temple will pass the chalice of shaddows milk to the third, fifth, and seventh Pillars, who in turn will perform the 'Kut of Life'. The Chalice will then be passed back to the 1st Temple who will invoke Bloodline.

Quertezia
Montesk
Fragnated
Laternix
Perpgastic
Banile

The Solar will then perform 'Kut of Life' with the Dagger of Traggia for the Solar to finish the Bloodline ceremony on the Solars twenty-first Birthday.

Blocarta
Intonix
Cufram
Jastix

The Solar must then consume the chalice which binds the Shaddow to the Solar.

"What does this mean?" I asked baffled "What is the 'Kut of Lif...'" as soon as I spoke I realised what the 'Kut of life' was and putting two and two together coming up with four; James had performed this. There was not a mark on his hand though. Why not? Was this how strong the magic was? Who was the Shaddow?

I re-iterated my questions to Suzi who listened intently, she didn't have all the answers but now we had identified the ceremony we could ask Nancy, who might know, or would certainly know someone who would be able to shed more light.

Arrangements were made for both of us to meet Nancy on Wednesday night. We were uneasy about leaving things so open with James, because of all of the events that had happened, so we set about trying to make it that for the next two nights James was kept busy. That in itself was not going to be easy as we couldn't watch him twenty-four hours a day.

After much persuading on Suzi's part he agreed to come out with us Monday night. In the meantime we scanned the relevant pages from the book and emailed them to Nancy so she could at least look at what we had found. Monday was back to work so we headed to bed as it was nearly midnight although neither of us could sleep.

Work for me was becoming boring and frustrating, the silence in which I found myself everyday set in a tedium that would be difficult for the hearing to comprehend. I watched as colleagues laughed and joked with each other, sometimes they'd catch me looking on and stop, they'd look awkward but what could they do? Sometimes I had to sit and watch everyone around me just so I knew I wasn't on my own in the office. Doing only half my job made my time there go slowly. The company had done their best to fit in with their obligations and my new disability. I couldn't complain but the zest for my occupation was diminished, so much so that I didn't want to be there.

In just a matter of a few days most communication with me about anything other than work, was just signalling a good morning greeting or goodbye. It was a lonely place to be, social email was frowned upon between colleagues.

Customers I was used to speaking to were using email, which kept up the banter but it was not the same. Those that needed to speak to someone were passed onto to other colleagues. I was feeling next to useless, stuck with the mindless task of inputting information into the computer or surfing the net for other details, never properly being able to follow up any of it with phone calls, which could have expedited matters. I still had appointments with my specialists to discuss my future and possible ways forward, including Cochlear implants which scared me witless. Further talks with an Occupational therapist were arranged to make sure I was integrating properly with my team. I knew they wanted me to talk about my feelings and how things were but most times I just said I was fine, it ticked the required boxes, they couldn't do more if I didn't open up. I wondered if maybe I should ask if they could point me in the right direction to a job that would be more rewarding for my new condition.

Monday at work finally drew to a close and I slunk off home looking forward to being in company of Suzi and James, where I didn't feel so different and isolated. We all headed to the pub, this held its own ghosts for all of us, as it had only been about two weeks since the accident but we had to carry on as normal though. The Pub was more than half empty which was expected for a Monday. James seemed his normal self whilst we played a couple of games of pool and drank a couple of pints, nothing unusual at all. Yet something obviously tugged in the back of Suzi's mind because when James went to the toilet she pointed out that he kept checking his jacket, I hadn't noticed, which was now slumped over the back of a chair. Before I had time to stop her she had dived into it, feeling around all the pockets. Nothing! She checked again and still found nothing. I tapped her on the shoulder as I saw James heading back, he looked very serious.

James grabbed his jacket and made the excuse that he wasn't feeling too good before promptly leaving.

Suzi and I looked at each other perplexed but immediately both had the same thought, to follow him, if we could without him noticing. He was on foot as we had picked him up in Suzi's car. This was another strange thing; he hadn't wanted a lift home. His house was nearly a mile away and mainly up hill, he didn't enjoy walking at the best of times.

We were in Old Leigh, The Smack Inn; he had turned right once outside and gone across the footbridge heading up the Church Hill steps. We stopped at the bottom and watched as he went up the sixty or so steps which were interspersed with high gradient cobbled slopes. I suggested that Suzi went back and got her car whilst I would follow on foot and text her to keep her posted on our whereabouts.

Keeping close was not easy but I hugged the dark shadows of the fences as much as possible, occasionally ducking into a gateway, just in case he turned. It was ten o'clock and I couldn't tell how quiet I was being although he didn't turn round to glance back, just marched on, so I guessed I was doing okay. I felt like a spy in a movie which in turn gave me a buzz.

When I reached the top of the steps James had vanished. 'Damn' I whispered. If he had gone straight across the road towards Elmsleigh Drive at the junction with Leigh Broadway then I knew he would be heading home. I couldn't see him there and it was a fairly straight road. There were shops on either side until St Cedrics Church and then only the odd shop after, mainly houses. I text Suzi my location then searched every nook and cranny in that direction, ending my search at the junction with Progress Road standing on the triangular island that diverted traffic either left down Elmsleigh Drive or right towards The Broadway, turning through 360 degrees all the time searching for James. James had not been out of my sight for long when he reached the top of the steps. I couldn't understand how I could have lost him. Some spy I'd make.

I saw Suzi's car coming towards me and directed her down the right side of the traffic island back the way I had walked, which was a one way street. She pulled up outside the chemist on the right and I got in.

"I lost him."

"Lost him." I guessed she said, her facial expression helping me decipher her words.

"I don't know... he wasn't that far ahead. Maybe he saw me and ran."

We both shrugged. Suzi started driving off back towards Leigh Broadway going left at the second triangular traffic island outside St Clements Church which was directly ahead of us. As we turned the corner I glanced into the church graveyard and saw someone standing in the shadows. Mentioning it to Suzi she pulled up in the next lay-by just past Woolworth's whilst I kept an eye on the figure; it was too dark to see clearly but from the outline it could have been James, the figure certainly had his bulky frame and moved like him. I wanted it to be James. Whoever it was, it was not clear what they were doing, but it involved a fair amount of bodily movement.

Without saying anything I got out of the car and headed back to the church. The graveyard only contained a maximum of about fifty or sixty graves as it wasn't very large. A small stone wall barely four feet high surrounded the church and its graveyard.

Crossing the road I slowly made my way closer, trying to avoid being spotted. In the light of a street lamp near the Church I saw James's face, he saw me and for a few seconds, although it seemed like longer, we stared at each other before he grabbed an object from the ground and ran off, placing one hand on the wall he leapt over it in a single bound and into the depths of Elmsleigh Drive.

I stood motionless letting indecision catch me. Did I give chase or go back to Suzi? By the time I had chosen it was too late, James was out of site and I knew he would be too far ahead to catch so I walked into the Church yard to look at the gravestone where I had seen James.

Using the dim light from a nearby street lamp I squinted at the headstone - 'David Smith 1945- 1969, In loving memory'. Under a blanket of moss there was a word, or words, hidden. Scraping it away I found a solitary word 'KRAKNAMI'.

18

Caressing the letters carved into the headstone I studied the word as though inspiration would give me an inkling of what it meant and some reason for it being there, searching the indentations, reassuring my mind they were there. What significance did the word have? Someone had taken a great deal of time and trouble to do it, great care to make it look as though it should have been there from when the headstone was first carved.

A thought occurred that we should check out some of the graves of the other children who had been murdered? But I knew they did not when Sarah had shown me them I didn't recall seeing it, although I hadn't been looking at the time. Was it possible that I had missed it? Maybe over the course of time this 'sign' had been eradicated, washed away by the ravages of the weather. We would have to do some more investigating. Nancy, possibly, may have answers, an idea what this word signified or meant? I took some pictures on my phone then ran back to where Suzi was parked, briefly explaining what I'd seen, showing her the images on my phone.

Back at my flat we viewed the image again, 'KRAKNAMI'; staring at it for ages flicking between the images of just the word and the whole headstone. I grabbed the book that I'd taken from my dream and started to search through it, looking for the word, hoping to shed some light on its significance. Page after page I skimmed not paying attention to what they said, just searching for a clue. The book had only 150 pages, the paper was dense and stiff which gave the book its bulk, it took barely half an hour to look through.

Nothing!

Suzi searched the web using my computer. For the first search she used the word on its own enclosed within speech marks, "word not found" was the message that was returned. She tried changing the spelling of it to see if it had been known as anything else, then breaking it into two words, hyphenating it and finally putting a dot between each letter as if it were an acronym.

Still nothing!

I poured us both a glass of wine.

The evening was drawing to a wasted end, we hadn't managed to keep tabs on James and now we hadn't even managed to find out what 'Kraknami' meant. I toyed with the idea of searching where Sarah's body had been discovered to see if it had been carved into a rock or tree as if it had been part of some ceremony. But on second thoughts, something didn't feel right. On the grave stone it had been carved meticulously as though it belonged. If we found it near Sarah's burial place, the two still wouldn't be connected; the circumstances didn't gel together. After explaining my ideas to Suzi, she quite rightly pointed out that there had been various landslips over the last twenty years so she didn't think it likely that we would find anything anyway.

The police had done a pretty thorough job of scouring the area, if there had been anything unusual she was sure they would have found it. I played devil's advocate and pointed out that they wouldn't eek out any significance from it even if they did see it. However, she was sure they would still register it.

Being nearly midnight we called it a night. I picked up the book and took it with me. Turning off the light, neither of us were in the mood for sleeping, both wide awake, curiosity keeping our thoughts churning, yet we knew we had to get up for work and needed our sleep. We shared a little quality time before drifting off exhausted.

Proper restful sleep evaded me. Strange images swirled in front of me, bright light, then darkness, hands pulling me, strange faces, symbols, alternating in quick succession, they appeared randomly, but I knew I was meant to make some meaning from them.

I was again in St Clements graveyard, standing by the grave where I had been earlier that evening only now it was daylight. I was running my fingers across the headstone. Looking over the retaining wall of the churchyard I saw Leigh Broadway, it was different, older, but new, the shop facades painted a different a picture from that which I knew and it stood deserted.

In my hands was a Stone Masons hammer and chisel. Looking again at the headstone, only the first three letters 'KRA' were there. I was marking the stone! A pair of feet appeared in my peripheral vision to the left, a black cloak hanging down almost touching the well worn sandals. As I looked up I saw a preacher reading from a book and splashing the stone with water, it was holy water. The water was held in a chalice suspended by three gold chains.

When my work was complete I turned to face the preacher, suddenly, he threw some of the water over me, it burnt, like a million tiny Bee stings.

Sitting bolt upright I put my hands to my face where I had felt the burning. Nothing. I scanned the room, searching, it was almost pitch black. Nothing stirred. Suzi remained motionless next to me her naked arms protruding from the duvet, her long dark hair sprawled over the pillow.

I remained quite still trying to recollect the images and place them in some sort of order to decipher the story they were painting. Maybe we had been trying to work this out from the wrong angle. We assumed that 'Kraknami' was to do with the Drysidium Faith, when, if I judged my images correctly it had more to do with the church and Christianity? That posed some questions that needed answering. Where was I going to find the answers? Obviously not the web, we had already tried and if the word appeared in any shape or form it would have been found during our search. I suppose we could ask a vicar, but how much would one want to tell us if this was a dark secret that the church wanted to keep quiet?

Anyway, I didn't know any vicars, and I certainly wasn't a regular church goer, I wasn't even an irregular church goer.

Suzi's parents were!

That was a possibility and something I would have to speak to her about the following day.

Over breakfast I explained my dream and thoughts about speaking to a vicar. Suzi agreed and said we ought to go to church with her parents on Sunday, I was not entirely happy about that but knew that it might be the only way to get an answer. She used to go regularly so knew the vicar by name and was sure that he would help if he could. Apparently a nice chap, friendly, trendy and bonded a lot with younger people, creating some extraordinary results.

On Tuesday evening, James managed to evade both Suzi and myself, refusing to answer our text messages or phone calls. Waiting for Wednesday was like being stuck in limbo, but when it finally arrived we were filled with new enthusiasm. Suzi had asked her parents about 'Kraknami' but they had never heard of it. They were pleased when she announced that both she and I would be coming to church on Sunday.

My original misgivings about Nancy I had let subside, I was still wary and put it down to the fact that I didn't understand a lot of what I was experiencing. Nancy was still eating her dinner when we arrived and as she ate we explained the events of the past couple of days. Suzi had emailed the pages of the ceremony on Sunday so at least if she had a chance between then and now she could look for more information. We had brought the book with us again, with the page earmarked for 'Bloodline'.

Nancy finished eating then made us some tea and we went and sat in the living room. Nancy had not said much, choosing to listen to everything we had to say until we mentioned 'Kraknami'. At that she had stopped chewing for a second and looked up quizzically before resuming eating, but her face was set in a peculiar frown.

At times likes these I found my silent world infuriating, I wanted to ask so many questions without it taking half the night to get the answers, just wanted to have a normal free flowing conversation, where things didn't have to be written down so I could understand them.

Nancy took the book from us and opened it where the 'post it' note marked the page and read. Suzi and I watched. As she read she asked Suzi questions. I was kept out of the loop, again, not intentionally I knew but I couldn't hide my frustration. I realised it was probably just questions confirming what we had already told her, but still, I wanted to be involved.

Nancy got up and went to the book shelves in one of the alcoves beside the fire place. She eyed the many spines of the books so neatly placed in size order.

"What's going on?" I asked Suzi:

NANCY THINKS SHE REMEMBERS SEEING KRAKNAMI IN HER BOOKS.

she scribbled on a small notepad she had started to carry round with her, just in case.

"Is it connected to the Church?"

NOT SURE.

We watched Nancy as she searched through book after book after book. She put one book open face down on the floor and resumed her search, kneeling as she browsed the lower shelves. She was engrossed in her search for a good twenty minutes before returning to her chair with the book she had turned face down on the floor. She then looked at me and started to explain what she knew. I watched her lips move and felt the words turn to sound in my head.

"Bloodline is the ceremony to invoke the Shaddow. The Shaddow is the spirit of the person who has been dormant for twenty-one years. Not dead, just dormant, inside the body of the Solar. In this case your friend James.

"The spirit of the Solar would normally be passed into an unborn child in circumstances where the physical death of the Solar was imminent. The child would be totally unaware of the Shaddow throughout its life until a few hours before the twenty-first birthday, when the Shaddow would be waking, trying to master its carrier. It is important that the Kut of Life be performed within seven hours of the twenty-first birthday in order to bind the two spirits together as one. James would be The Solar.

"The Temples are the High priests so to speak" she raised her hands to signify speech marks with the first two fingers on each hand "They are the ones that start the process by invoking bloodline, awakening the Shaddow. Your friend James would find it very hard to fight it as it is very powerful."

"So in theory this 'Shaddow'" I emphasized using my fingers as speech marks "Could have been wandering around through the centuries?" Nancy nodded her agreement that it was possible "But what is so important about this one person? Why doesn't someone else simply takes his place?"

Nancy didn't answer the question but got up and left the room returning a few minutes later with another book already open, she pointed to a passage which read:

PREFACE

Many Faiths have followers. Faiths are led by the few who hold key positions. Many different terms are used for these and a few will be touched on in this book. These masters believed that in order for the faith to continue and prosper, it was vital for themselves to go on living. Living out an almost eternal life, normally upon their death bed a suitable vehicle for their extended life would be selected and a ceremony or incantation invoked.

There are many different theories that exist for the many different faiths, they all have their own particular quirks, but the one thing in common is the ability to continue to live and hide through the centuries.

When, through the centuries, the presence of such faiths was out of favour with the ruling family then sanctity would be sought, a hiding place where they could be safe. Many faiths died out over the centuries as people were slaughtered without the chance of invoking the immortality giving incantations, so very few faiths still exist in modern day society. The few that do, appear to be less active and fanatical than when they were first started.

In this book I plan to discuss some of the faiths I have discovered, from the earliest writings to their apparent endings, exploring some of the more bizarre rituals which have been carried out, and the reasoning behind them.

I looked at Nancy and handed the book back to her, she could see I wasn't sure what she was getting at.

"It is just the Shaddow that occupies James, a reincarnation. You may find there are others like James within the faith. Many, if the followers have been around for a long time in one guise or another. James will now co-exist with his Shaddow until James's physical death and then the Shaddow will be passed on yet again. James will never exist as you knew him before.

"The advantages for the faith was that if certain members needed to disappear to avoid recognition they could do so for twenty-one years and no one would be any the wiser. Then after twenty-one years they would physically look different anyway"

"Until now! Until I...we discovered the body of Sarah after the accident and she started leading me on this merry body count."

Nancy smiled "Sarah's spirit obviously wants justice for the cruelty she and the other children suffered. Sometimes you come across a spirit which doesn't want to pass over until it is satisfied that justice has been done."

19

"But what's Kraknami all about though?" Finally exacerbated at the thought that everytime we found something new it led us nowhere.

"No mention of it anywhere. Not in any of the places I expected to find it. I'll ask a couple of friends."

I had expected Nancy to know everything. I'd painted this picture of an oracle type witch and felt a little disappointed when she didn't produce the answers. Maybe that was to do with the impression that Suzi gave. She certainly held Nancy in high esteem. Conceding at least she took things seriously and was prepared to help. We knew now that James was just one of the few that were an incarnation of the Drysidium Faith. We didn't know how many there were? Or how were we going to stop them? Whatever we did I knew what the outcome would mean, losing a friend. My best friend. There was no turning back. He wasn't one of us anymore. This was the first time it had really hit home what the outcome would mean. The accident, which I had thought caused the events with James I now knew had been inevitable, I just had a pre-warning due to the loss of hearing caused by the accident, the damage had been done and there was no going back. Life moved on regardless and I was caught in the crossfire.

"What do we do now?" I asked reflectively before adding "There must be something we can do to save James before it's too late." My voice almost pleading.

Suzi turned and looked at Nancy, Nancy's eyes gave away that she knew something yet she paused before speaking as if looking for the right words then facing both of us in, she stated:

"There is very little we can do."

I stood up. Rage building up inside, I was so helpless.

Nancy got up and looked deep into my angry eyes and said calmly, "The Kut of life has secured James's fate. One way to look at it is to say that it isn't really James anymore, just his shell. I know that doesn't make it easier. His destiny was like this from the moment he was born. You couldn't have changed it even it if you wanted to." Her eyes said she was sorry!

I was numb and had hoped beyond hope for a more positive response, that there would be a glimmer of something that we could do. Nancy's continued to stare into my eyes and they seemed to have the capacity to pacify my anger.

Suzi then said something. I saw her lips move out of the corner of my eye but didn't understand. I sighed and walked over to the window, looking forlornly out, surveying the street scene below. Some kids were playing football in the road and I started to think about James and myself and how we used to play football. I let the thoughts consume me, cascade through my mind allowing me to escape the realisation of the evening's events.

I felt a hand on my shoulder and turned, it was Suzi. She indicated that we should leave. As we stood at the front door Nancy put her hand on my shoulder and said 'Sorry'. I understood the sentiment but it didn't make things any easier or better.

It was only half past nine and I asked Suzi to drive me to the scene of the accident. She looked at me apprehensively but obliged without questioning my motives.

A big part of me wasn't ready to let James go yet. I had to do whatever was necessary and going back to the beginning seemed logical to me.

With the exception of the tramlines left by the car down the grass bank, all evidence of the crash had been removed. It now just looked like the piece of waste ground that it had become after the landslips. The image of the night of the accident was still vivid in my head. Gingerly, I made my way down to the actual resting place of my car. Suzi followed a little way behind, sceptical of my reasoning, but allowing me this quirk.

Scanning the ground, my thoughts questioned why all this had happened to me. Searching for clues, answers, anything. I just didn't know what. Anything, something that could help solve this situation, turn back time. I so desperately wanted to turn back time get back to my life before the accident.

I sat on a big rock that still held its scars of where my car had hit it. Closing my eyes I tried to picture the scene as it had been that night, my thoughts as we went cascading down the hillside. The sudden stop as we hit the rock upon which I now sat. Opening my eyes I overlaid the picture on top of how it looked now, in my mind it was clear.

Moving over to where Sarah's remains had been found I pictured the canvas sack and knelt in the dirt convinced I was going to find something else. In reality I knew it was futile. The ground around me was soft and loose, easy to move with my bare hands. I shifted piles of dirt from one area to another as if on a mission. I didn't look at Suzi for fear that she would think me mad.

I wanted a clue to jump up and bite me, a sign, anything that we could use. I stood up and turned round on the spot, unconcerned that I was getting my jeans and shoes dirty. The light was beginning to fade as dusk fell. I hadn't noticed Suzi move down to the rock and stand just behind it; but then out of the corner of my eye, I saw her gesticulating wildly. She was waving for me to come over having discovered a piece of what looked like broken driftwood, on it were the letters, roughly scratched, 'AKNAM'. Looking at each other we both smiled. We knew what was originally spelt out.

It seemed so minor, yet it was another part of the puzzle, and made me feel like there was a chance to change things, put things right. I carried the wood back to the car feeling happier.

Now we had proof that on at least two of the graves the word 'Kraknami' appeared, the only question that remained was what it meant and the significance of it. Another problem we had to deal with was James and the Drysidium Faith, neither Suzi or I were murderers so trying to wipe out the entire membership was not something we were going to entertain. On the other hand, we couldn't leave it alone to manifest with more innocent lives being taken.

As we lay in bed I could feel the warmth from Suzi. I sensed the gentle rise and fall of her chest as she slept, it was almost rhythmical helping me drift into an uneasy sleep, ravaged by dreams of the Drysidium Faith walking the streets wearing their robes, snatching children, openly without a care, an unstoppable machine allowed to roam free and kill at will.

In my mind I tried to stop the images and concentrate on Sarah, hoping she would break my restless slumber. I had questions I wanted to ask. Things I thought – hoped – she might know. Why I thought she might I wasn't sure, all she had done so far is guide me in the right directions, allowing me to find out first hand everything I needed to know. The warnings she gave were mere riddles. I had the book but that was only one piece of an intricate puzzle. Were we looking at it wrong? Were we not reading between the lines correctly?

How had this Faith remained secret for so long? What was their purpose? Most cults, faiths, had a belief, a reason to exist whether for the cleansing of the human race or to raise the devil. I had not read anything that pointed to a view that could establish grounds for their existence.

I was startled from my slumber by a hand fighting its way into mine, it unnerved me at first but then I realised it was warm and inviting. I thought I had been sleeping, maybe it was dream. I rolled over towards Suzi and squeezed her hand tenderly, her body moved in towards mine. I felt her smooth naked legs intertwine with mine, her toes gently playing with my ankles, slowly our arms embraced each other and all the worries dissipated into a throng of pleasure as our lips touched.

Sleep came easily as we lay swimming in a myriad of nice feelings.

Thursday – we were up as usual getting ready for work. Suzi had put the TV on and was watching GMTV but I paid very little attention, I couldn't be bothered to read the subtitles as they flicked up on screen; my thoughts were of the day ahead at work. The isolation. The monotony. I knew the time was coming when I would have to seek something else to do. I couldn't stay where I was, it was driving me nuts. I sulkily ate my Frosties and drank my orange juice before taking time with my coffee.

Suzi gave me a tap on the arm and indicated for me to look at the TV. It took me a couple of seconds to catch up with the subtitles. The picture I recognised as the house behind Blenheim Park, this time it had police tape cordoning it off from the public and, it seemed the occupants. The summary of the subtitles was that a body had been discovered in the grounds and police were questioning the occupants although they were not believed to be connected.

Suzi I could see felt as contented as me about this, finally another soul had been laid to rest. William.

Suddenly her smile vanished and she looked sorrowful.

U DO REALISE THAT ALL WE CAN DO IS LEAD POLICE TO THEM ONE BY ONE?

she scribbled on the pad on the coffee table
"But what about James?"

JAMES IS A PART OF IT NOW. VERY LITTLE WE CAN DO.

Her face looked distant. She obviously felt as sad about it as I did.

"But he still looks and sounds like him."
Suzi looked thoughtfully at me:

YES BUT WE BOTH KNOW.

Despondent, I turned back to the TV. I hated this situation, my best friend gone as such and what I had to do was to set him up to fall. The embarrassment his family would face. Suzi's hand on my shoulder told me she was ready to leave for work. I kissed her gently goodbye on the lips and sat contemplating the future.

This was another time when I wanted Sarah to come. I had more questions I wanted to ask. I wanted to know if there was something that we could do, I didn't want to give up on my friend like that. I couldn't.

I closed my eyes and tried to feel her presence. Concentrating hard, I knew it might mean I would be late for work, but I held no enthusiasm for it anyway. Stretching out on the settee I made myself comfortable, slowing my breathing and relaxing, waiting for sleep to take me under. Taking deep breaths through my nose and exhaling out slowly through my mouth.

Patiently I stayed still. Nothing. Even though I was completely at ease. Still she didn't come. I began to feel that there was something wrong it had been a couple of days now that she hadn't come to me. Maybe we'd found all the undiscovered resting places and there was no longer anything for her to do. Yet somehow that didn't sit right, she'd started this, led me into danger - in my dreams - allowed me to touch history. To disappear so suddenly, wasn't right. What could I do though? I couldn't demand to see her. Was she gone forever?

20

Defeated I gave in and left for work with Sarah plaguing my thoughts. The more I thought about it though the more I sensed a strange kind of peace around me even if something wasn't exactly right. Taking my time, I didn't care that I was late I knew what was waiting. Sure enough the Thursday monotony set in almost immediately as I sat at my desk. I couldn't stop my mind drifting, re-evaluating events since the accident, trying to piece together explanations, reasons, facts, and other bits of information we had gathered.

The only thing that actually felt real anymore was the book, the one piece of physical evidence that meant I wasn't going completely mad; even then that posed more questions than answers. How on earth had I managed to pull the book from my dreams? It wasn't impossible, was it? Then again, that whole dream sequence had proved to be real, the fight with James, when I'd fallen back on him I'd hurt his ribs, heard the crack. Yet he showed no sign of the cut on his hand from the ceremony that he had performed. Was my friend really gone now? It appeared so. Since Monday, neither Suzi, or myself had heard anything from him, he didn't return our text messages or phone calls. We had even tried calling him at his work, his colleagues would just say he was busy and after a few calls they asked us not to call anymore, getting quite stroppy about it.

What did Kraknami mean? Hopefully, we would find out Sunday when we went to church and spoke to Suzi's vicar.

At last, Thursday afternoon ended and I could leave work, life started to ooze its way back into my being, the energy crawling into every sinew that had been desolated by the day's stagnation. I didn't have any more answers but I wasn't at work either. We were going to the pub tonight and even though it held its own demons with my new disability – it was a welcome relief from the day.

Thursday night, Friday and Saturday drifted by and I was growing more concerned by the loss of Sarah. She was solace in my peaceful world despite the riddles she sent me. Suzi was one good thing to come out of the accident. I'd found someone special. I was relaxed and happy with the relationship, even though I hadn't realised I missed the companionship before, I had been content with our little group, and with no one in particular; funny how life deals its hand.

Saturday night I stayed at Suzi's house so we could walk with her parents to church, St Mary's on the main road. I had suggested we turn up after the service as I didn't fancy sitting through a Sunday morning ritual. Suzi quickly pointed out that that would have appeared rude, especially as we wanted the vicar on our side. Not being a church goer, in my mind I knew this was going to be boring, even more so now I couldn't hear what was going on. Suzi had last attended the church two months previously. Her parents had always taken her to church as a child but when she became old enough, she was allowed to choose for herself what she wanted, out of a sense of duty, she explained, attending regularly at first, until the first time she missed it due to homework. When she hadn't been told off for not going she began to miss it more regularly, always stating homework as the reason; gradually she just stopped going. However, one day she had just felt the need to go and from then on had gone intermittently, when the inclination took her.

I expected a lot of old people and was surprised to see so many younger couples. The vicar stood proud in his pulpit as he gave a lively sermon, looking at ease, as he addressed his congregation. His body language was larger than life, emphasizing points he was making, he gave a real sense of belief in his words and he obviously enjoyed it, interjecting humour to hold his congregation, judging by the signs of laughter I saw. Suddenly I wanted to be part of it, hear the passion. A couple of people got up to do readings, they looked far more serious, even scared of making a fool of themselves. Suzi tapped me on the leg when it came to pray ànd I bowed my head in respect but out of the corner of my eye I would watch other people around me. When it came to the hymns I read the words printed in the hymn book Suzi was holding and was surprised that I knew a couple of them like 'Morning has Broken' and 'Rock of Ages', but others I had never heard of, 'Majesty, worship his Majesty', and 'There is a green hill far away'. It was like being back at school in morning assembly, even then I didn't sing.

When the service drew to a close everyone started to leave and we held back, waiting in the pew. The vicar stood at the back of the church and spoke with his congregation as they left. We wanted to make sure we would be last so we could ask him about 'Kraknami'.

As we approached him I noticed that one side of the vicar's mouth looked as though it had slipped, he had been too far away in the pulpit to even attempt to read his lips or take in the details of his features. He greeted Suzi with a big lopsided smile and friendly hug. I couldn't follow what was being said but he held his hand out and I took it, I guessed Suzi had introduced me. His mouth drooped on his right side sometimes when he spoke.

Suzi slipped into easy conversation with him as if they were old friends, this seemed to make sense as Suzi's parents had been going to his church all of her life.

I watched his expressions carefully since I couldn't follow what was being said, the eyes changed from joy to puzzlement and I surmised that Suzi had mentioned 'Kraknami'.

Watching them speaking made me realise how vulnerable I could be when I couldn't follow the words spoken, how heavily I relied upon the honesty of others to look out for me. I was totally at their mercy. I had picked up very little lip reading skills in a week and a half and I wondered if I would ever be able to hold a normal conversation with a complete stranger, not giving away that I was deaf.

My attention wandered around the church, as Suzi and her vicar engrossed themselves in conversation, taking in the ornate details of the carved pillars, the painted ceiling, the elaborate stained glass windows; marvelling at the skilled craftsmanship that made all this possible in times when power tools and modern technology wasn't available. I walked towards one of the pillars close by, it had an inscription on it and I let my fingers caress the letters gently, feeling every indentation.

Feeling a tug at my arm I turned. Suzi was still talking with the vicar. Looking around I saw no one else.

I let my fingers continue caressing the white speckled stone pillar until I felt the tug again. Again no one was there, I shivered, and all the hairs on my arm stood on end. I took a step to the side of the pillar and lurched forward expecting to see a child standing there, someone having a joke with me. Then stepping forward again I was around the back of the pillar.

Nothing!

Out of the corner of my eye I saw movement but couldn't pinpoint it. Walking to the nearest pew I looked underneath. Nothing! I checked some of the other pews. I could feel I was being toyed with.

I looked back to where Suzi and the vicar were, they had moved off slightly, heading towards the door. I could see no one else in the church.

I knelt on the floor to look under all the pews on my side of the church. Nothing!

"Excuse me dear; can I help you?"

Surprised, I looked up. A tall, thin lady, dressed in a light blue cardigan, white blouse, long pale green pleated skirt and wearing slippers was standing there looking at me.

"What? I mean, sorry."

"I said can I help you dear? Have you lost something?" she inquired politely.

"No" then I paused for a moment "I...I thought I saw someone. I was just trying to..." it occurred to me that I could hear her. I made to stand up and banged my head on the seat of the pew. "SHIT!" it came out too quick for me to stop it. "Sorry I didn't mean to swear" rubbing my head.

"That's okay dear. I have heard worse" her voice was just like a favourite granny.

"Who... are you?" I asked cautiously

"Arthur and myself look after the Rectory and the Church."

Still rubbing my head "I don't understand. You see.. I'm deaf so how can I ..." a realisation dawned "... you're dead aren't you?" As the words came out I wanted to grab them back, I didn't want to cause offence "I'm sorry."

"It's okay dear. You can say it. You've lost something haven't you?"

"No. I just felt someone tug my arm. But when I turned round there was no one there."

The lady appeared to move closer, her voice soft. "No dear, you misunderstand me. You've lost something!" she repeated.

I frowned "I don't understand."

"I know many things dear. Something tells me you've lost something that was personal."

I saw something move behind her, she saw me glance to her side "Oh don't mind him that's just Jack, he won't hurt you."

"He's dead too?!" It was more a statement than question and then it was more for my benefit than anyone else. "What happened?" Another tinge of sadness gripped me, another young person dead. Was he connected to Sarah?

"He died from a disease of the heart when he was just six years old."

"Why hasn't he moved on?" and then with a sudden thought "Why haven't you moved on?" I found myself drawn into this conversation, almost forgetting I was actually talking to ghosts.

"It's not everybody's destiny to pass over, and", she paused thoughtfully "I like to look after the church, it's all I know how to do. Jack, well he has another purpose to fulfil before he can move on. He has just been waiting for the right opportunity."

With that Jack appeared from behind the old lady. He had no shoes and was wearing plain brown, thick woollen pyjamas. He looked long and hard at me with his big innocent eyes. Then he spoke.

"Sarah says she's okay but something's blocking her." His tiny voice almost hidden behind the teddy he held in front of his face.

I was stunned yet relieved. What could be blocking Sarah? Who could be blocking Sarah?

The little boy suddenly and shyly sank behind the lady again. She looked up and smiled.

"He has done his task. Now he can rest peacefully." With that the lady made the figure of a cross, forehead, chest, right, then left.

"Amen", she finished.

I stared at the lady "It's rude to stare Peter."

"Sorry. Has he gone then?"

"Yes, finally he is at peace. You were his task."

"But how? Why?" thoughts tumbled from my mouth "When did he die?" I was curious to know how I could be his task as he looked as though he died in the 1960's, a good twenty years before I was even born.

The lady smiled "Ah, the complexities of life…and death shall never be explained. It is best just to accept it as written."

There was a tap on my left shoulder. I turned and Suzi was standing there. Without warning I was brought out of the hearing world I had just been part of, where I could have sworn that I had heard every noise inside the church. Now I was back into my silent world with a thud that made me unsteady on my feet. My arms flayed outwards as I tried to steady myself. I lost everything that Suzi said. My mind in turmoil and feeling dizzy, I put out a hand to support myself. It was too late, I went crashing to the floor, dazed and confused.

My body was a stranger to me nothing would work as I wanted it to. I lay where I fell between the two pews. Suzi was trying to say something to me, but it was like watching a movie through a camera. Next I saw myself being lifted up onto my feet, but was not part of it. I was helped through to a chamber where there was a couch. Surrounding me stood the vicar, Suzi, Suzi's parents, and the old lady behind them all, looking on with a warm, caring smile.

The old lady spoke, it sounded like it was only in my head "Be careful who you trust". With that she was gone.

I could see myself still getting attention from the people surrounding me, but not feeling anything. Slowly that feeling changed and I felt the glass of water that was being placed on my lips. I drank in small gulps and hesitantly sat up.

I looked at Suzi. "What happened?" she mouthed.

For an instant I recalled the events in my head only, I wanted to tell her, something inside prevented me from letting out all I'd seen and I lied, feeling alone in the roomful of people. "Don't know just suddenly felt weird."

The vicar spoke, and all the faces in front of me, half smiled as if they knew some piece of information I was not privvy to.

21

Feeling a little subdued by the events of the morning I remained deep in thought all the way back to Suzi's. I wanted to know what or who was stopping Sarah from communicating with me. I wondered who the old lady meant when she warned me to be careful who I trusted. She couldn't have meant Suzi. Suzi had helped me so much. James, I knew about him and he seemed to be keeping his distance anyway. She might have meant Nancy, who I didn't know and had niggling doubts about anyway. However, Nancy had been Suzi's mentor and part of me knew I had to trust Suzi's judgement; she hadn't let me down.

I had almost forgotten about the Amulet I was wearing around my neck. It could be that that was preventing Sarah from contacting me. No. It couldn't be. I'd been wearing it when she had contacted me before. It had to be something else. What?

As the days had gone by I didn't seem to be getting closer to a resolution, just more and more questions and facts to deal with that didn't necessarily appear connected, directly. If it hadn't been for the crash, would I have been so concerned about James's behaviour or would I have just let our friendship go by the wayside as time went on and as so many friendships do? However, if it hadn't been for the crash would Suzi and I have got together? Life and destiny had a funny way of working, it was perplexing. A part of me wanted to move away, start afresh somewhere possibly where my parents had relocated. There appeared to be no obvious solution here and perhaps, there was never going to be. Just the way my life was destined to play out and I couldn't change it.

Shaking my head in disgust, I was curious how I could even think of walking out on my friends – that was low. Suzi and I were close now and I had a lot to be thankful for. Did I love her? I didn't know.

James needed me. That's what I wanted to believe and I couldn't walk away from him regardless of the outcome, whatever that would be. James was involved in something that was not of his doing and I couldn't leave him to get on with it I had to help him even though I had no idea how.

The local free paper was sitting on the doormat when we arrived back at Suzi's, a few days late, no surprise there. It sat folded in half with just one word of the headline showing, it was in large bold type; 'DISCOVERED'. There was a photograph of the house where William had been buried, sealed off with police tape. Martin, Suzi's dad, picked up the paper and threw it onto the table in the hallway along with his keys. I didn't give it anymore thought and went upstairs with Suzi. We sat on the bed while she told me what the vicar had said.

The vicar, Marshall, had never come across the word 'Kraknami', but there were still many things about his church and faith that he did not know and upon hearing the approximate year when this inscription was made it had triggered some piece of history he'd forgotten about.

He had said that around the sixties, in this area, there was strange goings on within the church. It appeared that some of the local reverends belonged to something that was not altogether welcomed by the church. In 1967, thirteen of them were ex-communicated, which decimated the local congregations, leaving them without spiritual leaders for a time.

Marshall reckoned it might have had something to do with that, but would have to make enquiries, how fruitful this would be he was not sure. Sometimes his superiors didn't like to be asked questions about things that were not 'okay' with the church. Suzi had given him her mobile number and he was going to ring her when he knew more.

Suddenly Suzi jumped off the bed and grabbed my hand pulling me into a standing position, "Dinner's ready", she mimed then she kissed me on the lips before heading off downstairs. Her lips were so soft and warm and I could have stayed there and forgotten about dinner but Suzi was already at the bedroom door.

At the dinner table I noticed the free paper lying on the end of the table, open. I glanced at the upside-down headline and tried to read the accompanying story:

The body of a young boy, thought to be William Thorpe, aged nine, was discovered earlier this week buried under the garage floor of a house on Blenheim Crescent. The grim discovery was made after Police acted on an anonymous tip off. They are appealing for that person to come forward and contact them again to help them further with their enquiries.

The boy was reported missing in June 1964 whilst on a day trip with his family. Dental records were used for identification purposes and his parents have been notified. The parents, Andrew & Anne Thorpe released the following statement via their solicitor.

'Today the police have notified us of the discovery of the remains of our son, who disappeared over thirty years ago. This has resurrected painful memories for our family. We had been forced to accept that we may never find out what had happened to William all those years ago and whilst he has always been close to our hearts, we have had to move on. We are thankful that we can now, finally, lay William to rest.'

The police are now hunting the original owners, who it is believed built the house, records are missing and they are asking for anyone with any information to come forward.

Police are concerned that this may be connected to the body of a young girl found in Bonchurch Park last week, she was also believed to have been murdered around the same time, the young girl has not yet been identified and police are searching missing person records of the time.

Thinking long and hard about the situation; the police had now made a connection that we had not expected; even so what could they do, there can't be much evidence left to point to who the murderer was. I knew forensics were good, but there must be limits.

I felt a tap on my arm, it was Suzi.

"You alright?" I pointed to the paper and she picked it up and read the article.

After dinner we went for a walk along the Cliff gardens opposite Leigh Station, not far from where the accident had happened taking time to sit down on a bench to bask in the hazy sunshine. Kneeling on the bench Suzi faced me, straddling my legs her arms draped around my neck her bum resting on my knees.

I sat staring through Suzi, trying to think of a way forward, wondering who was keeping Sarah from my dreams. It took me a while to notice Suzi waving her hands in front of my face to focus my attention. I looked into her beautiful hazel eyes.

"Sorry. I was just thinking of how we can move forward."

She hurriedly used her phone to write something behind my back forcing her chest into my face as she did so, I didn't try and stop her, then pulling back she showed me **CUD TAKE ME TO URS**

"If only we could find out…" I hadn't registered what she had typed, I smiled.

"I could do. But what would we do once we got there?" I said stupidly missing her point.

She sighed heavily then typed another message on her phone **SURE CUD FIND SOMETHING**. She leant forward to kiss me, in case I needed a hint of what she meant. Letting the moment linger I held her tight, wrapped up in the warm feeling that had started to race between us.

"James's aunt and uncle built there own house in the sixties didn't they?" I broke away from our embrace.

Suzi looked perturbed, sighed then pulled her body closer to mine again gently grinding her hips into mine.

I pushed her back by placing my hands on her shoulders "Well surely it would have been a big thing then to build your own home, maybe there was some sort of club or association they belonged to."

Reluctantly she sat back, resigned to the fact that whatever she did she was not winning with her powers of seduction. She typed on her phone **AND?**

"If there was an association then maybe they have a list of builders that were recommended at the time. They must have used someone – they wouldn't have literally built it themselves. If there is an association there would be a list of houses self built in the area. There can't be that many."

PROB JUST THEM. WASN'T HE A BUILDER?

"Can't remember."

Suzi leaned into kiss me and this time I didn't resist, however, this time it was Suzi who stopped just before our lips touched. She looked at me.

WOT HAPPENED TO UNCLE?

"Not sure, he never really spoke much about them except for that, cos he wanted to build his own house at some point. Why?"

MAYBE Suzi paused then shook her head No!

"What?"

MAYBE THEY BE PART OF FAITH? DEPENDS ON AGES OF HIS PARENTS.

MAYBE SPIRIT PASSED ON WHEN JAMES MUM PREGNANT WIU HIM.

"Then his uncle would be dead now."

Suzi nodded her agreement.

"We'd need to look a bit more closely at James's family tree."

SURE POLICE WILL FIND OWNER THRU LAND REGISTERY. BIG THING IN PRESS RECENTLY BOUT IT.

"That's only for recent sales and new builds. I think."

WE CUD CHECK BACK AT URS and she smiled and moved her body provocatively against mine so I knew what she had in mind.

"Okay but wouldn't the police have done that?"

WONT TELL US THO. COME ON TAKE ME BACK TO URS.

I could feel the urgency in her body and we walked quickly back to mine.

By the time we had got back to mine she was focussed on the search and it was my turn to have my attempts at seduction rebuffed. Reluctantly I searched the net for the land registry service and then entered the details of the address. As it had not been purchased after 2003 it only detailed the current owners who bought the property in 1989. Another dead end.

Suzi sat on my lap and started typing in the friends reunited web address. I looked at her, puzzled and watched the screen as she clicked menu after menu until she came to the 'find your family tree' she was a fully paid up member. I had never used the site before.

She punched in name after name, first James's parent's names, including his mum's maiden name, she didn't know their birth place so left that detail out, she knew their birth dates. She also knew James's grandmother's name and maiden name which she entered and his father's parent's names and siblings.

She pressed enter and waited whilst the system confirmed the information she had input.

"Now what?" I asked, feeling that we should be doing something rather than just sitting there.

WE WAIT. GET EMAIL IF ANYTHING FOUND

"So what do we do now" With that she stood up, spun the chair round so we faced each other, took my hands, placing them on her hips and mischievously looked me in the eye.

22

Not bothering to head to the bedroom, we sank down on the lounge floor pushing the table and chairs out of the way with our feet in the passion of the moment.

Afterwards, we lay on the floor breathless allowing the moon, which shone brightly through the window, to light us. I just wanted to lay there in the twilight having a conversation like two normal lovers might, but I wouldn't be able to read her lips in the half light and to switch on the table lamp would only break the mood. Besides the moon accentuated Suzi's sexy curves which I gently caressed taking in the softness of her, the excitement.

Out of the corner of my eye I saw something flash. At first I wasn't sure if it hadn't been a light source from outside until I noticed the pop up box on the computer screen which had broken the screen saver from its routine. Dragging myself away from Suzi I hit the return key to see what it was. In the back of my mind I hoped it was news about James's family tree.

The mail opened; it was from my parents asking me to go and stay for the weekend, my cousins from America were over and they were trying to gather as many members of the family, however distant, together. It was in two weekends' time. I had told my parents about Suzi and she was invited as well.

I lay back down beside Suzi trying recapture the moment. I mentioned the date to her, I couldn't see what she replied, but then she planted her lips firmly on mine and I felt her nakedness against mine and we just lay there amongst the cushions where nothing seemed to matter anymore.

Sometime during the night, Suzi must have dragged the quilt

from the bed and spread it over us. I didn't notice her leave or come back.

We were up and out to work by 8am. Changing my job was now becoming a serious necessity; the satisfaction I got from it had waned considerably now that I couldn't hear. What else could I do? I couldn't think of anything off the top of my head that didn't involve some sort of verbal communication. Realistically, it was more likely just the way I viewed it as that is all I'd ever known. I needed to skew my perspective and think more clearly; there must be loads of jobs available.

Sarah was no longer coming through in my dreams and that concerned me, especially as I didn't know what I could do to change it. The Drysidium Faith was a conundrum, we needed proof that they were up to no good but there wasn't any physical evidence to connect them to any murders. Everywhere we turned seemed to be a dead end, their tracks so well covered. We had dates of deaths, we had the remains, but no connections.

I missed James in a way. No matter how much I text or phoned him, he didn't answer, Suzi had no success either. It was like he never existed, wiped from our lives – except for memories.

The door to work loomed in front of me and I stood looking at it pre-occupied with other matters. My heart sank. The will to live was draining from me as if I'd sprung a leak. Eight hours of nothing stretched out in front of me, like a straight road that divided a desert in two, disappearing beyond the horizon. Two works colleagues brushed past me smiling their greeting, I reciprocated half heartedly and followed them in as they held the door open for me.

Switching on my computer I drank the rank cup of tea I had got from the machine, and watched as my computer whirled into life, going through its monotonous routine, the same as every day. I ploughed through the twenty-seven emails, a few of them spam. The day continued in that vain and by the time I left I didn't ever want to go back. I had my first 'sign' class tonight, a suggestion made by my specialist, who thought it would help me adjust. The class started at 8 o'clock and Suzi was going to do the course with me; she was so supportive. The way the day had gone I was not particularly in the mood for learning but I knew Suzi would not accept that attitude.

Whilst I waited for Suzi to pick me up, I played 'Freecell' on my PC. A pop up box flashed up on screen asking whether I wanted to view a new mail. I clicked 'no' then felt a pair of hands on my shoulders which nearly made me jump out of my skin. I'd allowed 'Freecell' to take focus completely.

I saw a person like outline on the screen and started to close my game down. I put my right hand on the hand that was on my shoulder.

It wasn't Suzi's as I expected and swivelled round sharply on my chair to see James standing there. For what seemed an eternity there was a stand off while neither of us spoke, just staring at each other. I tried to speak but for the briefest moment couldn't find any words, there was something strange about him.

"What you doing here?"

He just stood there not answering looking distant, his mouth quivered as if to speak. As I took in his face I could see that he was flushed, hot, as if he'd been running. He still didn't move. His eyes then inexplicably rolled back in their sockets and he slumped to the floor.

Astonished I was momentarily lost for what to do, too bewildered to check if he was alright. Then as rationality came flooding back I kicked his foot lightly expecting a reaction. He remained motionless on the floor and slowly I went to my friend's aid, kneeling beside him, checking his vital signs. He was still breathing although very faintly.

James opened his eyes, making me jump, staring intently at me. I watched his lips move but didn't know what he said. Damn, I wished I could hear again; his eyes closed and he lay on the floor as if asleep, peaceful.

A thought occurred – I didn't know how he had got into my flat. I ran and checked the front door, it was closed. I opened it to see if I'd left my keys in the lock. Nothing! Closing it, I went and stood by my friend who still lay on the floor. I walked to the front bay window to look for an answer, maybe I had left a window open, but my windows were one floor up and there was nothing nearby to use to climb up. I saw Suzi walking up the path to my front gate, she stopped when she saw me in the window, waiting for me to join her, I beckoned her in. She looked puzzled and pointed at her watch.

I opened the window and shouted "James is here". With that she rushed in. I explained what had happened. Suzi re-checked his vital signs then placed a cushion under his head, before we both went into the kitchen.

HE LOOKS OK! SEEMS OK.

I went to grab the pad from Suzi, momentarily forgetting she could hear me

"I just don't understand what happened. I don't know how he got in, I'm sure I didn't leave the door open and he doesn't have a key. There's no windows he can climb through either."

HE DOES NOT HAV A KEY?

"Positive, I've never had reason to give him one. It never occurred to me really."

Suzi got up and walked back into the lounge, I followed and watched as she searched James's pockets. She produced a bunch of keys, checking each one. Another email flashed up on screen and I went over and hit the return key. It was from my mum confirming the visit of my cousin from America. It reminded me of the previous one that I had received, I clicked on my inbox, there were two emails sitting there unread, one was a spam, and the other was from friends reunited. I opened the latter.

Suzi tapped my shoulder and I turned to see her pointing at a key in amongst all the others, it was an exact copy of my front door key, she also pointed to another one, hers.

HE DOESN'T HAVE A KEY TO MY PARENTS PLACE. NEVER GAVE HIM ONE

Suzi typed on a word document.

"Why and how did he get our keys then? Who's are all the others?"

I showed Suzi the email from friends reunited. It was regarding the family tree she had set up for James's family. There were four possible matches. We clicked on the first but further details didn't match. The second was also a non-starter. The third one rang true, names and dates. Further information showed that James had a distant cousin, who had also been trying to trace the family tree. She had had quite a bit of luck. There appeared to have been a name change in the sixties which was when the family first became known as Sullivan, the exact date was a bit vague.

We added the details and viewed the new family tree James's distant cousins Phillipa had produced. She wanted James to contact her but we replied, she wouldn't know any different. From the family tree there was nothing too significant although the name change was strange. Phillipa had said she'd tried to find out why some of the family had changed the surname but had met with a blank wall. Phillipa had lived in Southend until the family relocated to Cornwall in 1972.

No legal documents were available confirming the name change within the family. It appeared that one day the surname was 'Day' the next it was 'Sullivan'. It was not apparent how the legalities of it all had been addressed, such as deaths – a birth certificate would have been needed to register the death, the different surname would have become apparent. Still, now we had more information to work with.

One question still remained 'What was up with James?' He was still asleep on the floor, neither of us wanted to wake him up but there were questions to answer.

Patiently we waited, watching him. Occasionally one of us would check his pulse. He just appeared to be in a deep sleep. At one point we tried to lift him onto the settee but he was too heavy. It was starting to get late, we had missed my sign class – which didn't bother me – and we needed to go to bed. It was nice in a strange way to have him there but we had to find out the truth. I gingerly nudged his shoulder. It took a fierce nudge to shake him from his slumber and as he did he yawned, stretched his arms out above his head, hands flexing to get the muscles working again. Suddenly his eyes opened wide and he sat bolt upright. Staring at us like a cat caught in the headlights of an oncoming car, shuffling back towards the wall behind him on his backside. I stood up perplexed. He said something, I didn't understand.

I looked at Suzi, who was approaching James, talking to him, I didn't know what was being said. By the time I was standing next to her, she had stopped speaking. She was staring at James intently waiting, expectantly for his reply. He sat frozen against the wall. Suzi waved the bunch of keys at him. Her face showed anger, her eyes wide, cheeks slightly flushed. James struggled to his feet, using the wall as support. Pearls of sweat formed on his brow, he was trying to back through the wall.

Suzi moved closer to him, fire in her eyes. I had never before seen James frightened, I couldn't understand why he was acting like he was.

James's demeanour gave way and he struck out at Suzi, catching a flat hand across her left cheek. With the power of the strike Suzi went flying backwards, falling over the back off the settee. The keys left her hand and landed on the seat of an armchair.

I lunged forward trying to pin James to the wall. He had always been able to overpower me but now he seemed twice as strong and easily managed to hold me back. With a swift movement he hooked his right foot behind my right knee yanking it towards him. I collapsed in a heap on the floor, releasing my grip. James tried to step over me as I fell. I grabbed for his ankle which he tried to kick free but only managed to stumble into the computer table, hitting the corner on his left thigh.

Recovering quickly he lunged towards the armchair to grab the bunch of keys. Suzi had managed to right herself and launched herself at James and the keys, trying to intercept him. With one strong swing of his left arm he knocked her out of the way. This time she went crashing to the floor hitting the edge of the armchair on her way down. James grabbed the keys and headed to the front door. Without thinking, I picked up the nearest object I could, which was a mug I had been drinking from, and hurled it at him catching him on the back of his right shoulder before falling to the floor and smashing.

I got to my feet using the arm of the settee to pull myself up. James turned to face me. We were in a stand off. Staring into each others eyes. Waiting. Trying to pre-empt the others next move. I saw his mouth move but didn't understand what he said. Suzi was still on the floor, clutching at her stomach.

From nowhere James suddenly produced a knife. I stood frozen to the spot, scared that my friend could resort to such tactics even though deep down I knew this wasn't my friend anymore. He would never have pulled a knife on me but it didn't stop me trying to reason with him.

"James. What's going on? Why did you come here tonight? We're your friends. I'm your best friend." My voice was filled with anger and desperation.

He replied and again I couldn't follow the words. He looked at Suzi, who was now just starting to get up, then at me. James reached out with his free hand to the internal door that helped create a lobby between the front door and the lounge. Stepping back, he opened it and stepped through closing it without taking his eye off either of us.

I lunged at the door but was halted in my tracks as the blade of the knife came through the paper thin door about head height, before being retracted. I was stunned. Suzi stood by my side, staring at the hole left by the knife.

I went to the window and watched as James disappeared down the street.

23

Standing speechless, my breathing still heavy, I was amazed by the events of the previous five minutes. Deep down I knew it wasn't James but that didn't make it any easier.

Suzi was still holding her stomach and I put my hand on her shoulder to ask her whether she was alright. She nodded even though she still looked a little winded. I was not going to argue with her as I knew what she was like when roused, instead, I straightened up the lounge, picking up pieces of the broken mug. Suzi walked into the kitchen.

My curiosity was aroused. Why had James come round? And how did he get my house keys? Even Suzi's house keys? Tidying the cushions I realised that Suzi been gone for a long time. Becoming concerned, I went into the kitchen. She was laying doubled up on the floor, holding her stomach and crying, obviously in a great deal of pain. Kneeling down on the floor beside her I gently tried to ease her over so she was facing me. She was reluctant as tears streamed down her cheeks. It dawned on me that this was far more serious than I had first thought and didn't wait to be asked, I rushed to the phone to call for an ambulance. Picking up the receiver it dawned on me that I wouldn't know when the phone had been answered. Damn! This was so infuriating! How do people cope?

I rifled through Suzi's shoulder bag that she always carried with her and found her car keys. I would have to drive her to the hospital myself, it was only five minutes away. Picking her up effortlessly and as gently as I could I carried her out to her car, with every movement I could see another grimace of agony. Getting her into the passenger seat was tricky.

Driving as fast as her little Burgundy Fiesta would allow I slowed at all the speed cameras. 'Damn those bloody things!'

I knew full well that I wasn't insured to drive her car and was torn between getting her to the Hospital and not breaking the law. I always thought that in this sort of situation that I would act recklessly, but I still held back.

Suddenly, after one of the many cameras, a car pulled out in front of me and I had to brake hard to miss it, ironically now I was grateful for the camera – if I hadn't slowed down there would have been a ticket and an accident.

Pulling into the hospital A & E I double parked. Lifting her out of the car she seemed heavier than before; there were still tears in her eyes and she helped as much as she could by putting her left arm behind my neck to help support her weight. I pushed the car door shut with my foot and didn't bother to lock it.

Carrying Suzi to reception my arms started to feel weak even after the short distance. The receptionist spoke but before she finished what she was saying I told her I was deaf. Her facial expression showed acknowledgement and she listened without getting angry that I had interrupted her. I explained what had happened, leaving James out of it, preferring to say she just fell. Quickly, two porters rushed up and took her from my arms placing her on a trolley. As I went to walk after her, the receptionist grabbed my arm. The counter was low but she still had to stretch, the hand was firm but gentle. On a piece of paper she'd written:

SHE'LL BE FINE, FORMS PLEASE.

I looked at her. I wanted to go with Suzi, make sure she was alright but I knew forms had to be filled in and contact details taken. Suzi, I wanted to go with Suzi. The receptionist's eyes showed empathy and this placated me. Reluctantly, I conceded. The receptionist, Laura, according to the name badge, contacted

Suzi's'parents for me after I had given as much information as possible to help her locate Suzi's Hospital records.

Suzi's parents turned up within twenty minutes by which time I had parked the car properly, no news of her had been given to me in that time, I just sat and waited. I was worried, angry that James had put her life in danger. I repeated my story to them.

Suzi's mum, Vanessa, went to speak to the receptionist. I could see she was concerned for her only daughter and Laura tried to placate her. A & E had been fairly quiet but was starting to get busy and Laura was doing her best to deal with everyone. Suzi's dad, Martin, tried to comfort Vanessa before going to get a cup of tea from the machine. They sat down again and we all waited. Doctors came in and out. Ambulance crews came and went. Patients came and went. It seemed like an eternity.

Eventually a Doctor came out to the receptionist, and she directed him to us. We were then escorted to a quiet corner. I tried to follow what was going on, but couldn't even make out one word of what was being said. Vanessa burst into tears whilst Martin comforted her and chatted to the Doctor. My heart sank, obviously it was far more serious than I first thought. I wanted to ask what, but before I could speak we were ushered further into the depths of the hospital. Corridor after corridor we walked following the porter the doctor had assigned to take us to where we needed to go.

At the end of the journey was another waiting room, Suzi's parents sat down and the porter left. I stood, looking and feeling awkward, I asked what was wrong, Martin wrote down 'APPENDIX'.

Time passed like watching paint dry, the tedium set in, intermittently one of us would get up and stroll round stretching our legs, reading the notices, the adverts, picking up a magazine, anything to while away the time. A Doctor eventually saw us and judging from the relief on Suzi's parent's faces she was okay. Vanessa was allowed to see her daughter briefly before we were ushered away and asked to allow her to rest until the following day. She would be in for about a week.

Martin drove Suzi's car, and dropped me off at home.

My flat had a tainted atmosphere about it. It was early morning and I was tired, but my bed wasn't inviting, nowhere was, yet I knew I needed sleep. Dragging the quilt into the lounge I settled on the settee only managing a few hours before I had to get up for work. I contemplated pulling a 'sickie', decided it was the obvious choice; I didn't even feel guilty about it. I sent an email and snuggled back up under the quilt, I didn't feel so tired anymore.

Switching on the TV I flicked through the channels, early morning TV was bad but slowly the pictures blurred before my eyes and I was taking in less and less of what was before me.

"Help me."

It was Sarah's voice but I couldn't see her.

"Where are you?"

"You must break the Octagon of Garia. It's holding me back."

"The What? Of What?"

Her voice faded as she struggled to communicate with me. I tried desperately to recall what she had said. She was gone.

I opened my eyes 'Octagon of Ga...Sarah!. Sarah!' I shouted. What was the last word she said? How was this holding her back? Who possessed this thing? Would it be easy to locate?

Suzi was out of the equation, I was on my own. I could ask Nancy, even if I did feel a little uneasy about her.

I thought back to James and his behaviour the night before, it was niggling me. It was strange how one minute he'd appeared normal and then he was gone, taken by another influence. I really believed he was actually there last night, at one point, not just in body but in spirit to, trying to get out, trying to break whatever or whoever it was that was taking control of him. Nancy had said that he was now lost and there was no hope for the James as I had known. My only question was "Was he fighting from within?"

I decided a visit to him at work was in order to try and talk to him. See if I could find anything out.

By 11.30am I was outside James's work place, I couldn't see his car parked anywhere but that didn't mean anything. I marshalled my thoughts together for a few moments then walked into the reception area, expecting a frosty reception after all the phone calls I had made. I was greeted by a middle-aged man wearing paint splattered overalls. I asked to speak to James Sullivan, quickly explaining I was deaf and couldn't lip read. The man fidgeted whilst he thought for a second then scribbled on a pad.

JAMES NOT HERE. NOT SEEN SINCE LAST MONDAY. IF YOU SEE HIM TELL HIM TO CONTACT US OTHERWISE HE WILL HIS LOSE JOB.

Taken back a little, I thanked the man and decided to head round to James's house, figuring he should be there, his parents out at work.

Catching me unaware, his father was in, working from home and James had not been home for a week or so, saying he was staying with friends. Impulsively, I asked if I could have a look in his room as he had borrowed a couple of DVD's that I needed back. He hesitated only briefly before letting me in to find my own way to James's room.

The room looked neat and tidy, unusual for James, as I knew him to be quite messy at the best of times, his mother was obviously taking advantage of his absence. It was often the case when he was out, infuriating James no end.

I looked around the room, not sure what I was searching for; anything, hoping something obvious would jump out at me. We had spent many hours playing computer games and watching DVD's over the past few years, the main things he possessed besides his stereo and TV with full surround sound. Books and ornaments weren't his thing. He liked football and was an avid Manchester United fan.

I checked underneath his bed, except for shoes, it was clear, his mother had carefully arranged the shoes in their pairs. His sleeping bag was gone though. I checked his wardrobe and noticed his rucksack was also missing. I checked his shoes again, his hiking boots had gone, he didn't wear them very often and when he had I had commented on the fact. James had bought them to go on holiday to Scotland and had hardly worn them in the three years since.

I hadn't seen the door open but felt a hand on my shoulder. Mr Sullivan was standing there. I watched his lips move before he shook his head and went to James's desk and wrote on a pad:

FOUND THEM?

I shook my head and quickly made my excuse to leave. Mr Sullivan eyed me suspiciously. I ignored it.

I knew James was not into camping. The sleeping bag had been an unwanted gift from a previous Christmas, his parents had misheard him, he'd always joked about it, how his parents didn't really listen to him. It had lived under the bed gathering dust. I was still no closer to finding out where he was. I thought he was staying somewhere he wouldn't normally if he needed the sleeping bag.

At a loss I went home.

As I sat ploughing through the facts, scribbling them down on a pad as if that might organize them. 'Rochford' kept springing to mind, nagging at me, drawing me to it. I grabbed a snack and thought I would head there to see if I could find the barn where I had confronted James in my dream. Firstly though, I would visit Suzi and make sure she was alright.

Suzi was sleeping so I left the flowers I'd bought her. The nurse said she was recovering well.

I racked my brain trying to remember the location of the barn, things looked so different during daylight and I couldn't recall all the details accurately. After walking around for what seemed like hours I eventually saw the barn hiding behind a large farmhouse. I walked past, not wanting to arouse any suspicion by staring at it, surreptitiously eyeing the grounds, looking for clues. It looked picturesque in its location on this bright sunny day. The wide road frontage with its neatly manicured gardens looked imposing. Heavy net curtains covered the windows concealing the inside. To the right of the building, tall trees added to the thick hawthorn bush made the boundary and these trailed off towards the distant horizon. An empty field sat to the right of this stretching as far as the eye could see, it was recently ploughed.

The road changed to a single track country lane shortly after the farmhouse which was the last house along this lane. I was shaken from my study by a vehicle whizzing past, making me jump.

I paused to regain my composure, before walking further along until I came to a gate that led into the field. Checking to make sure I wasn't being watched I climbed over, ducking quickly behind the hawthorn bush that marked the boundary to the road. Slowly, I headed back in the direction of the house. It was hard going trying to keep low and out of sight whilst retaining my balance in the ploughed soil. I watched for signs of life in the house when I could.

Behind the house, just visible through the trees was the barn. Last time I was here the barn hadn't looked quite so large and formidable. The outline stood proud even though it tried to hide behind the trees.

The house looked peaceful, as if deserted only hours before. No vehicles that I could see. I was now level with the barn. Through the trees and bushes I could make out that the barn was well maintained not like the ones I had seen so many times on car journeys, ramshackle and falling apart.

I was tingling with apprehension as I watched for movement, aware that I was in fact trespassing. The warm breeze became a tad cooler in the shade. Further up from my position I could make out a break in the bushes, where one part had died, this would give me the access required. Making my way through I snagged my shirt.

Once on the other side, I scanned the area, still no sign of human occupation. Squatting behind a tree and just peaking out I saw where I had struggled with James that night in my dreams.

24

With trepidation I crept forward, crouching, keeping low to the ground. My deafness gave me an unusual sense of safety, tricking me into believing that if I couldn't hear anyone then I couldn't be heard either. Every step I took my confidence grew, the thought that I was trespassing was inconsequential. I wanted finality to this whole grotesque situation. Ever since the accident, turmoil had destroyed my otherwise plain life, only now did I realise how much I valued that simple life. If I was going to be deaf then I wanted there to be some purpose that would give me a positive reason to move on and accept that the rest of my life was going to be like this.

I moved to the wooden clad wall of the barn, the south side. A knot had fallen out of a feather edge board leaving a peep hole. I peered through. It was as I had seen it the night I had stolen the book, empty except for a makeshift altar, the floor covered by a layer of straw.

Making sure the coast was clear I made my way to the door, which would not budge. Only a latch was visible on the outside and I guessed that it must be bolted from the inside in which case there had to be another way in. I skirted round the outside of the barn, completely engrossed in my task, forgoing glances to check I was not being watched. Looking for another entrance firstly I followed the timber clad wall to the east side of the barn that was nearest the trees and not far from where I had come through the hawthorn bush. I didn't recall seeing a door there but I hadn't been looking.

Nothing!

Then I rounded the north side, still no sign of another entrance. I rounded the west side of the barn and expected to see two large barn doors, there wasn't; if there had been at one time they were gone now, all trace erased. I went back past the locked door on the south side and re-investigated the east side again convinced I had missed something. No change still nothing. Perplexed I became absorbed further in my task.

The north side again, again there was no visible entrance. How could there be a door locked from the inside and no way in other than that. I liked challenges but ones that were solvable. I walked around the barn yet again engrossed by this intangible problem. A simple four sided barn approximately thirty-five feet tall to the lowest point of the roof, no windows, just the door below the roofline on the south side. Flummoxed, I tried the door again, pushing it, pulling it, then pushing it again, using my shoulder to bolster more pressure, it did not budge. Standing back I was sure there was something I was missing from the larger picture.

Suddenly there was a cold metal object on my shoulder.

'Shit' I thought freezing, expecting something to happen, to feel a sharp pain somewhere as someone struck me. A thousand excuses zipped through my brain. I gulped and turned slowly round to face a man, over six foot tall, stocky, wearing jeans and a knitted orange jumper. In his hand he held a single barrelled shotgun pointed straight at my chest. He had short hair and cruel grey eyes. My legs became like jelly and I stumbled backwards.

The gun became my only focus as I struggled to support my weight. I knew I would have to do some fast talking. There was no escape. The man spoke his mouth barely moving. When I offered no reply his face showed anger, cheeks turning crimson. Still I stood there, stunned. Common sense to utter the words I was deaf had left me. There was no one else in sight.

Slowly the man raised the shotgun, holding it like a familiar friend in both hands and pointing the barrel towards my face. My eyes widened in terror as I took in my pending fate. Panic engulfed me with droplets of sweat forming on my forehead as my body temperature rose sharply and my heart pounded like a tattoo inside my chest. Words failed me yet I needed to offer an excuse before it was too late.

The man scowled at me, the gun still hovering in front of my eyes, then slowly and purposefully he pulled back the hammer on the gun, cocking, ready to fire. My bladder was feeling the tension and any second now I was expecting to feel a warm sensation coursing down my legs. I had never faced a real gun, the terror it produced was new to me. Two figures locked in a silent dual. In his eyes there were questions he wanted to ask.

He uttered another few words and I expected this to be the end. I stood transfixed and helpless, every notion of running gone, expecting to feel a searing pain and then nothing. I closed my eyes in readiness. For longest moment I wondered what had happened but then he nudged my shoulder with the barrel and pointed to the road. Was I dreaming? He nudged me again. Tentatively I started to move slowly lifting my right foot, it didn't feel like my own. Then my left. Was he going to change his mind? Was this a game? Slowly it registered that I wasn't going to get shot and picking up the pace I ran as fast as my scared legs would carry me. Before I knew it I was at the entrance gate, then out into the road, I didn't look back; I just ran, ran back into the safety of Rochford.

I couldn't believe I had gotten away with it. My leg muscles were burning screaming at me to stop and finally I came to rest at Market Square. It was just like the dream when I ran from James. Déjà vu.

My heart pounded hard, every breath hurting. The adrenalin alone had allowed me to push my muscles further than I had ever done before. The greater the distance I had put between the man and me, the safer I felt. Bending over double I wanted to vomit, release everything that was inside me. I was sweating profusely, people stared, I didn't care I was safe. I knew how lucky I had been.

What I couldn't understand was why he had he just let me go? How long had he watched me? Did he know that I knew what went on inside? Surely he couldn't have, otherwise he would have held onto me. What was his role in all this? Was he just a keeper?

My phone vibrated. There was a message from Suzi.

'Hi sorry I missed u. Thanx for flowers there beautiful. Feel ok. B gd 2 c u. Luv Sx' I replied that I would call in that evening. It was 4.17pm and I still wasn't making much headway. The Barn really had been my only lead.

Maybe it wasn't used all the time? Maybe it was only used for ceremonies? I could stake it out but I could be there a long time without success if it was just an occasional location used.

I needed to locate James. I could ring up his other friends but I had a feeling that would be fruitless. A thought occurred, it was risky but, I believed, my only chance to try and end this. I sent James a text asking him to meet me at the barn at 10pm that night. I only hoped he'd read it. That would give me time to go home, visit Suzi, and let her know what I was doing.

What was I doing? Playing into the hands of a murderer? No, he is, was, my friend.

I ran over the previous night in my head as I headed to Nancy's. It didn't make sense for James to turn up at my place like that, not now. Some strange sense of hope gripped me; was James fighting back? Inside, was the real him trying to break through. Nancy had said that once occupied that was it. Maybe I had misunderstood. I had hope and that was all I needed.

I rang the doorbell of Nancy's flat at just about 5.30, she answered wearing a dressing gown, I quickly apologised for disturbing her. She explained that she'd been off ill but let me in, again her words came alive somehow, if only everyone possessed whatever she had life would be easier again. Maybe she could explain how to Suzi and we could at least have a normal conversation. I said that

I had some questions and she was the only person who I thought might know the answers.

Telling her everything that had happened in the last twenty-four hours she listened without interruption. She didn't believe it was possible that James was fighting back but she was not an Oracle. I mentioned about the Octagon of Garita or something that was holding Sarah back from contacting me. Nancy went and grabbed a book from a shelf, opened it and placed it in my hands, then left the room.

Octagon of Garia – Used to bind an unwanted spirit, destroying the link they may have with the subject.

There was no diagram to show me what it looked like and I flicked through the book while I waited for Nancy to return. The book was a dictionary of terms and symbols; I read a couple to pass the time. Nancy was gone ages. I thought maybe she had put the kettle on to make tea. I casually looked around the room, the curtains were drawn blocking out the early evening sun. Everything appeared to be in its place except for a rucksack on the floor. It looked familiar. Nancy entered carrying two mugs, offering me one, which I took taking a sip. Up to then I hadn't realised how thirsty I was. One sip couldn't abate my thirst and I drank more, even though it was hot, it didn't matter and in just a few seconds the drink was gone.

Nancy sat and watched, slowly sipping from her mug, she smiled at me and took the book from my hands. I explained that I was going to confront James at the barn. I thought if he knew I knew about the barn and where it was, he would meet me. She didn't look surprised just sat there as if waiting. I carried on. I told her about the man with the gun and asked whether they would have a watcher as such. She just smiled again.

Suddenly I became queasy and light headed, my hands and feet were not my own, the room was starting to spin, and then to blur, everything moving in slow motion. Nancy took the mug from me. I did a double take. It wasn't Nancy who was taking the mug from me, it was James. James smiled and my eyes rolled back in their sockets, everything went black.

Had I just landed in the lion's den? Had I really been that stupid? I always thought there was something unsavoury about Nancy but had allowed myself to be convinced otherwise, against my better judgement.

When I came to, James was in the armchair opposite me. I tried to speak but couldn't form words. My body still didn't want to function as mine. Then I realised I was actually completely paralysed. Panic pulsed through my fuddled brain, fear making my heart beat faster, all I could do was view the room from the slumped position I was in on the settee.

I could see Nancy and James talking and laughing. Everything inside me worked fine, emotions in turmoil at this situation I'd allowed myself to fall into.

I willed any part of my body to react. Thoughts rambled, questions remained unanswered. What was going on? I thought Nancy was Suzi's friend.

James and Nancy stood up and came towards me, smiling in their victory. They'd won their game. James grabbed my hands and dragged me off the settee into the middle of the floor, not caring whether my head hit the floor or not, it did – I think – I didn't feel anything – I was face up. Nancy placed objects around me and when she finished leaned over and spoke very slowly.

'My Uncle's barn. Thank you. You did exactly what we needed you to.'

She smiled then picked up a book that was sitting on a side table near my feet and standing over me made arcs in the air with her arms. All I could do was look up at the ceiling, helpless. Was this the end for me?

James was out of sight and I was powerless, a stuffed toy that had been discarded on the floor by an angry child.

I saw a glowing light that appeared to be emanating from my chest. Straining my eyes I only managed to see the arcs of my cheeks and the glow of the light. Then a slight burning sensation grew just below my neck, at first it was warm and nice but soon it grew in intensity, and with that so did the pain. Internally I was battling, my thoughts trying to form some sort of clarity, if I could feel this then surely I would be able to feel the rest of my body. I caught sight of Nancy, the smile had gone from her face, replaced by concentration. James was still nowhere to be seen.

The heat source burned even brighter, filling the whole room with its glow, I fought the pain. I still could not move any part of my body but at least I knew I was still alive – but I wished I wasn't, the burning produced a horrible stench that sank itself into my nose.

A sudden bright flash of light lit the room, I couldn't blink and thought I was going to go blind. Then blackness embraced me.

Except for the warm sensation on my chest all my senses were numbed, no vision, no sound, no smell, and I couldn't move. I remembered the amulet. How had that fitted into this scenario? I wanted to get up but couldn't.

I was stuck. What had happened to James?

25

Wracked with emotions I lay incapacitated on the floor, the lack of vision and sound fuelling my emotions. I hoped the paralysis was only temporary. Desperately I tried to relax my mind until it had worn off but I felt so vulnerable stuck on the floor and this sent pessimistic thoughts coursing through my mind. My frustration tore at me, screwing every fibre. Double crossed by Nancy!

Damn I should have trusted my instincts.

How was I going to tell Suzi? Would she believe me? Would I ever get the chance to tell her?

All I could do was breathe and hope that with each breath my body would repel the potent sedative they had given me, if indeed it had been just a sedative. The panic would come on me in waves and just when I thought I had tempered it, it was there again beating at the door like an unwelcome friend.

Time lost meaning. Every few moments I willed my limbs to move. I had to try something. The minutes passed like hours. Nothing! My brain tumbled through all the possibilities, the connections between Nancy and James. Did Suzi know? It was my only distraction from my helplessness.

In my current state I could understand what it must be like to be left in a coma, the brain still functioning and alive. Were people aware of their situation in a coma or was it an endless dream. I thought coping with deafness was bad, I had no concept of what it must be like for people who would remain alive like this for the rest of their lives with bodies that could do nothing. Then in the darkness of it all, a familiar voice resonated:

"*Thank you, I'm free again. You are safe.*"

"*Sarah*" relief rose in my voice.

"*Yes.*"

Mentally I smiled.

"*What's happening to me?*" *For the first time in what seemed hours a sense of ease coursed through me. I regarded Sarah as a friend and it was good to hear her voice, even more so now I was incapacitated.*

"*Your friend, she is in danger, you have to help her. Only you can save her.*"

"*Do you know how long before I can move again?*" *a stupid question I thought after I said it. There was silence* "*Sarah! Sarah!*" *I shouted in my head, there was no reply. I was alone again. Empty and alone. I couldn't tell if I was awake or asleep or dreaming in some sort of drug induced coma.*

I started to run through all the events of the last couple of weeks since the accident, the graves we'd found, how my life had changed, what had happened to James. And now, how Nancy had turned. My friend – I scoffed. What had Sarah meant by the fact that she was in danger and I had to help her, Why? My mind flitted back to the last time we had visited Nancy and how I'd felt betrayed by her and Suzi. Maybe my gut instinct was not incorrect. Is Suzi in on it? No, I found that hard to believe, she wouldn't. I was just tainting her with the same brush as Nancy, and that wasn't being fair whichever way I looked at it.

I needed to do something instead of laying here being useless. I had so many unanswered questions. I pushed the thought of movement as hard as I could through every fibre of my body, willing it to move.

"*Get up, you are in danger. You must leave now.*"

"*I can't.*"

"*You are only asleep. Wake up. You can move.*"

I was taken aback. Had I really just been sleeping? I tried to wake up, willed myself to wake up, but I was gripped by a strange reality. I thought I'd been awake. But how could I doubt Sarah? She had never let me down.

I struggled with my indifference between reality and dreaming. How could I tell if I had feeling in my body? I had nothing to gauge it by.

All I could do was try to stir myself systematically, try to send messages around my body starting with my hands, focusing every effort; first my fingers. Were they moving? I really couldn't tell.

"You must get up. You are in danger."

"I can't."

A sudden coldness took my heart. My lungs tightened, constricted. With a powerful release I sucked in a massive gulp of air my lungs hurting with the strain.

Immediately I sat bolt upright amazed by the ease with which I had moved. I was back in Nancy's lounge, a blur of thoughts computing in the foreground, trying to decipher what had happened and what I was meant to do next. In front of me Nancy lay spread-eagled on the floor. All my limbs were like lead taking an enormous amount of effort to move each of them in turn. I could have fallen a sleep again, my eyelids were so heavy and they kept closing as if spring-loaded. My head was unsteady on my shoulders.

Sluggishly I pulled myself up on my knees, the effort was almost too much. I stayed on all fours for a time willing my energy to come back. It was as if I had gone twenty rounds in boxing match, finding it difficult to comprehend that it was so hard to move, like moving through treacle. In the back of my mind was Sarah's warning that I was in danger.

Every movement was slow, and cumbersome, like a puppy taking its first steps, its paws and head too big for its weak body.

I crawled over to where Nancy lay, motionless, glancing up at the window to gauge roughly how long I had been out. No light shone through the heavily curtained window, I surmised that it must be late evening or possibly night. I had a drowsy recollection that James had been here. Where had he gone? The ecstasy of feeling starting to course back into my body creeping through my veins and slowly I became more sure footed, my head still felt like a hammer drill was going off in it, with a cloud of dust spinning around inside. I found Nancy's pulse, she was still alive.

I staggered to a standing position, my knees nearly buckling immediately and I had to steady myself on the nearby chair. Light headed and dizzy I moved to the window and pulled back the curtain slightly. It was night time. The street outside was quiet, many of the houses shrouded in darkness because the few street lamps that were there didn't work, typical for this part of town. I turned to face the room, something was different from earlier. What was it? I took two steps toward the door and stopped – The book Nancy had been reading from. I scouted the area around her and I saw it hiding underneath the low coffee table in the alcove to the right of the chimney breast.

I went to pick it up. Voices broke the silence of Nancy's flat. They were in the communal lobby downstairs, I recognised the distinctive echo, similar to the lobby outside my own front door. I grabbed the book and made my way to the lounge door. My head still pounding its disapproval but quickly the adrenalin pumped and became an anaesthetic numbing the pain, allowing my mind to become alert, shrugging off the drowsiness. I listened to the voices, they were a mumbled hush and I could not make out any words.

I heard the distinctive sound of keys being tried in a lock, I had two choices: hide and hope I wasn't found, or see if Nancy had a backdoor out via the kitchen which so many of these conversions did. I scurried from the lounge along the hallway, past the top of the stairs, keeping as close to the wall as possible as the glass panel above the front door would not conceal me. The only light in the flat came from the lounge which left the hallway in a kind of half light. I didn't want to take any chances though. I passed the bathroom and into the kitchen/diner. There was a back door and the keys were in it. I unlocked the door, sliding the bolts back then taking the key with me I locked the door from outside. That would hold them off for a few minutes at least if they were after me, and after they saw Nancy on the floor, that was a strong possibility.

I hurried down the rickety wooden steps to the back garden jumping over the last few. A bright light suddenly illuminated the whole area. 'Damn security lights!' I muttered under my breath. 'Go out' I willed it, as if by magic the bright light faded showering me in darkness.

I took a couple of seconds to get my bearings in the blackness after the blinding light. Most of these flats had alleys running along the back of the gardens with inter connecting passageways to the streets that ran parallel to each other. I clambered over the fence at the back as quietly as I could and trundled through the undergrowth and rubbish that littered my path. It was pitch black and a couple of times I stumbled as I tore on blindly. Eventually I had to concede and slowed down to take more tentative steps, even though I knew I had to make progress as quickly as possible.

Emerging a short while later in the street behind Nancy's where I waited a few houses down from the alley to make sure I wasn't being followed. The minutes passed and no-one came out after me, I guessed I was safe. Casually I started to walk home. Glancing at my phone I noted the time was '04.53' and I had two messages.

The adrenalin had started to ease now and hunger was making itself known. I hadn't eaten since lunch, and my energy levels were getting low. Dawn was not far off and soon the morning chorus of birds would sing their welcome.

I stopped abruptly. It hadn't registered. In all the excitement I could hear again. I had to put my hand on the nearest wall to steady myself. The relief that pulsated through my body was unreal, an end to my silent world. I wanted to shout my jubilation, but knew I couldn't. A smile beamed across my face as wide as the Grand Canyon, there was a new spring in my step, hunger faded into insignificance. Relief; I had my hearing back.

'Yes' I allowed a muted shout to myself.

The walk back to my flat turned into a casual stroll, life was normal again, all my problems forgotten and work would now be what it always was. And for that brief moment I completely forgot about James and the Drysidium Faith, even Suzi.

'Suzi – shit I was meant to see her', I exclaimed rather more loudly than I intended. I quickened my pace.

Once back at my flat I couldn't control my excitement and went straight to the stereo to play my favourite Madness CD, throwing the book I was carrying into the armchair. It was blissful, how much I had missed the wonderful sound, every beat, every word. I grabbed a bowl of cereal and sat on the settee, enjoying every clink of the spoon against china, every slurp as I ate. Turning on the kettle I listened to its song in the background as it ran its course. Everything in life seemed a thousand percent better. I couldn't stop smiling. I remembered the text messages and had a quick read, both were from Suzi.

'HI LOVER, WEN R U COMING IN?'

and

'NITE, HOPED I'D C U. U OK? XX'

There was so much I needed to tell her and there was no way I could tell her in a text. Leaving the CD playing quietly in the background I wandered into the bathroom to freshen up, if only I could turn the stereo up to full blast, but it was too early in the morning. I felt a cloud had been lifted from my existence.

I looked in the mirror, the awful reflection that came back at me didn't reflect how I felt inside, I shaved, stripped, and showered. In the full length mirror on the wall outside my bathroom I noticed the red mark about three inches in diameter on my chest under the amulet, a reminder of last night, the burning that I had felt. The amulet must have been working overtime to protect me.

I walked into the bedroom without turning the light on, going straight to the imitation pine chest of drawers and pulling out clean underwear and T-shirt, I was humming along to the words of 'Rise and Fall'.

Violently I was wrenched backwards onto the bed, losing my breath and dropping my clothes on the floor. Before I knew it I was face down in the duvet, hands held half way up my back.

I screamed in agony as one arm was pushed even higher.

"What the...." I tried to say but my face was pushed further into the duvet.

"Shut up. Just shut up. How did you get away? What's happened to Nancy?"

The voice I was hearing was that of James. With my new found hearing I felt more confident than before and I started to goad him as I tried to extricate myself from the duvet to answer the question "Wouldn't you like to know". It was very childish but I couldn't help myself. Anger, frustration and deceit, were all inside me.

"You think you're so funny?" James pushed a knee into the base of my spine, his grip was strong and he had both my hands in one of his. He shifted position and rested his knee across both my arms, making me cry in pain as I felt his shin bone cut into my flesh and then into my bone. Next my wrists were bound together, with what felt like a tie. I thrashed my legs about as much as I could. James dug his knee deeper into the base of my spine, the pain spreading around my body. A tear ran from my eye, my ankles were being tied together. I tried to kick them free, amazed at how strong James was.

Both the ties on my ankles and wrists were then linked together. With satisfaction James stood back to admire his handiwork

"That should do it. I'd like to see you get out of that."

"No. You wouldn't, you bastard." I spat out.

"Ooh. I'm frightened, what makes you think I'm going to keep you alive long enough for you to try and free yourself?"

"So why don't you end it now then? Go on."

"I have my reasons. But your time is limited, don't worry about that. One last thing, I can't have you shouting for help." With that he gagged me.

26

In the space of a few hours I'd managed to go from the delirium of getting my hearing back to being overshadowed by my imminent danger, possibly death. As I lay naked on the bed bound and helpless I still found it difficult to comprehend that the person who looked like James wasn't actually James. Cramp was starting to set in I could feel it tormenting my muscles. I wriggled as much as I could to try and keep the circulation going, occasionally pulling against my bindings to see if I could loosen them. My stomach started to growl letting me know that I had only had a bowl of cereal in what seemed like days but was in fact hours, the feeling of sickness biting into me. My mouth ached from the tightness of the gag, the skin at the corners of my mouth was sore from continued attempts to move it and my tongue felt raw from the continued contact.

Turning my head to the right, I could just see the tie that bound my legs and wrists together; my favourite saxophone tie, bought for me by my father as a Christmas present and now used against me. It hurt my neck to look but I was determined to try and release myself.

With all the remaining resolve and strength my limbs could muster I tried to break the tie by stretching it amazed by how resilient things could be when you didn't want them to be. My leg muscles gave in to cramp quickly, leaving me writhing around in agony with limited movement to do anything about it. Eventually the pain subsided.

For a while I listened to the murmurings from my neighbours above and below, people getting ready to go to work, early morning alarm calls and general muted hubbub of TVs. In a strange sense it was bliss and on any other day I think I could have enjoyed listening to it. I tried to relax but for the second time in two days I found myself incapacitated.

Ideas flitted around my head. All of them involved something to cut my bindings. Cramp caught my leg again and the searing pain brought tears to my eyes causing me to put more pressure on my arms which in turn made my shoulder start to cramp. I rolled around the bed just to try to get the blood flowing again but the cramps only eased a little. No one could hear my muffled cries, no matter how loud I shouted, the gag did its job. No one could see the tears of pain. Out of shear desperation I pulled my legs and arms apart again, battling against the restrains. Something tore, I half expected it to be a muscle and waited for the ensuing pain; nothing, except for the muted pain of the cramps my brain was desperately trying to shut out.

I pulled again, shutting out the burn of my muscles. A few seconds later I was rewarded with success as the tie gave way. The relief was ecstasy. Blood coursed through my veins giving relief to the muscles. I could at last straighten my legs. Every joint was stiff. I took my time to relax; even though my arms were still behind my back, they were not under so much pressure, at one point I tried to slip my hand below my feet so I could use my teeth but I was not that agile. I needed a knife. I listened to the flat. Was it empty? Had James left me on my own believing I was secure?

After a couple of minutes I decided it was safe to move from my bedroom. Manoeuvring myself to the edge of the bed I attempted to sit up, placing my still tied feet on the floor using them as a pendulum to counter my torso. It took four attempts before I could finally hop to the kitchen.

I reached the block of five knives that sat near the toaster and grabbed any one I could. It was awkward but eventually I cut my hands free and removed the gag before cutting the bonds around my ankles. Hurriedly I got dressed before indulging in some breakfast, but not before first securing the front door by moving an armchair in front of it so at least I didn't have to worry about James coming back and catching me unawares.

First thing on the agenda was to visit Suzi to let her know what was going on and that I was safe. Switching on the TV was such a pleasure again. I had only experienced hearing loss for two weeks and although part of me felt guilty I wanted to dwell in my own relief. GMTV were discussing Clint Eastwood's new movie 'Million Dollar Baby', I revelled in the voices, music to my ears. Then they talked about last night's TV, then the news, World and Local. There was a report on the body found in Bonchurch Park. Police believed it to be of a young girl, Theresa Williams aged eight, who disappeared in 1971 – her parents had been notified. The police were concerned that this could be linked to the body of the boy discovered under the floor of a garage in Leigh, who is thought to have disappeared in 1964. Police were also concerned over the safety of Paula Dowden, aged nine, who disappeared on Sunday, whilst playing in Priory Park, Southend. There had been reports of a man, fitting James's description, hanging around the area looking suspicious – there was an appeal for witnesses to come forward.

In my mind James's free days were numbered. I was not going to let things go on much longer, this had to end. I left the house and made the short walk to the hospital.

On the way I contemplated why I just didn't go to the police now; I knew where James lived, I could at least tip them off to when he was last seen? So why didn't I? Loyalty? Perhaps, but he wasn't my friend anymore, not as I had known him. I was sad inside for that one reason alone. Time had moved on and this character and the Faith seemed to be getting careless. All the other deaths and disappearances had left no clues and if it hadn't been for Sarah guiding me then the others would have remained lost souls forever.

As I neared the hospital I wondered what Suzi would make of the news about her mentor, Nancy.

It didn't occur to me that she wouldn't believe me, but after our initial greetings, I replied to her question of how I was and I told her about Nancy and James - this was met with a torrent of recriminations against me. I was staggered; I had told the truth of how it was and Suzi denied it all saying that it was not possible and I must have misunderstood what was going on, insisting I had been so small minded after she had tried to help me. We were told at one point to quieten down by a nurse or I would be asked to leave.

I tried almost in vain to argue but Suzi was adamant. Then out of the blue she clicked that I could hear her. Her face contorted in surprise, her temperament changed for that instant and I almost saw her smile again looking on me with affection but she stopped mid smile.

There followed an awkward silence. Two friends who had betrayed each other, at least that's what it felt like. I sat there looking out of the window; it was dull and miserable outside, reflecting the mood inside. I nearly got up to leave. I had never lied to Suzi, I had never had the need and I wasn't going to start now. I just wanted her to believe me. Deep down I knew if she didn't want to believe me then I would not be able to make her. Almost nonchalantly I stated that I'd seen James, if you can call it seeing him. She stared at me for a long moment then asked me what I meant. Her voice was short but level. I explained what had happened.

She drifted off into her own thoughts, I nearly got up and left but finally, out of the blue, she reservedly apologised for not believing me about Nancy. At first I wanted to berate her for not believing me then I saw that she looked confused - she couldn't understand why Nancy had turned. I couldn't help but feel sorry for her; her mentor had let her down.

"Oh by the way, I had a phone message from Marshall. I tried to call him back last night but he was out" Suzi's tone was matter-of fact.

"Maybe he has some news on 'Kraknami' " I replied trying to remain upset with Suzi, but not succeeding.

"That's what I was thinking, I'll give him a ring later."

"What do we do now?"

"I don't know."

We sat in silence, both knowing it had to be brought to an end once and for all. It wasn't as easy as just contacting the police since they probably wouldn't believe a lot of what we told them, even though we could provide facts and figures. They'd almost certainly want us committed. Suzi broke my thoughts.

"Have you still got the book?"

"No. You took it to Nancy, she still has it so that's going to be no help. Maybe I should just burn the barn down at least it would temporarily scupper their immediate plans."

"Would it? It's just an altar."

An idea came like a light just blinking into life.

"Nancy said it was her Uncle's barn."

"Her Uncles Barn! She hasn't got an Uncle." Suzi sounded incredulous.

"What do you mean she hasn't got an Uncle?"

"She hasn't got an Uncle. That I do know."

"How?"

"I've seen the article."

"What article. What are you on about?"

"Her whole family died in a car accident when she was eight years old. Her mother, father, twin sister, her fathers' brother, and his wife. It was some sort of miracle that she survived. She was brought up by her Gran, who I've met. She told me about the accident. Are you sure she said her uncle's barn."

"Yes she leant over and mouthed 'my uncles barn'. Well that's what it looked like to me."

"It just seems rather strange that she would say that. She'd know that the first opportunity you got you would tell me and I would know that she doesn't have an uncle" Suzi looked puzzled.

"Maybe it was something else then. I'm not exactly an expert at lip-reading although when she moved her lips it always seemed easier for some strange reason."

Between us we ran through all the possibilities that it could have been which wasn't many and most were absurd jibberish making us both laugh. Again we got asked to keep the noise down, this time the nurse gave us one of those 'You two' looks, as we had gone from arguing to laughing.

Suddenly Suzi's face went very serious. A rye smile appeared and slowly spread across her whole face, her eyes sparkling.

"Mia Yonkel Sparn!" She stated with a positive energy.

"What?" I stated as if she was insane, trying desperately not to laugh.

"It's a piece of nonsense, but it's a clue."
She stopped and thought some more.

"Hello? Are you going to tell me or do I have to call a psychiatrist?" I stated playfully.

"When Nancy was teaching me about..." She looked around the ward and beckoned me closer. Whispering, she continued "When she was teaching me about white witchcraft, she dabbled with some black witchcraft that she had come into contact with, and that I might possibly have to deal with sometime, and was always useful to know. I was only thirteen at the time and the way I said it made it sound like "my uncle's barn", I remembered she joked about it a lot at the time. It's a joining spell used for protection, very simple, and very effective. It's great if you want to hide yourself in another."

"Woah! What?"

"If you want to hide yourself in another person."

"Sounds too bizarre and just like the Drysidium Faith."

"No it's not quite the same thing."

"If that's the case who's hidden in who?"

"She has hidden herself inside you."

I stood up sharply, feeling a bit peculiar "Insi...what?....Inside me?"

"It's okay." Suzi indicated for me to sit again and to keep my voice down "She obviously thought she or her talent was under threat so she hid herself."

"What about her body? What happens to that? Won't she die?"

"No it remains in a state of suspension, for all intent and purposes in a coma like state. This is fine for about five days, after that, yes, the body will start to shut down and die."

"Shut down and die! Then what happens to her. Isn't that a bit dangerous? I mean someone could kill her."

"Yes it can be, but she obviously thought it was worth the risk. Now her spirit mind" I nodded "that remains hidden in you until it is unlocked."

"Unlocked! How do I do that? And why?"

"You don't" she paused "I do. Don't look so worried it won't hurt you, but she obviously thought it was necessary."

"How do you reckon James comes into it? He was there if you remember and she certainly didn't seem to mind. In fact it looked quite the opposite."

"That I'm not sure of. Once we unlock her inside you we should be able to find out. Maybe they were trying to use her powers against her. Or even against you or us."

This was all very strange and didn't sit comfortably on my shoulders. I knew I had experienced some weird stuff in the last few days.

"How do we unlock her?" I conceded, knowing once again I didn't have much choice.

"I need a few things, if you don't mind getting them for me? It's going to be a bit difficult here. We can't exactly perform it on the ward and they're keeping me in for a few more days yet."

"How about if we close the curtains?"

"Nice idea. Won't exactly conceal what I've got to do unluckily. Let's think."

The hustle and bustle of the ward washed over us as we thought of a place where we could perform this task discreetly. I didn't know what to expect but we obviously needed privacy. In a public hospital that was not going to be easy, if possible at all.

"The only way we, you can, is if we do it during the night when everyone's asleep, if that's possible. Is it a quiet thing to do? Also, how am I going to manage to stick around that long? What time do they kick guests out?"

"Guests!"

"Visitors, you know what I mean."

"I think it's nine."

"I could hide in the toilets? I suppose."

"Yeah. Night would be ok. But you still have to get past the nurse."

"True. Can't you smuggle me in?"

"I'm bed bound for a couple of days whilst everything sorts itself out inside."

"What are we going to do then?"

"I don't know yet but if you can go round to my house and collect a few things then that would be a start. Bring them in tomorrow?"

Suzi gave me a list of things and the locations of where they were in her bedroom and I left her to rest and work out how we were going to perform this task discreetly.

27

I had no problem gathering the things Suzi wanted, her Mother was very helpful. They were aware she was a white witch and trusted her judgement. To me, it seemed strange that a family were quite so open; I doubted my family would be so understanding. 'The book of Kees' sat on a shelf inside her wardrobe; a silk handkerchief and her Enclypta Crystals nested on her bedside table. She asked especially for a box at the back of the second drawer down in her chest of drawers, hidden amongst her socks – apparently very important; she said she would explain later.

As I was about to leave I received a text from Suzi **'CAN U BRING P COK FETHER ON DRESSER. S X'**

I put all the items into a rucksack I had brought with me, careful not to break the feather or crystals politely declining her parents invite to stay for dinner.

Back at home, I spent the evening indulging in a couple of DVDs, it was so nice to wrap myself up in the hearing world again, like a warm blanket on a winters day. My experience had been a mere drop in the ocean compared to the lifetime of adjustment most deaf people faced. I was thankful that I didn't have to make that adjustment, already forgetting how difficult the world had been without sound.

I'd taken the extra precaution of barricading the front door as I didn't want any unwanted surprises, again, but was still restless after watching the DVDs, wondering whether Sarah would invade my dream world now. Switching off the light I let the darkness take over, savouring all the night time sounds, even the ones that had annoyed me before, the ticking of the central heating pipes under the floor, the wind outside whistling around the roof, all made a welcome return. It was nice to feel normal again. My sleep was so restful that when my alarm went off the following morning I was refreshed and raring to go. Upon switching on my phone two messages immediately flashed up:

'CUM IN BOUT 11AM. NITE. S xx'

'ARE YOU OK? NO ONE HAS HEARD FROM YOU FOR TWO DAYS. FIONA X'.

Fiona was a work colleague and it made me feel good, finally someone at work actually cared, that's how it felt. I couldn't blame them. It must have been difficult for them as well. Some of them, Fiona being one, had made the extra effort, but she still hadn't come to my desk to chat as often as usual. I dwelled more on that and realised that I had been guilty of it too, not making the effort. I'd allowed my confidence to be knocked, let myself slip into the easy path of keeping myself to myself because then I wouldn't have to deal with the harsdship. Maybe I had made my temporary deafness harder than it ought to have been? Now I will never know.

Melancholy slipped over me for a brief time as I knew I would have to ring the office and explain my absence. I decided telling my version of the truth was best, that although my hearing had come back, which would be obvious, I had appointments with my specialists to make sure that it was permanent, and in all the excitement had forgotten to ring in. I hoped I was a convincing liar.

In the back of my mind I decided to keep up the 'sign' classes as a reminder of how fortunate I was.

It was surprising how genuinely pleased my manager sounded when I called he acquiesced to my request for the rest of the week off so I could see my specialist and confirm everything was alright. I was pushing my luck, but it did give a few days clear to sort everything out. He was more than accommodating, quite bafflingly so in fact and agreed that that was fine even asking if I thought that was enough!

GMTV was on in the background as I got ready to go out and after the interview with Val Kilmer, who was promoting his new play 'The Postman always rings twice', I caught some of the regional headlines picking up on one story.

Police are hunting a man after a woman was found unconscious in a flat in Southend. The woman, in her 40's, was found on the floor of her lounge. Neighbours became concerned after seeing bright lights. The woman who has not been named is in a coma in Southend Hospital. Police are hunting this man.

A sketch appeared on screen, it was barely a good resemblance of James.

He was seen entering the flat earlier that day. If anyone has any knowledge, would they contact local police on the following number.

A number appeared on screen.

Things were not going well for James or rather the person inhabiting James. Instinctively, I knew this person would be looking to disappear again.

I thought about how busy James had been the last week or so taking more and more risks. Previous incarnations all seem to have been more opportune and discreet. Maybe society had just changed so much that we were now much more vigilant. We had internet, TV, Phones. Maybe we were more wary of one another. One thing I did know and that was that if he wanted to move on, he would have to find a pregnant woman and soon. Before he was caught.

It was strange that all the other members of the Faith had managed to conceal their identities. Were they cleverer? Was it just the way it was? One person acted as the face of all evil. In all this time Suzi and I had not uncovered anyone else who was involved. Why was that? There had to be links.

Suzi had specified 11am and given the impression of precision. I found out why soon enough; all the beds on Suzi's ward had been vacated, with the exception of hers.

"What did you do? Send them all off to meet their maker" I announced my arrival sarcastically.

Playing along "Well! We needed privacy, I had to do something. It took a while to dispose of the bodies. The nurse was a bit suspicious though as I carried bags of bats, bits and body parts past her. You know what I mean."

I smiled "Cool! Yeah, at least you managed to clear up the blood stains" I looked around the floor pretending to look for traces of blood.

"Well, I did think it would give it away." We both smiled, this was so much better than my visit yesterday. "I think they'd all decided to leave because of the food."

"It's that good eh?" I sat down on the edge of her bed.

"It's alright, certainly not as bad as everyone makes out."

I gave her a kiss on the lips, placing the rucksack by her feet.

"You got everything?"

"Yep. I think so." I started to empty the contents on the bed whilst Suzi sorted through them.

"Can you pull the curtain round the bed, please?" Suzi sat up. She looked to be in pain but didn't say so, just concentrated on her task.

She laid the silk handkerchief out as a diamond, placing two Enclypta Crystals, the red and the green ones, on the east and west corners respectively. The Book of Kees she had open in front of her, it was a small A5 book no thicker than a children's Ladybird book. The peacock's feather she placed between the two crystals.

The remaining seven crystals she placed in an arrowhead on the north point of the diamond.

"What's in the box?" We heard voices and sat silent listening intently, concerned that someone was going to interrupt us. They voices stopped and their footsteps faded into the distance.

"Close call" I said "Why did you specify this time anyway?"

"Last night I just started asking a few general questions, you know. Anyway, the two opposite were leaving today, and the one in the next bed was going down for his operation at 10.30 this morning so I thought this would be the best time, and my doctor was coming about 9am."

She carried on setting up.

"Normally I'd ask you to sit at the arrowhead but under the circumstances…"

"I'll stand at the end of the bed" Suzi smiled, she picked up the box "What's in that?"

"Something precious of Nancy's. Every white witch has a Companion which they trust and you enchant a token. Can be anything, usually a crystal or pendant and this acts as a focal point should anything happen, like now, allowing the companion to make contact and bring back the spirit from the carrying vessel, yourself, and return it to their own body. However" she sighed "under the circumstances we can't complete that, but we can bring her forth to communicate with us, or more importantly through you" I must have looked nervous "It's okay, you'll feel a little funny, but it won't hurt. Promise." She smiled "What will happen is there'll be a channel between you and Nancy. Don't worry, you'll have full control and be aware of everything that's going on."

"Mmm…Okay" I said hesitantly "But how will we return her to her own body?"

"When I get out of here we'll go round and sort it."

"Shit!"

"What?"

"The Police discovered her body, it was on the news this morning, not her body that is, just that they had discovered her and were looking for James."

Suzi thought for a second "In that case!" she muttered to herself briefly "She would have appeared to be unconscious so in theory there'll bring her to the hospital" she paused in thought "yes, that's good." Then she spoke to me again "That's fine. That'll probably make things easier."

I was baffled and accepted what she said, shaking my head nonchalantly.

"Right, let's get on" she continued.

Suzi, waved the feather around marking out the perimeter of the curtain and whispering to herself almost inaudibly. She placed the feather on the bedside table and read from the book on her lap. "Accuma Remerata Ji Kooklan. Channel me to thee. Let the voice speak freely using the vessel to channel energy to the designate here." She touched the ivory figure of a bird which Nancy had chosen for her vessel, resting her thumbs lightly on it, and then placing her index fingers on the last Enclypta Crystals at each side of the arrowhead.

A visible pinpoint of white light emanated from the tip towards Suzi, which astounded me as I expected it to affect me. Then Suzi's eyes locked on mine, there was a definite sharpness about her pupils and I became very whoozy, my legs becoming wobbly, having to grab hold of the end of the bed to support myself. My vision blurred and a strange heat struck at the centre of my head, spreading every second until my head was warm and tingling.

Suzi concentrated hard, her lips were moving but the delirium I was in prevented me from coherently hearing her. The Amulet started to burn but immediately stopped. Quietness came over me and for a split second I thought I had lost my hearing again and my heart sank.

Imminently the strength returned to my legs and I could hear Suzi again mumbling to herself, relief soared – sound.

"You alright?" Suzi enquired

"Yes, I think so." Mentally checking my body. "Has it worked? How do we know?"

"Yes. And I have just spoken to her"

"You have? Wow! What did I… she say?"

"She can help. The Book is at her place, hidden. If you go to her flat she will guide you to it. You can trust her. She knows what it must have looked like before, but she had no choice, she wants to make peace with you. There is a way to resolve this but it will be dangerous. You are going to have to go to the barn."

28

The only times I was ever brave was in a group of people knowing they were behind me, a kind of bravado, on my own I would shy away from most challenges. Apprehension at the thought of revisiting the barn rose inside. I was just one person and the last time I had been there had left an indelible mark on me. I knew the man with the gun had been lenient and inside knew that would not be the case if caught again.

My head still tingled slightly from the joining spell, a strange kind of pins and needles that I couldn't touch physically. Would I come out of this with my sanity intact? That was a good question. Although I hadn't heard from Sarah for a while, I believed she was still there waiting for the right time, a blind faith I had. Relieved that Nancy was actually on our side, I put my doubts of her to one side once and for all.

As I was leaving the hospital I joked that we had been lucky to get away with completing the 'joining spell' without being disturbed. Suzi simply smiled nonchalantly stating that it hadn't been luck; the peacock feather was in fact to cast a simple spell creating a temporary mirage in people's minds making everything appear normal: it only works from a distance and at short glances, breaking down on close inspection.

Suzi would locate Nancy's physical body in the hospital so when I returned she could make everything right; in the meantime Nancy's spirit was my guide and after some lunch at home I headed to Nancy's flat. On the way I became aware that Nancy might be able to see and hear everything I was doing, possibly even know things before I did. Trying to stop myself thinking only made it worse and I was fast becoming paranoid.

"Can you see and hear everything I do?" I asked aloud and got some strange looks from a couple walking nearby. There was no reply. How was this going to work?

As I neared Nancy's flat things started becoming more peculiar. The strange tingling amplified sending shivers through my spine. A momentary spasm checked my body and I steadied myself on a nearby garden wall until it passed. Working on the theory that Nancy would instruct me verbally to locate the book I headed to her front door but an overpowering intuition kicked in and I took the alley to the back door, where there was a key hidden in locked box screwed to the wall which required a six digit code to open it, to my surprise I knew it. Nancy said nothing. This must be the way it worked, intuition. But what if I needed to ask her a question? She hadn't answered my last question.

All seemed normal in the kitchen. Walking past the stairway I noticed the front door had been broken in and a temporary repair made, I guessed to enable the emergency services to get in. An overwhelming urge sent me into the toilet to my right which was separate from the bathroom. Closing the door behind me, I sat on the lid looking towards the back of the door. For a few seconds I sat there then leant forward carefully pulling back the carpet and underlay from the edge of the door. A floorboard held firmly in place by two flush catches, was visible. I struggled to get my fingers under the hoops of the catches and after some gentle persuasion I managed to lift and twist them, releasing the board.

Hidden underneath were two packages wrapped in newspaper. I was just about to reach for one when intuitively I reached further into the darker recesses for a different package hidden from view forced to get off the seat to grasp it. Part of me wanted to be nosy and look at the others but my curiosity was mysteriously curbed. Replacing the board and carpet I left the toilet.

I thought it strange to have a secret hiding place in such an odd place but then intuitively answered my own thoughts. *'It could be quite clever in the right circumstances.'* Obviously that depended on what else was hidden there. *'Never mind'*. I was never going to find out.

"Is this how it works?" again my question remained unanswered.

In the lounge I was spooked slightly by my last experience here. *'Sorry about that'*. It was a weird sensation knowing the answers but not actually hearing them spoken, like having a split personality manifesting inside. Sitting down I opened the package and indeed it was the book. Next I was guided to the bedroom which was between the toilet and the lounge. Pushing open the door I was immediately flung back against the banisters with such a force I barely prevented myself from going over it backwards. Recovering my balance I saw James. He launched himself at me grabbing my shoulders before trying to get his hands around my throat, forcing me back onto the banisters, my spine grinding against the hard wood.

"Don't you ever just give up" he hissed at me.

I heard a crack and felt the banister give a little. It took all my effort to counter James's force and drag him to the floor. We landed heavily on our sides facing each other, kicking out he caught my right shin, I howled in pain. Adrenalin pumped through my veins taking the edge off the pain. As James went to get up I wrapped my arms round the lower half of his legs causing him to crash back to the floor, barely having time to break his fall. Thrashing his legs he tried to break my grip. I in turn tried to crawl up his legs, my body receiving the blows from his feet in quick succession, every one hurting, but I had to fight it.

"No I don't. You...?" His right knee caught me on the chin and I went reeling back against the spindles of the banisters. The taste of blood filled my mouth and before I could do anything about it James had broken free and was sprinting down the stairs, taking three steps at a time finally crashing through the broken front door which gave way easily. Pulling myself off the floor I stood at the top of the stairs. My first thought to run after him – I was held back and guessed it was Nancy.

"Are you going to talk to me or what?" still no answer. "Is this how this works then?...Hello?...Anything."

In the bathroom I rinsed my mouth out, finding nothing more serious than a split lip. Well at least I would have a nice bruise to show off.

Back in the bedroom Nancy guided me to her bedside chest of three drawers and pulling out the bottom one I lifted out the false bottom. Nancy liked her hiding places. So much secrecy for one person I thought. *'I have my reasons'*. 'Okay didn't mea....hold on if you can answer that why not answer my other questions?' this time I only thought it. *'My energy is limited, I have to be careful how I use it'*.

Placated I grabbed the wooden dagger and the flat wooden decorated disc that were visible. What are we going to do with these? *'Just let me guide you when the time comes.'* I was just a vessel, an important vessel. Taking the book from where it had fallen during the struggle with James I left the flat to catch a bus to Rochford.

My phone vibrated. I had a message:

NANCY. LET ME NO WEN U NEED ME 2 PROCEED. SUZ X.

On impulse I text back 'OK', I felt like a spare part.

The barn stood like a beacon to me, I had been here twice, once for real and once in my dreams, even though that had been a very real experience.

Turning I walked away from the barn back along the road I had come along.

"Are you going to enlighten me as to what we are doing? And what we are going to do?" I paused "Oh yeah! How do you know so much about these people?" like lightning my distrust had returned. I asked the questions out loud as it seemed natural. To anyone listening they would probably have thought I was mad.

There are lots of things that need to be explained, please just trust me for now I need to save my energy.

Trust! Such an innocent word but one I questioned after so many twists and turns. I was a pawn in a game I didn't know how to play. Deep down I knew I had to trust Nancy if only because of Suzi.

Once back at the main intersection, I took a right turn to head out towards Stambridge following this road until I came to a sign that read 'Rush Farm Private Road, Keep Off'. Somehow I knew it was the back entrance to the barn. Walking along the half made road lined on both side with bushes, I wondered whether I was doing it because I wanted to or because Nancy did; the edges seemed fuzzy.

On the horizon, buildings loomed up, some large, some small. The closer I got the more cautious I became despite the fact it all appeared deserted. Approaching the first building just off the track, a modern built barn made from iron girders and plastic corrugated material, I crept round the side until I came to the doors and looking through a gap where the padlock and chain were I could see nothing but farm machinery.

Next to this barn was an old stone built piggery, mud stained and equally as deserted, looking a little worse for wear. The area in front had been concreted, forming a sort of parade ground. A low steel gate secured the area and ran from the barn with the farm machinery to the stone built wall, this gate prevented vehicle access to the piggery. Buildings of varying shapes and sizes then surrounded this parade area.

Making sure the coast was clear I climbed over the gate to take a closer look, still cautious at how quiet it all seemed to be. All the buildings were empty except for one containing straw bails stacked to the rafters.

A narrow alleyway ran between two of the buildings diagonally opposite the gate and piggery opening onto a field, in the distance

I could see the original barn and farmhouse just down the gentle slope that ran away from where I was.

I heeded a compulsion to go left towards the hawthorn bush that marked the edge of the property, this was the same boundary I had snuck through before; in the distance I could see it ran all the way to the road at the front. A strip of land occasionally mowed lay between the back of the piggery and the hawthorn bush perfectly secluded from site of the house.

Wait there!

"For what?"

Just wait.

Luckily the evening was warm; intuitively, I had brought some provisions with me in anticipation of a wait, and also my denim jacket to help keep me warm, providing the temperature didn't drop too much. Finding a large flat rock half buried in the ground I lay down to let the warm rays of the late afternoon sun wash over me sheltered from any breeze. Slowly I drifted into a restful slumber.

Awoken sometime later by the clang of a metal bolt and to the sound of voices talking jovially followed by sounds of car tyres scraping across the concrete, stones caught in the treads, clipping the surface 'tap tap'. Hearing quite a few cars arrive one after the other I thought about taking a look but was stopped.

You will see from here.

Sure enough, I found myself watching a procession of people meandering towards the barn, chattering as if on a ramble through the country, all very relaxed and informal, each carrying a large carrier bag. I ducked behind the rock just to be sure that I couldn't be seen and was surprised how calm I felt; for now.

The sun was low in the sky, a vibrant orange on the horizon. The more people arrived, the more apprehensive I became, not knowing what we were going to do. I hoped it was good, because the odds were definitely against us. 'Now would be a good time for some words to pacify my nerves' I muttered hoping Nancy would reply but it was met with silence and no intuition.

Continuing to watch the stream of people it was half an hour before all had disappeared around the edge of the barn and, I guessed, into it.

Darkness was descending rapidly. I was waiting for a signal or intuitive command from Nancy. I looked at my phone, it was 9.30. The warm night air was cooling and putting my jacket on I left my guarded position to cross the expanse of ground between it and the barn.

Voices from inside the barn hummed in the air before falling silent in an instant. Looking at my phone it was. 9.37. The last sign of daylight vanished, night took its place.

'READY' I text Suzi then waited for a reply 'OK' which came back a minute or so later. I was baffled by the fact that I was acting out actions without a preliminary thought process.

Creeping around the barn I stuck my eye to the knot hole I had found before, this was all too weird. Inside, the people were dressed in the same robes from my dream and kneeling on the ground in front of the altar. Three figures stood behind it, one reading from a book, one holding a chalice and another 'The Dagger of Tyse', I knew what it was!

Making my way to the barn door I hesitated as if gathering my thoughts.

In my mind I asked the question 'What are we going to do?'

Trust us. Trust us! A pang of panic swept over me and I knew I was not going to like what happened next, but as much as I tried I couldn't resist the compulsion to enter the barn as bold as walking into a crowded room and shouting a greeting at the top of my voice.

Dread filled me as I faced the barn full of people all staring at me as though I was mad. I felt mad, insane.

In the middle of the sea of faces I saw James's parents and another part of the puzzle came together. The end was imminent and it wasn't the end I had anticipated.

29

I wanted to disappear, the ground to open up and swallow me. All eyes were upon me. In my stupidity I had allowed myself to be guided into what I had tried to avoid. All my misgivings about Nancy I had pushed to one side, but Suzi, to be betrayed by her hurt me to the core. The instant I walked through that door I had been betrayed, a mere puppet on a string. My legs would not allow me to turn and run, powerless to the witches that controlled me. But why?

The Barn was silent. The door shut behind me, the soft click easily heard in the deathly silence that hung over the barn. A glance behind left no doubt in my mind that this was the end. A man had moved into position by the door, poised should I try and bolt, standing calm as though he had just let in a friend.

A man behind the altar spoke "Let us welcome the new member to our gathering Brethren." I looked sternly at him, astonished, "Please joins us, do not be afraid. The initiation will begin shortly."

It was surreal. I tried to fight my body's motions but resistance was futile. Unnerved and unsteady I joined the front row of people kneeling down. I was obediently being a disciple, as if my will was not my own. Inside I cursed Nancy and Suzi. I had never felt hatred like it in my life. A life which, I became aware would probably be cut short.

I eyed the barn door, making plans for an escape. It became clear why I could not open it from the outside; there was an electronic locking system, like that in a car, obviously operated by some sort of infra-red release from the outside.

The man spoke again "As you are aware, the service of Johia is upon us", his voice masterful and calm. "The quarter moon of Tagria is nigh. The blood line must continue, the Drysad is chosen. We merely await alignment. Let us prepare for Johia."

A door behind the altar opened and two more robed figures walked in carrying an object. No, it wasn't something it was someone, a child. She wasn't struggling, merely subdued. Her eyes roamed around the barn, turning her head slightly her gaze locked onto mine. Her eyes showed fear, yet she was calm and quiet. 'Fight it' I wanted to say, willing her to struggle, to break free. My voice remained silent by the will that was not mine.

Laying her on the altar like a rag doll, she did not try to move. I guessed she must have been drugged, the two robed figures let go of her wrists and ankles. The two men walked to the wall behind the altar where there hung huge curtains at least thirty feet tall, dark rich purple velvet. Each man pulled a cord and the curtains parted easily, revealing a sign drawn upon the wall.

A large circle fifteen feet in diameter was overlapped by a nine pointed star – the points of which barely broke the circle. In the area between the arc of the circle and the points were drawings, in sets of three, three had the mark of an eye, three with three horizontal lines and three with the crescent moon exactly like the moon that shone tonight. In the centre was a giant pair of eyes drawn with five pointed stars as pupils.

The figure I thought of as the Master of Ceremonies turned to face the wall, "Etiecarta Etiecarta Monil Grueffa."

Raw energy filled the room, a power surrounded me electrifying the air. The Master of Ceremonies knelt down before the diagram on the wall and put his hands on the two lowest points of the star, each with the crescent moon in them, and continued to speak.

"Enlighten us with your presence and accept our gift. Grant us eternity to provide servitude to the greater good of the Drysidium Faith to which we give ourselves. Watch us as we grow in your shadow and protect us from the evil without."

The two men standing by the back wall came forward to the girl. They began to cut the girls hands, deep cuts, one slice across either palm, letting the blood flow into two chalices which they held.

Inside, I was fighting, trying to break the will that held me captive. I wanted to get up and take the girl away before it was too late but I was glued to the spot. The anger that boiled inside me would not break the bonds that were keeping me against my will. I had to stay and watch as the cruelty unfolded before my eyes. Whatever they hoped this appalling ceremony would achieve I wished with every living morsel of my body that it failed. I caught the girl's eye again and deep within me I was saddened to have to watch this atrocity take place, the pain I could see in her eyes though she kept silent throughout. How had I allowed myself to be manipulated in such a way? What was my role to be now? I could feel the girl pleading for my help.

My hands screwed up into fists, my finger nails digging deep into the sensitive skin of my palms. I would explode if I didn't do something soon.

Two candles were placed at either end of the altar.

Suddenly the room resounded with the voices of the congregation. At first I couldn't make out what they were saying. The more I listened, the clearer it became, "Asnara Asnara, Kiltempian Heroto" The united voices grew in volume finally reaching a crescendo. Then silence.

Unbeknown to me the congregation had divided and formed two parallel lines on either side of the room. I now stuck out awkwardly at the front. I looked round at the two groups of people, their hoods showering their faces in dark shadows. Each head bowed in prayer. I shuffled quickly to join the back line on the side of the barn nearest the door. I was about to settle when two pairs of hands grabbed my arms and I was hauled to my feet. I guessed whatever the initiation ceremony was, I was about to find out. The rucksack I had carried with me was snatched away by the man who guarded the door.

I was placed in the middle of the barn and forced to kneel in front of the altar, facing away from it. The Master of Ceremonies walked towards me. I eyed the crowd of followers, all neatly turned out in their robes. I looked for help, a saviour and caught James's father's eye, it was cold. My heart sank. It seemed no-one I trusted was innocent, everyone I thought I knew was not who they portrayed. He'd known about his son all the time, how could he let this go on. He had always seemed a nice man, the whole family had. How could he support these grotesque goings on? Where was James?

Where was James? I hadn't seen him enter the barn, unless he was well concealed under one of the hoods. No. I was sure I would have recognised his posture, he was my best friend, I knew him like I would know my own brother.

Rage burned inside but I was still helpless, Nancy's power was too strong.

The Master of Ceremonies and his two cronies approached, each of the cronies carrying a chalice with the girl's blood in it. In my mind I conjured up images of what they would make me do. Two more of the followers were now attending to the girl, who still lay motionless, scared, and silent on the altar. The Master dipped his index finger into one of the chalices and drew a mark on my forehead.

"Astencia ha Johia Klanest – My brethren welcome you."

I wanted to spit out my rebuke yet couldn't.

There was a chorus of voices, I lost what they said. I wanted to move, break free but couldn't, I was held on the spot. The Master continued.

"The Drysidium Faith is one of purism, as one of us you will uphold the nine segments of life, represented by the Ocara Star. Do you concur to be bound over by Johia."

Inside I was screaming 'No' but I could not make the sound, I was being overpowered, limply and obediently, I said "Yes."

The atmosphere in the barn became alive, electric with energy, a feeling of power not noise. Everyone around me was quiet, all looking on with pride and excitement. I felt a warm buzz where the mark had been placed on my head, then a strange sense of ease and all the anger drained from me, the angst and frustration disappeared. I was succumbing, enjoying the warmth of the bonds with the Drysidium Faith. Compassion and sympathy for them. An understanding.

In an instant I knew what I had to do and confidently I walked to collect my rucksack, as if I could have done it at anytime. From within it I drew out the book and the wooden knife. It all seemed so right, now.

I stood behind the altar. I had the full attention of the Faith, all eyes upon me. The Master of Ceremonies watched from his place amongst the followers who were now in a group around him. Behind I felt the power of Johia boring into me.

I opened the book at the page marked 'Giving of Blood'.

The words in front of me on the page didn't make any sense, they became a blur. I held the wooden knife firmly in my right hand. My grip so tight it was burning my palm.

A warm sensation pulsed from the Amulet round my neck. I could feel all eyes upon me. Every pair boring themselves deep into my soul, willing me on, commanding me to continue with this sick ritual. Slowly I raised the wooden knife so it was level with the girl. I started to cut the girls T-shirt. What was I doing? I had to stop. My will wouldn't let me. Was I really going to let another innocent life pass by?

The point of the knife hesitated just above the girl's heart, just creating the first indentation on the skin, without breaking it. I looked at her, into her eyes. The fear, the desolation rang like a silenced alarm bell in a vacuum.

"Johia. Johia…" was repeated, firstly by the Master of Ceremonies, then gradually by the rest of the followers, in a low hum. The pressure was mounting. Pearls of perspiration formed on my forehead and one drop rolled into my left eye where it stung and the pain lingered for a long moment. The candles at each end of the altar flickered.

The picture was becoming clearer in my head. The words on the page made complete sense now, I knew what they meant. I placed the book on the altar and gripped the knife with both hands raising it off the girl's skin, her innocent flesh. This was going to be the final strike.

Like a concentrated voice I heard the Master speak to me "Go on my brother, Johia waits to welcome you."

Inside I was fighting the battle. The lines between my beliefs and the Drysidium Faith were losing coherence. I needed an inner strength to fight, a strength that was deserting me. My thoughts returned to Suzi and Nancy, a mixture of hate, trust, love and betrayal.

Readjusting my grip on the knife I gripped the handle tighter as the voices around me echoed inside my head. I knew now what I had to do. With one big thrust I brought the knife sharply down. The girl's eyes widened in terror and although her scream was silent, I could hear it reverberate around my head. I felt the shudder as the point of the knife hit the hard surface of the altar. My eyes locked onto the Master. The followers had slipped into silence, the Master smiling his approval.

A split second later he was revelling in the full course of my actions. I leapt over the altar and was heading directly for him, knife in hand. I didn't care what happened to me now, I had to do something. It had caught everyone unaware as they all stood in silence bewildered at this, almost futile action. As I reached the Master I didn't actually know what I was going to do, a wooden knife was hardly a dangerous weapon.

I hit the Master at full speed, his two cronies unable to react in time to stop me. We crashed to the ground, knocking the wind out of him. Next thing I knew I was being pulled off him by the cronies and I surveyed what lay in front of me. The Master laying there, dark red blood soaking his robe, near his stomach, the knife still in my hand, covered in blood.

The followers were still, eager not to interfere with proceedings. The Master just laughed, and got up as if not injured at all "You can't fight Johia. You have failed and now you will become 'Dekara'.

30

The two cronies dragged me back towards the altar; I knew I was doomed. Nancy, who had guided me here and into these endeavours, I believed had deserted me. 'Dekara' What was that? I would become 'Dekara'.

Trust. Out loud I shouted 'There's a limit'.

The Master turned to me and looked inquisitively his eyes seeming to pierce my inner being.

"Is there something you would like to tell me before…" he smiled a sinister smile and didn't bother to finish his sentence.

I spat out my distaste, "There's nothing I'd want to tell you." A second later I regretted the words; I had to try and delay, in hope that a way out would present itself "So what's your purpose?" it sounded feeble.

"Our purpose?" the Master paused, then smiled crookedly "Our purpose is Johia."

"You're sick. What are you really trying to accomplish?" All this delaying seemed futile. I didn't know where my escape was going to come from.

"One would only say that… if one didn't understand. You have to understand Johia and believe." He was almost mesmerising.

"You kill innocent children for what? As sacrifices. That is sick! They've done nothing to you." I turned as best as I could to face the group of followers. "How could you let this happen? Some of you are parents. You have children." I found James's parents in the sea of faces just visible under the shadows of their hoods. Nothing registered. It was blind faith; not one of them questioned what they were doing. Not one believed they were doing wrong.

"You only waste your breath. Our belief is real and true. Is yours?" The words floated as if on a warm summer breeze.

I knew I was wasting my time trying to reason, trying to talk my way out. Inside I pleaded to Nancy to put into action whatever she had planned before it was too late.

The men forced me to kneel down in front of the altar by kicking the back of my knees. The girl still lay there, quiet, still and peaceful, the blood on her palms dry and crusty. There was a wet patch on the red cloth around her waist where she had wet herself as I had thrust the knife down onto the table missing her. If only I could end her suffering for her. I still had the wooden knife in my hand, but my arms were firmly held. I was not strong enough to break free.

A third person from the followers came forward and took the girl from the altar into the room from where she had come. The men forced me to drop the knife and placed my hands on the altar, palms up. I could feel the tension in my elbow joints as they were twisted uncomfortably round.

The Master started to speak and straight away I felt my life force ebbing from me, my whole body became heavy and cumbersome, my breathing instantly laboured. I was losing feeling in my limbs, my brain shutting down. The Masters' words were just a blaze of noise that was fading.

"Denar Hirani, Denar Hirani…" I repeated again and again; I had no idea where it came from. It took a while to register it was me. Energy coursed back through my weary body, slowly at first and then it became a river of raw unleashed power, I was alive and strong. The cronies had loosened their grip as the Master had overpowered me and I found it easy to break free from their hold, shaking their hands away. Standing up I continued to repeat the words "Denar Hirani, Denar Hirani…" my voice growing in stature. I turned to face the Master. Our eyes locked in a mortal mental combat.

My strength almost overwhelmed me, every fibre of my being was electrified and pulsed with renewed energy. I knew I could win this battle of wills, the followers around faded into insignificance, this was an exclusive fight. The air was fused with the power on display. I could see the Master's eyes were weakening, his voice waning. His body seemed to physically shrink. The two cronies who had held me backed away from me towards the Master looking terrified of me.

A blinding flash of light lit the barn and I was thrown backwards into the altar, knocking one of the candles over. A massive whoosh could be heard as the flame ignited the cloth that covered it, sending flames two feet into the air.

The Master had fallen to his knees, he looked weak and powerless. Facing the nine pointed star his eyes were vacant. Waving my hand in front of them, he showed no recognition. I was strong and had won. I didn't know how or what I had done exactly. The Master was an empty shell. I looked around at the followers. Their expressions showed amazement and hatred, hatred for the one who had defeated their Master. Yet none came to his aid.

I stood proud and a little concerned in case they decided to attack yet they remained still, was I missing something. I hadn't noticed the heat from the flames growing more intense as the fire took hold, the cloth acting like a wick, and the straw, like dry tinder, igniting within seconds the area behind the altar. The two cronies stood contemplating their next move, the Master defeated, their leader. Again all eyes were upon me, I could see revenge in most, others looked lost – their leader slain.

Suddenly a flame leapt from the altar to the master, hitting him square in the chest. He didn't flinch, just knelt, as if it was just an effigy of him. What had I done? What spell had I cast?

The fire was spreading rapidly, the altar was well ablaze. The wooden planking underneath the straw was catching alight. Almost instantaneously, everyone in the barn had the same idea -

to leave.

A throng of people headed to the door, a mild hysteria breaking out, there was only one exit and the fifty or so people who were here all had to go through it. A part of me wanted them to burn in hell, but it wasn't my job to take human life regardless of how bad they had been. I joined the throng at the door, the heat building up quickly as the fire consumed more of its food.

The disc. I found myself fighting to get to the other side of the crowd to where my bag had been discarded. I pushed past people elbows flying, everyone was panicking, the fire was already up into the rafters above us and it would not be long before the roof came crashing down. I tripped and fell to my knees. People stepped over me and on me in their rush to get out, loud screams started to emanate from the crowd as all their efforts looked to be in vain. I tried to get up but no one would allow me to do so, more concerned with getting out. I edged my way forwards on my elbows and knees, occasionally feeling the weight of someone as they stepped on me, I would scream in pain, the adrenalin would kick in and I would pull myself forward out of the trampling mass of feet.

Finally, I made it to my bag and away from the crowd. I briefly lay, gathering my breath. As I did so I realised how much smoke was starting to fill the barn.

I grabbed the disc and let Nancy guide me, heading me back towards the altar and the start of the fire. "Are you mad?"

Trust me.

"Jee whizz, you trying to kill me or something?"

Trust me.

This was fast becoming a suicide mission yet Nancy would get out alive.

The knife.

I knew where I'd last had it. The fire was raging, the Master was still kneeling where I had left him, alight yet the flames didn't seem to be burning him, his clothes and features all looked exactly the same as they had done before. Not one of the followers made an effort to save him. I bent to pick up the knife which was just under the altar. The heat from the fire was intense. I had a task to perform and could feel Nancy guiding me. Picking up the knife I dropped it instantly as the handle was hot from the surrounding heat. I grabbed at it again, trying not to hold it too tightly, hoping it was cool enough but time was against me and I just had to grin and bear it, any longer and it probably would have gone up in flames. I ran to the wall with the nine pointed star on it.

Time was running out. Kneeling before the star I placed the disc on the floor between myself and the wall. The heat from the fire behind was slowly roasting my back. I coughed as the smoke started to penetrate my lungs. I didn't know how long I had, the roof was already ablaze and I knew my time was nearly over. How long was this was going to take?

Trust me.

"Jesus, what are you trying to prove? I need to get out of here now." I looked around, nearly everyone else was out.

We are nearly there.

I tried to shut the fire out of my mind and concentrate. I looked up at the star.

"Demarg Histut Fugama Lifdut. Johia your time has come to an end, I offer you poison from the knife of life." And with that I made a small cut in the palm of my right hand, just enough to drip a few drops of blood onto the wooden disc. "Leave this world. Brikata Ghangia Jukit Loten." I felt a sudden surge of power from the wall. My life force started to leave me, my body was not my own, my lungs exuded all the air they contained. A crushing pressure gripped my heart. I tried to repeat the words, "Demarg Histut Fugama Lifdut." I could hear them in my head, but there wasn't any volume.

The smoke was getting in my eyes, making them sting. The noise from the spitting fire was a triumphant fanfare as the flames licked there way round every timber. With every last morsel of strength I threw the wooden disc at the wall, splattering the drops of blood over the star and fell forward onto the floor.

I remained there for a short time sure that I was going to die. I attempted to kneel but struggled to get up, my body weak. I could just see the Master through the smoke filled barn, still in situ, like a prisoner held by an invisible force field, the flames still having no affect on his physical being. Abruptly, he disappeared under a blanket of white heat and I fell back to the floor coughing from the smoke, my strength gone, my fate sealed. Although the pressure on my heart had been released, my lungs were still burning. I heard a timber crack followed by a whistle as it fell feeling the vibration through the ground as it landed somewhere in the barn. I remembered the little girl and deep down knew it was too late. All seemed doomed.

I knew it was only a matter of time before the barn collapsed. I was losing consciousness choking on the thick black smoke, I could not muster the strength to will myself to move, the exertion would only cause more pain in my lungs. I felt myself drift, this was the end. I closed my eyes and left this place behind.

"Thank you. But it is not your time. He is still free."

"Sarah. Is that you?"

"You can't let him go free. He must be finished."

"I can't help any…"

My body suddenly jerked. Wearily I tried to open my eyes, all I could see were shadows, and bright lights, nothing was real anymore. My eyes closed again. All went quiet and still.

31

Opening my eyes I blinked as the bright sunlight hit my pupils. Was I in heaven? It took ages to shake the grogginess enough to realise I was not actually dead, my mouth felt dry, my tongue like it had spent the night in a bowl of plaster dust, my head ached and my stomach had a putrid vile feeling about it. I coughed as I breathed in the clean air, as if I had smoked eighty a day for my whole life and was suffering the effects. Trying to sit up only made me dizzy, so I rested where I was.

Slowly a picture of what had happened appeared in my mind. Whenever it happened. I didn't know what day it was. I just knew I was in a hospital on a ward with sixteen other people, guessing it was mid morning judging by the daylight. I laid there for a while before a nurse saw that I was awake and came to speak to me.

"How you feeling this morning? You had quite a lucky escape by all accounts."

"What day is it?" The words like strangers in my dry throat, my voice merely a rasp.

"It's Saturday. The doctor will be around later to see you're alright, nothing a few days rest won't cure, I'm sure."

"Could I have some water please?" my voice barely audible.

The nurse took the jug from the bedside and poured a glass of water, then helped me sit up. The fogginess slowly cleared from my head.

As the day drew on and my strength started to return I recalled some of the events. By the afternoon I felt well enough to look for Suzi; although my legs still didn't quite feel like they were my own, almost detached.

Southend Hospital is a large place, a mix of new and old. This was not the first site of Southend Hospital, but the longest running. The original site had had limited space with no room to grow, this new site provided everything under one roof with a labyrinth of corridors. It took me forty minutes to get to Suzi who was in Thomas Ward in the Desree Wing. I had been placed in the nine storey Tower Block on the eighth floor; you could definitely tell this was the old part of the hospital; the décor left a lot to be desired.

Tiredness had kicked in and I had been forced to sit in one of the many small waiting areas en route where I could get a drink of water.

"Hi ya" I croaked approaching Suzi's bed, she had been sitting up reading.

"Hi. I heard you were in. They ought to get us our own ward, with Nancy as well."

"Maybe we could all ask for transfers." As more memories of the barn came flooding back my legs went a little wobbly.

"You okay?"

"I'll be fine" I coughed and spluttered.

"You did well by all accounts. Have you seen the local headlines?"

"No. I've not long woken up." Suzi grabbed a copy of the Evening Echo from her bedside table and showed me the headline

GIRL FOUND DEAD, CULT BLAMED

it continued in smaller bold type underneath:

Barn burned to the ground – arrests made

I sat on the edge of the bed to rest and read more.

After I had passed out, the fire brigade had arrived rescuing me. Although, initially, it was thought I had been part of the cult; it was later discovered that I had been trying to help the girl. Police were still waiting to talk to me about the events. The fire brigade had not been in time to save the girl or the Master and one other who had perished in the inferno. Police had made various arrests in connection with the dead girl who it appears had been abducted two days before from Chalkwell Park. The police had arrived shortly after the fire service and the robes the faith wore had aroused suspicion. After further questioning, arrests were made and they were now all being held for questioning.

Police believed there were connections to other cases of missing children dating back thirty years or more.

"So we dunnit?" jubilation coursed my tired limbs and my voice cracked making my eyes water.

"No we haven't!"

I looked at Suzi surprised and she just nodded knowingly at me.

"James!" we spoke simultaneously

The joy dissipated. James was a key to the cult "I don't understand why James wasn't there that night." A myriad of images struck me. "But his parents were!" I stated "I saw them. I don't understand why. If it was such a big ceremony then surely everyone would have to have been there?"

"That's what I would have thought." Suzi agreed "I haven't had a chance to talk to Nancy yet."

"Is she still..." I couldn't think of the correct word "...you know...inside me?"

"No, I came to see you last night. I put things right. She is okay. Oh! I've spoken to Marshall" she finished matter-of-factly.

"And?" I asked

"'Kraknami' was an ancient term used by Christians to lock the spirits in the place of burial. Apparently there was a strong belief that spirits could communicate with the living, so if ..."

"...then the murderer would lock the spirit down so they couldn't let on who had done it" I interrupted her.

"Well that's not quite what it was intended for. More, when and if, bodies of murderers were buried it was to stop their spirits breaking into the realms of the real world again."

"A spiritual prison then."

"One way of looking at it."

"So what abou...So because Sarah's resting place had been disturbed, by me, the prison had been broken. And... she communicated with the one who broke the prison. Obviously this cult firmly believed in spiritual communication so they used it for their own ends. But surely that would mean that..."

"...Someone in the church was involved somewhere along the line, as we found out there were those vicars who were excommunicated, can't remember when exactly. Anyway, the only way to break the spell is to break the lock 'Kraknami' which you did" Suzi suddenly looked melancholy, "It's ironic really when you think about."

"What?"

"Well, it was James who sort of caused the accident in the first place"

We let that settle.

"How about the spirits of the other murder victims? If they all had the prison, lock thing, then surely they wouldn't have been able to talk directly to me."

"That's as I understand it from Marshall."

"How about the little boy buried under the garage? He communicated directly with me."

"Wasn't it through Sarah?"

I thought for a second. "Not really. Well. I mean she was there. Maybe they hadn't put the prison in place. Could have got disturbed before hand, I s'ppose."

"Could be" Suzi agreed.

"Anyway what are we gonna do about James?"

The mood changed. James had been our friend but it was still hard to believe all that had happened and that he would no longer be around.

"I don't know" Suzi reflected. "I suppose we've got to find him. We need to speak to Nancy as well. The way I figure. Unless there is another... part of this cult somewhere in the country then I guess he'll just fade away, start a new life. If there is another part of the cult then the only way he can carry on is..."

"The Kut of Life" I finished. Suzi smiled her agreement. "Maybe we should contact the police?"

"The police are already looking for him, remember?"

I nodded "So there's nothing really for us to do except get out of this place and have some fun." Suzi understood the underlying message in that comment but our mood showed the opposite. We missed James.

Life went on, everything had been done that could be done. I'd lost my best friend, through no fault of his own. He was gone. Caught up in something that was destined from birth, his life had been planned without his knowledge. All I had now were the memories. The holiday to Majorca, the Friday night drinking sessions that had lasted until sun up. The pranks we used to pull, the laughter.

The time I pretended to give his phone number to a girl behind the counter of a McDonald's restaurant. Suzi had been there; I had written down James's phone number, mobile and home, on a napkin and walked into the loo, putting it into my pocket. When I came out I went straight up to the counter and spoke to the young brunette asking her to play along, handing her the napkin in full view of James. The young girl, Natalie, at first looked embarrassed but she smiled and took the napkin. There was an instant, when I caught her eye that I wanted to ask her out for myself I believed she would have said yes, judging by the smile on her face and her disappointment when I asked her out for my friend. I think she was surprised by my confidence.

I had walked back to where James was seated. James had been quite shocked that I'd gone through with it. To this day I never did tell him that I had swapped the napkins in my pocket and passed a blank one to Natalie. I couldn't help contemplate the fact that I should have asked her out, it wasn't very often I had that sort of confidence when sober. It was a cruel joke on James as it made him feel rejected as well because she never rang. I always knew he'd get his own back sometime.

Life had changed now. I had Suzi and we had a future for as long as we wanted it. For all the time we'd known each other it seemed an unlikely pairing as we had always considered ourselves friends and that would be how it would stay. So out of something bad, something good had happened and for that I was grateful even if, at times, life felt a little hollow.

I left hospital the next day after the police had visited me to take a statement. I told them what I knew, almost every detail, leaving out the talking to ghosts and anything that I couldn't explain. I had known the interview would be coming so had discussed it with Suzi to help get the story straight beforehand.

I contacted work and was returning on the Monday of the following week, my immediate manager, and his manager, wanted a meeting at 9am on the Thursday before to discuss my future and return. I sat in my flat and viewed the scene. I could see James and me playing computer games and drinking 'til the early hours. Flat and disheartened, I sat and drank a beer.

Suzi came out of hospital on Monday. I visited her at home - she had lost a lot of weight but was eating normally now, her strength returning.

Nancy had been kept in. She had only woken from her mysterious coma after a visit from her friend Suzi, the nurses said that friends could sometimes be the trigger, but little did they know the truth. Nancy was due home Tuesday.

The weekend passed slowly, I was nervous about my meeting on Thursday. Would I still have a job? I was doubtful although circumstances had been difficult. I had not treated them with respect by keeping them informed of what was going on. Then again, what could I have explained? Still, my name had been mentioned in the local and national press and after the field day they'd had about murders involving a cult I suppose I could be considered a hero of sorts.

That didn't sit comfortably on my shoulders.

I sat in front of my boss and his on Thursday as arranged and was pleasantly surprised by their relaxed attitude. They had felt that this meeting was needed to grasp the full picture of events and where things were going to go from here. They were happy to give me my full responsibilities back now I had my hearing again.

My job was full of all the interest it had had before, it was nice to be back in the throng of things, work colleagues, clients, and suppliers. I saw Suzi in the evenings and my first week back at work passed quickly. At the weekend we went looking for a holiday for two, somewhere quiet, hot, and, importantly, cheap.

It's surprising sometimes how quickly you can move on when faced with the realisation that you can't change events and what will be, will be.

I checked the newspapers regularly to see whether James had been arrested but after a few weeks it seemed he had just disappeared. The police had come to see me once asking if I heard from him, which I hadn't, I assured them that if I did I would contact them straight away.

All there was to look forward too was our holiday to Corfu, Dassius, a three star self-catering apartment in a quiet, family run complex a short walk from the beach. This was perfect.

32

Twelve weeks had passed and life was good. Suzi and I had just come back from our holiday where the temperature had remained around 112 Degrees Fahrenheit which meant we spent most of the week in the pool, just to keep cool. The holiday managed to cement our relationship and when we got back Suzi moved into my flat. Things were great. It helped take my mind off losing my best friend.

Subconsciously, one weekend I found myself walking down James's road. I had no particular reason to do so, deep down I still missed him. In the distance I could see a 'For Sale' sign and as I got closer found it was outside his parents' house. Glancing through the windows; the rooms had been stripped bare, the gardens which had been so well loved, were now looking neglected.

A pang of sadness hit me, but this was just a small chapter in the course of my life and something I couldn't change. The house where William had been buried did in fact belong to James's Uncle and Aunt and they too had been arrested. What I hadn't realised was that they were there the night the barn burned down.

I hadn't received another visit from Sarah in my dreams so I guessed everything was okay and she had finally moved on.

Suzi had certainly made her mark upon my flat, it wasn't a bachelor pad anymore it had become our small home, she had even brought up the subject of moving to a bigger place, getting a joint mortgage. This was scary stuff, the sort of stuff you would normally talk to a best friend about and they would entertain themselves at your expense for the rest of the evening, well that would have been how James would have reacted, although deep down he would have been happy for me, for us. The James I missed anyway. I was not totally against the idea of moving I just didn't see the need, I loved my little flat.

One night we came back early from one of our fortnightly trips to see Nancy, Suzi had not been feeling too well. As we opened the door, to what had become known as our flat, we picked up immediately on a strange sense of foreboding. Everything was in its place but something didn't feel right. Something we couldn't put our finger on.

It plagued us and made going to sleep difficult, every noise woke us from our slumber. The next three nights were equally as uncomfortable. Nothing ever seemed out of place, it was the atmosphere that was different somehow.

On the fourth night Suzi sat me down. I thought she had discovered what it was about the flat but instead broke it to me that she was pregnant. Dumfounded, I gawked at her with my mouth open, not quite getting my head round it, I almost felt sick to my stomach. I even asked 'How?'. It was not the response Suzi had wanted but after talking for a while jubilation settled in even if I was terrified of becoming a father. My life really had moved on, changing beyond recognition.

The following week work had organized a night out for the staff, due to good year end results, Suzi planned to spend the night in on her own checking the papers for larger flats. Leaving the do about half past eleven, rather worse for wear, I staggered home.

As I got close to our flat I noticed the lounge light was still on and guessed Suzi had waited for me to come home. I tried to sober up slightly by sitting on a wall and taking deep breaths before going in, which worked until I stood up and the cold night air hit my lungs, making me even more light-headed.

The noise of smashing glass from inside a house cleared the fogginess in my head temporarily, it had come from behind me. I couldn't see anything from any of the flats and all was silent again.

After a few more minutes I realised it was futile to sit here and went indoors. The light was off in the lounge by this time, I must have sat outside longer than I had thought. The flat still had a foreboding presence which we had not managed to clear, Nancy had even tried a cleansing spell to no avail. I stepped into the blackness that blanketed the lounge and heard the crunching of glass underfoot. In my drunken haze it didn't connect with the noise I had heard earlier and I just tried to be quieter, which I was not, every noise amplified by my clumsiness.

Throwing my coat over the back of the settee I walked to the kitchen struggling to hook the toe of one shoe on the heel of the other and kick them off. I stumbled into the kitchen as I fell off balance. Pulling the door to I decided it might be prudent to make a coffee before going to bed. The room was struggling to stay still, swaying and spinning before my eyes. The kettle was louder than usual and any minute I was expecting Suzi to walk in. Carefully, I stirred the coffee making sure the spoon didn't connect with the sides of the mug. The more I tried, the more it hit. Walking back into the lounge I sat down, leaving the light off.

In the silence the smell of coffee slowly started to stabilize my senses, my eyes gradually focussing on the dark objects within the room. The street light streamed in through the wooden blinds. I knew I was going to feel rough in the morning and rested my head on the back of the settee closing my eyes.

I heard a movement to my right and opening my weary eyes caught the sharp movement of a shadow near the kitchen door.

"Sorry honey, I didn't mean to wake you" I slurred.

As the words left my mouth I realised it wasn't Suzi.

In a nervous reflex action I dropped the mug of coffee, the contents spilling over the carpet and my socks, luckily the coffee had gone cold. Standing up, my right foot stood on the mug and slipped from under me making me fall awkwardly on the arm of the settee. Trying to break my fall; I only succeeded in twisting my shoulder.

The figure in the shadows moved towards me at great pace and I struggled to get up, my drunkeness impeding my success. A pair of strong hands gripped me round the neck and I was pushed to the floor face down. The grip changed position and a knee was placed firmly in the centre of my back. I put my hands out to try and get some purchase to push myself up against the weight that bore down on me. Something sharp dug into the palm of my left hand; the pain was only dulled due to the drink.

A strong grip fumbled at my throat, stopping me from breathing. Quickly, I started to panic, my hands flailing at the hands around my throat, grasping for anything. The pressure was building up in my face, my cheeks were burning, pearls of sweat were starting to form on my forehead and tears beginning to well in my eyes. My stomach was reacting to the copious amounts of alcohol and I could feel bile rising.

I grabbed an arm with my left hand, the grip around my neck released. I sucked air and tried to roll away at the same time, but the knee in my back was still holding me in place. Again I placed my hands in a press up position and tried to get free. The pain in my left hand shot through me like a bolt of lightning tears running down my cheeks, gritting my teeth and with an almighty thrust I pushed upwards at the same time releasing the contents of my stomach.

A hand grabbed the back of my shirt, the nails scraping the skin underneath, as the body of the person on top was sent flying backwards into the armchair behind. I turned sharply knocking the coffee table out of the way, staring at the figure in front of me for a split second before vomiting more. The bearded man was not familiar, the smell wafted to me, the body odour making me convulse again. The adrenalin had got me this far now it was deserting me fast. My limbs were weary and I fell back onto the floor half sitting. Another bout of nausea gripped me with an iron fist. It became almost a stand off as we stared each other out, the man holding his left arm.

Before I could react the man had got up and run towards the bedroom. My first thought was for Suzi and our unborn child. During the whole of the attack I hadn't even given them a thought. Now my worst fears ran through me.

I called out her name as loud as my crushed throat allowed, it didn't seem loud enough. I followed staggering to the bedroom, putting my hand out against the approaching wall, smearing it with blood from the injury to my palm. The bedroom door was ajar, I pushed it hard and burst into the room expecting to see the figure of the man. In the dim light I could see Suzi's body under the quilt. Stopping, I watched, fearing for her life and questioning whether I was too late?

Walking slowly in I watched the dark shadows for movement. As I got near the bed, I heard a noise behind and spun round in time to see the flash of silver heading toward me about waist height. Instinctively I clumsily moved out of the way, tripping over and crashing into the chest of drawers to my right. A searing pain came from my ribs.

I knew I didn't have time for pain and stumbled backwards to put some distance between me and what I guessed was a knife. The figure approached as I backed into the wardrobe holding my ribcage with my cut hand, the blood staining my clothes making them cling to my skin. I glanced around for something to defend myself with. Nothing was within easy reach. Edging to my left I kept one eye on the intruder and one eye on Suzi's body, which had not stirred at all. In my mind I guessed I was too late and this gave me the fight I needed. I was being backed into the corner of the room that was normally my side of the bed. Tripping over a shoe on the floor I threw my right arm out to steady myself, it touched the top of something hard leaning against the wall. The intruder lunged for me, knife thrust forwards. My hand grabbed whatever it had landed on and swiftly swung it round, it caught the man's left shoulder and the vibration rocked my hands. The thrust was enough to knock him sideways. I swung the weapon again, the anger inside giving me the force of ten men, quickly without aim, this time catching the man fully in the arm I heard the crack of the bone as it gave way under the force. The man let out a scream of pain

I caught the man again with the weapon on the return stroke. A splatter of blood landed on my face. Renewed energy kept me repeatedly hitting the man. He buckled and fell to the floor, knife still in his right hand.

Anger had replaced any reason, adrenalin had sobered me up and I kicked out, catching him square on the jaw. A second crack cut through the air and the man went flying backwards banging his head on a handle of the chest of drawers, another cry of pain. As I approached to land another blow on him, he thrust the knife up from the floor.

There was a momentary pause. I swung again with my weapon, this time at the knife. I missed. I was now side on to the man who was kneeling. I saw the flash of the blade and swung round to deflect the blow that was heading for my ribs before grabbing the hand that held the knife with both my own hands, letting my weapon fall to the floor. We fought for control of the knife, each struggling to gain power over it. I had no idea where my strength was coming from.

Suddenly all opposing force died and I fell in a heap on the floor, half covering the man.

Silence filled the room and slowly I slipped into unconsciousness, my body reeling from the effects of the drink and the wounds from the battle and that's how I stayed until morning when I was awoken by the full glare of the sun bursting through the crack in the curtains.

Wearily I blinked, every part of my body ached with stiffness, my stomach still reeling from the drink, my clothes sticking to my body. My head thumped with every movement I made. The recollection of the nights events were unclear in my fuddled mind, I remembered going to the work's do. Bits of information trickled back and an understanding of why I was on the floor. A realisation that I was laying on someone gripped my frantic throbbing head.

'Suzi' I said wearily standing up and momentarily forgetting all the pain. Immediately giddiness made me weak again, a sick feeling reeling in my stomach. I scrambled onto the bed where Suzi's body lay, panic taking control. She was still. I turned her gently by the shoulders, tears starting to find their way from the corner of my eyes. Her body was lifeless in my hands. My head pounded hard, my hands shaking. I held her body close to me.

It took a few seconds to acknowledge, to register, the movement of her hands as they stroked my back reciprocating the hold. Words could not express the feeling of joy that I felt. I let go of Suzi and retched over my side of the bed, coughing as the foul taste remained in my mouth.

Suzi stroked my back "You alri..." she stopped mid sentence her hand tense on my back, she had seen the aftermath of last nights struggle.

The rest of the morning was a blur of events, Suzi called the police and an ambulance. My clothes were taken away at the hospital by forensics and I gave a statement to the police.

In the myriad of things I hadn't taken a look at the body of the man I had killed. Although the police initially felt sure it was self defence they said that they would want to question me further. As a parting gesture they told me the identity of my attacker.

It was James. I retched but was empty. I had killed my best friend.